These are the strangely trou  omen, of failing light and da

Now is the time for the elders of the Kingdom of Rhye to perform their ancient rite on the barrow-grave of kings. Here will the destiny of the Triad-wielder be revealed: when the Dearth Hand rises, Eider, Lord of Rhye, will be condemned to the Shadow-Land, and to his fate.

Yet can he find Phoenix Fire and bring about the final redemption?

Phoenix Fire

Book 3 of
The Eye of Time
trilogy

LYNDAN DARBY

UNWIN
PAPERBACKS

LONDON SYDNEY WELLINGTON

First published in paperback by Unwin Paperbacks, an imprint
of Unwin Hyman Limited, in 1989

UNWIN HYMAN LIMITED
15–17 Broadwick Street
London W1V 1FP

Allen & Unwin Australia Pty Ltd
8 Napier Street, North Sydney, NSW 2060, Australia

Allen & Unwin New Zealand Pty Ltd with the Port Nicholson Press
Compusales Building, 75 Ghuznee Street, Wellington, New Zealand

British Library Cataloguing in Publication Data

Darby, Lyndan
  Phoenix fire.
I. Title
823.′914 [F]
ISBN 0–04–440153–1

Phototypeset in Linotron Times
by Input Typesetting Ltd, London
and printed in Great Britain by
Cox and Wyman Ltd, Reading

For Eve

Prologue

*Ragged feathers scatter black across the fathomless sky,
kites fly and from the remnants of dark a hooded figure
moves out along the ridge. At his back, the creak of old
wood and jangle of harness joins the stiff-limbed rhythm
of the aged horse who wheezes beneath the load. The
wagon, ravaged by the seasons, lurches drunkenly, its
lantern flare a smudge of light within the rain-heavy
gloom. The mute procession halts and as the windsong
chants its incantation, the canvas cracks in manic flight.
Within the wagon frozen travellers stir and peer without,
their faces stark beneath the thunderous sky.*

*The wagoner scans the landscape, his arm thrust out,
the long forefinger tracing the line of the ridge from east
to west; from sweeping crag to wooded hill where willows
brace their slender backs and knotted tresses drape the
rain-washed slopes. The wind-chapped finger draws the
contours, patiently it charts their rise and fall until within
its circle heathland is revealed. Flat and bleak it lies
beneath Nature's breath; yet at its heart the desolate earth
rises up in a gesture of defiance. Here the brooding
mound stands fixed against the moving sky, stilled
between the orbs of sol and luna. The narrowed eyes
focus bright and as the hefty stave meets flint shale, sparks
ignite beneath the circling wind. Here the journey will
begin. Here, where mists blur the boundaries and the
real and the imagined flow as one. The wagoner points
on . . .*

*. . . Far to the west there stands the ruined castle-
keep, blackened and bereft, yet within its grim shadow
life stirs, a weary stallion rears and clambers from the
rubble. On its back a rider, cloaked against the bitter
blast, raises a shredded banner against the churning sky.*

1

The ragged phoenix flies and upon the icy draught a desperate cry is cast. The rider hangs his head in sorrow and the night-black steed carries him away, far from the broken tower and walls of mourning, far, far away until they vanish into insignificance amid the hostile wastes.

. . . And to the east, slowly and in silence they come, a ghostly column weaving through the vapour, torches red as bloodstone, studding the ancient path, pre-empting the dawn sun. Eerie caravan of light, they make their solemn progress, a chimera of colour on the black carpet of the moor. In the shadow of the mound they halt; then as a fiery thread they climb until their flowing silks amass upon the barrow ridge, torches flaring as one great light atop the grave of kings.

Robes flap against the billowing wind and golden censers swing, the scent of musk cast upon the chill air. The ragged circle of shadows stands etched against the brooding sky, hands linked in silent invocation. They sway as one, summoning forth the energy of the elements.

Across the indigo sky an arc of star-fire flies and the gathering calls forth emblems of mystic lore. They move and breathe as one, heads bowed in homage to the Ancients as each raises up the bread, and then the cup, then incense and the Loric Key. All blessed by word and hand, the sacred tokens lie at the centre of the round stone which, carved by Nature's breath, becomes an altar for the Elders' lore.

Soon from their chanting column one emerges, stooped and silent, draped in robes of sapphire, his gaunt face lost within their silken shadow. White tapered fingers stretch towards the zenith, imploring universal light to bless and to receive. Bright steel cuts the frosted air, its glinting tip extended to the firmament, whilst cupped palms hold aloft the crystal prism. Mediator for the whispering of Ancients, he speaks in a voice no longer his, but Spirit:

> From every compass point we come,
> Summoned here by Ancient Lore,
> Bearers of the Sacred Key

With which to unlock future deeds . . .
We come, the Sower's Seeds,
Witness to those who came before,
And call upon the ancient light
To charge this crystal with the Sight,
That all may be revealed,
And in the past – the future sealed.

The moon breaks cover from the wind-blown clouds and the new-blessed prism absorbs its gaze. The shaded eyes of the Elders gleam and the censers swing aloft, until the Earth itself is set to flight; commanded by their invocation. Each one feels the power of Earth, trembles at unseen gods and makes reverence to the moving sky. In turn, they cup their hands about the mystic prism, searching out its pulse-light until mauve, blue and every pastel shade shines out and each beholds and speaks his vision to the other:

The land is white
The seed is black,
Dark musings seek
The light they lack . . .

The quizzing glass passes to the second Elder and he too speaks his signs:

The branch, the twig,
The woven bier.
A King of Light
Begets a fire.

The third grows taut as he receives:

Raise the cup and spill no drop,
Less the drum of life do stop . . .

The fourth in line embraces the sacred instrument:

Night of joy and day of black,
Draws the rod across his back.

The fifth gives forth a warning sign:

Taut bindings do the bindings part,
'Tis a dagger through his heart!

The sixth shakes his head in sadness:

When the heart begins to bleed,
This 'tis dead, 'tis dead indeed.

The prism pulses white hot within the hands of the seventh:

Heat of pyre, white of pall.
Birds upon the castle wall.
When the bird away doth fly . . .
'Tis an eagle in the sky.

All focus on the glowing glass, their voices raised as one prophetic chant:

Gold of feather
Then of mane.
Ice of water
Heat of flame.
First and last
Then last again
Gives the wielder his name!

Then did the sacred song vanish on the winds and the westering moon fall to the dark horizon, scattering stars, and changing the prism point from white to black. The mystics watched, their knotted throats silenced, each breaking heart willing a sign to seal the vision. Then, in a stream of fire the Gods gave token of the deed. Yet, as the great eye of the sun burst forth with rays of burnished gold, none saw the wagon etched black upon the distant ridge.

4

— 1 —

Upon the hill, in the cover of tall trees, the boy saw the straggling line of travellers as they trudged along the uneven road, their clothes heavy with the dust of days, their faces gaunt and grim. Three notes he blew upon the horn, his sharp alarm summoning the Elder from his hearth and soon before the wise man's lodge the weary travellers halted. The Elder greeted them with the warmth natural to northern folk and offered hospitality to all who would partake of it. Yet sorrow lay heavy on their faces and the leader of the company stepped forward to speak for all.

'Master, we are border folk and have travelled long days to seek your wisdom,' he explained, smoothing the brim of his hat between fingers and thumbs. He half turned and nodded to a young girl in their midst. 'We would you deal with 'er.'

All eyes focused on the silent figure clad in a tattered shift, her long, frail limbs the colour of alabaster. The headman ushered her forward with an impatient wave of his hat and as she moved amongst them, all shrank from contact with her gaze and touch.

The braided gold hair framed a gentle face and as she drew closer to him, the Elder read the signs that shone deep in the serene lilac eyes.

The menfolk moved back. 'Master, look not into 'er eyes so long!' the eldest warned.

'Aye,' their women chimed. ''Tis unwise to look at all!'

The young girl trembled at their hostility and lowered her eyes in submission, prompting from the Elder a concerned frown. He circled the child's thin shoulders with a kindly arm. 'Look not upon her so,' he chided them. 'Thy daughter has the gift of Sight.' He brushed the golden tresses. ''Tis an honour to your clan.'

Several shook their heads, but dark glances from their leader held fast their tongues and the Elder raised a questioning brow. 'You would seek advice on the matter?' he prompted. The border folk made no reply and the Elder flourished an open palm. 'Then you would have me take her in and train her in the Lore?'

At last the headman spoke out. 'Master, we would you 'eard 'er speak and then decide what must be done.' There was fear in his voice and sensing the growing agitation of the group, the Elder called forth his apprentice.

'Lead the child to my hearth,' he whispered. 'There make ready, spread the sand – lay out all that I would have to hand.' He bade the girl follow in the company of his aide and watched her taken to the safety of his lodge. The wise man turned again to her kinsmen and bade them take their ease, yet had moved but a few paces when their leader called out to him.

'Master, take precaution in the deed,' he warned sadly. ''Er fourteen springs 'ave brought us many cares.'

The Elder returned to him. 'Friend, I see no evil in the child.'

The eyes of the border man widened. 'Yet in 'er short time, where she has trod, strange omens, 'ave appeared,' he explained.

'There is nought that you should fear,' the Elder clasped his arm in reassurance.

The simple man fidgeted. 'Master, I would believe it so, but recent times 'ave seen the failure of our crop and now the withering of our livestock to the bone!'

The Elder shook his head. 'Friend, for these troubles there is some common cause. Such superstition has no place in seelie lore.'

The anxious face met the wise man's full on. 'Master, no disrespect to you I swear, but 'ear 'er speak and you will see 'ow well these 'appenings do fright us, one and all.'

The Elder calmed him. 'Fear not, I shall hear what thy daughter would say, but meantime be advised and keep an open mind.'

With a low bow the border man rejoined his weary company and the Elder left them to their rest.

Before the sand smoothed out upon the floor, the Elder drew her forth, yet the old man's incantation was barely at an end before the girl's fragile form grew taut and she reached out to take the Elder's sacred stave of fate. Though amazed by her gesture the wise man did not speak but let her take the rowan staff within her grip and watched as she, with wide eyes and trembling hands, drew mystic signs within the sand. First, 'Michael', the name of Good, she wrote clear, her silent thoughts racing far ahead of the clumsy movement of the stave. She strained for air, then groaned with each decisive stroke, flanking the sign of the angel, first with the viper and then with the dove. Again she gasped for breath, only half conscious, yet the lilac eyes were wider still and from the slender throat the disembodied voice of prophecy escaped.

'*The sun sinks low covering all in sulphur glow. The thunder cracks, rumbles as an avalanche. There is no rain to bless the earth; only lightning forks upward from the dust!*' The frail white body shook with the horror of her visions but as the Elder and his boy moved to aid her, she rallied and pointed the rowan stave clutched tight within her hand.

'*From where it leaps the ground bakes.*' The lilac eyes were half shuttered as she prodded at the sand. '*Great knuckles of parched wood push forth!*' Her swan-like neck rippled as she tried to swallow in the heat. '*Through the dry earth crust, through the sulphur light, they split as they meet air. They crack, and twist. They grow into a fist!*' Beads of sweat patterned the youthful countenance and she tried to wet her lips.

The Elder winced at the spoken vision, his face

7

registering growing disquiet as the girl flung down the stave as if it were her terror.

'*The wood is dead!*' She grew distraught. '*Its rotten timber flakes. 'Tis parched! 'Tis charred!*' She grimaced at the granted Sight. '*Yet still the deformed sapling lives!*' Now her strange voice quickened to a breathless chant. '*The fist unfolds. The twisted fingers spread. The knotted palm extends, as if it begged for bread!*' Her wan face was awash with tears as she stood transfixed before the climax of her vision.

The Elder was ashen. 'The Hand,' he breathed, daring to form the word as he turned to his bewildered apprentice. 'The Dearth Hand rises!' he gasped, his voice trembling with the realisation of his utterance.

As if released from trance by his spoken truth, the girl swooned and the apprentice rushed to save her. In an instant, the Elder had wrapped his cloak about her shivering form and plucked her up into his arms. 'Quickly!' he commanded the boy. 'We must remove her from this place.'

'Behold the child of Satan!'

She sat with her head bowed in remorse, a halter about her slender neck whilst her menacing captor raised a pitchfork above her head. Children perched on the boughs of the oak tree hid their faces, some wept as she was led away to horrors too terrible to imagine. At first, there was silence amongst the crowd of spectators, then boos and noisy catcalls, then at last, hearty cheers as the woman was returned free of her bonds. She tossed her blue-black hair wantonly and offered a deep curtsey, the low-cut blouse revealing an ample bosom, drawing appreciative leers from the ale-flushed faces. Alongside, her devil-clad captor took his bow and the crude wings that sprouted from his shoulders flapped clumsily as he acknowledged the crowd's jeers as if they were a shower of rare blooms. Coins tinkled into empty hats and outstretched skirts before the players disappeared and in their place a pot-bellied clown juggled with fruit while his fleet-footed squirrel monkey chased the juicy props and devoured them one by one!

Here at the crossroads the old wagon had halted and in the yard of the white-washed inn its inhabitants had performed their crude burlesque of moral tales, sold their talismans, their home-made cures for impotence, lovesickness and warts.

Having taken his rest at the scene, Lehon filled his waterskein from the pump and remounted. He prodded his horse on past the makeshift stage, tossing coins into the outstretched hat as he went, receiving a nod of thanks from the demon-wagoner and smiles from the garishly daubed faces of his company.

Lehon turned from the newly unfolding scenario, a wry smile creeping around the thin line of his mouth. He wrapped his cloak about him and scanned the road ahead: morning mists still lingered. About the open track, the air smelled of linseed and decaying leaves. He traced the line of hedgerows then looked beyond to where frost damp fields spread. Hollow corn-stalks spanned the black soil in brittle yellow lines to the far distance where, beside the stone walls, they rippled with heat. He watched the red glow of fire rip through the crop stubble, branding the earth's face with charcoal scars. The landsmen had lit their autumn fires to devour the harvest waste, had put to torch the bonfires of brittle wood and dry leaves.

Lehon turned in the saddle, the change of the seasons had spread as quickly as the dazzling lines of fire across Rhye's lands. His nostrils filled with woodsmoke and the icy wind set his teeth on edge, with it there came the sudden banging of a drum and cheers flew upwards from the gathering at the crossroads. The mortal kicked hard upon the stirrups: he must be gone before the castle-town closed its gates against the cold and the spreading dark.

The cry of the gateman drifted on the wind as Lehon galloped through into the confines of the castle-town where barking dogs sprang from the shadows, nipping at the legs of his mount. Their sudden ferocity sent doves tumbling from the sills in a chaos of wing and feather and Lehon galloped on until, free of canine pursuit, he drew his frightened steed to a halt. He wiped his brow yet felt himself shiver involuntarily as the dank air sucked at his skin.

'Go to, me lovely!' The drunken cry startled him and raucous laughter forced him to turn about. In that moment he heard the high-pitched battle-screech of a cockerel, the rip of claws and rhythmic flapping of wings. He saw blood on the hands of the men as torn feathers flew and the cock-fight echoed in the darkened alleyway. Lehon felt bile rise to his throat and glanced at the faces of those who stood in the half-light. His green eyes met no glimmer of joy and in their turn the townsfolk watched him as if he were a stranger in their midst. He pulled his cloak tighter against the chill but could not escape the cold gaze of the onlookers as he pushed his horse on up the steep cobbles towards the castle's glistening towers.

The thunder of his mount's hoofs upon the drawbridge set Lehon's heart racing. He was returned to Rhye, and at the thought of seeing his good friends, of knowing the comfort of his own bed, he smiled. Yet, as he entered the cobbled yard the smile vanished, for the clutter at its centre perplexed him.

'Lehon! Good friend!' Sounds of welcome came to him from the stables as Hariss stepped out into the evening sunshine towards him. 'Safe journey?' He beamed into the mortal's weary face.

'Aye,' Lehon replied as Hariss unsaddled the mount for him.

The good captain led him within and nodded to where the ale jug waited. With a grin Lehon hauled the leather bags to the oaken table and unbuckled sword and dagger. He poured some ale, and the two drank to friendship renewed.

'I've missed your company these long days, mortal,' Hariss said, wiping his mouth upon his cuff.

'And I yours,' Lehon agreed. 'Gaunt's hospitality is renowned, yet the days of the Council were long and tedious.'

'They brought together a Council?' Hariss frowned.

'Aye, and I the King's emissary,' Lehon replied. He drank deeply then nodded at the captain. ''Twas called to mull over the Elder's decree . . .' he began, but grew silent, knowing he must be discreet upon the topic.

'I heard it said the King must take a wife,' Hariss prompted. 'Can Elders dictate the King's fate?'

Lehon shrugged. 'It must be done. The Councillors of the Six Sees brought me seals, and likenesses of every eligible maiden in the lands.'

Hariss raised his tankard, 'Well I drink to it! May King Eider be glad of her he chooses!'

Lehon smiled at the man's enthusiasm. 'I hope he may.' He turned a serious look on him, 'But tell me, what is the King's state?'

Hariss frowned, ''Tis hard to give true answer, what with all the talk . . .' Lehon frowned as Hariss drew him closer, 'In the long days you've been gone the King has taken to unruly acts . . . and such a love of war-craft I never beheld in him afore!'

'The King has ever excelled in sword-skill.' Lehon laughed Hariss's care away.

The captain shrugged, 'There is no love in it. 'Tis obsession drives him now, and none must win but he!'

''Tis pride, no more,' Lehon urged.

Hariss shook his head. ''Tis the drink, and lack of sleep! The King talks of nought in these days but dreams and nightmares.' He took a long drink from his tankard, and Lehon saw the strong hand tremble. He saw in the grey eyes a look akin to pain as Hariss turned to him once more. 'I warn you mortal, the King is much changed.'

Lehon laughed, made uncomfortable by Hariss's unusual intensity. 'Excelling in swordplay? Drinking, and a few bad dreams?' He made to clasp the well-intentioned man's shoulder, but the moment was disturbed by sounds of much activity outside. Lehon moved to the door, there to see a line of servants and page-boys moving out across the yard. In their outstretched arms they carried mirrors and hand-glasses of every shape and size. 'What is the purpose of this?' Lehon asked of Hariss as he watched them halt before the strange structure at the yard's centre. There, the ostler and his boy added new panes of glass to the odd construction.

Hariss shrugged. ''Twill be destroyed,' he explained. He met the mortal's bewildered gaze, 'The King can no longer face the glass.'

'No longer face the . . . ? What is this you speak?' Lehon demanded, incredulous.

Hariss nodded affirmation. 'He will not have mirrors in his presence. 'Tis said he kept them draped by day and night, until, upon the middle-hour this night past, he ran amok, commanding every mirror in Rhye's Halls be banished from his sight!'

Lehon's brow creased with sudden anxiety, his mortal mind making no sense of the tale, yet seeing clearly the danger of its consequence. He turned quickly and went within to take up his pack-bags and weaponry. Hariss followed him. 'Lehon, I know no more than what I see, or hear in rumour.'

Lehon clasped his hand in friendship. 'It is enough, good Hariss. We shall speak more on this, but for now I must to the Seventh Elder with the seals, and then to the wizard to speak upon this strange decree.'

'The Lord Wizard has been much in solitude since the first day of the Solstice,' Hariss explained.

'The time of Consultation,' Lehon frowned thoughtfully. 'Then I shall find Regor, he may know more of this.'

Hariss said nothing, only drank deeply of his ale mug and watched the mortal walk away into the evening sunshine.

*

At the intersection where all corridors meet Regor halted, his pointed ears twitching at the sound of a clamour the like of which he had never heard within Rhye's corridors. He drew his sword, and glancing about him he paced on until, in the dim light of the dwindling candles, he saw them: an unruly crowd of court entertainers gathered before the great doors of the east wing. Actors, acrobats and tragic clowns, all draped in their outlandish garb; dancers too, with feet turned out and hands set firmly on hips. All quarrelled at once, all shouted and gesticulated, all demanded and admonished the careworn guard to grant them entry that they might settle the matter with the King, or at least seek the wizard's wise counsel.

Regor watched them all perplexed, for not only had their seelie manners been forgotten, but their entire demeanour was amiss. The elfin shook his head, bemused, for their theatrical attire was unusually bizarre, out of place, and lacking in its usual lustre. Regor scrutinised the chaos: were not the costumes all mixed up, or else back to front, or even inside out? The realisation turned to a wide grin which split the elfin face from ear to ear, for now he could see it all clearly – each face bore a smile that was painted upside down!

'What in the name of all that is seelie . . . ?' Regor laughed aloud.

At sound of his voice the gathering fell silent, but then exclaimed, 'Lord Regor, you have come!'

'And we must to the King in all haste!' said the sad-faced clowns.

'For we must not,' cried the minstrels.

'And we shall not!' stamped the dancers.

'We simply cannot perform!' They all shouted at once. 'Without greasepaint. Without dress. Without slippers. Without wigs.'

'Without mirrors!' the Harlequin cried at last.

At the forbidden word all fell silent and some guilty faces coloured red. Others hid their shame behind gloved hands, or pushed into the crowd to hide behind the rest.

Regor scowled his irritation at their temperamental display and was about to curse performing kind when Lehon came from the shadows of the western corridor into the dim light.

Regor greeted him, 'Welcome return, good Lehon!'

The mortal took his hand firmly. 'What disturbance is this?' he queried, nodding towards the colourful band.

'The dandies mourn the loss of their own reflections!' Regor sneered. He clasped Lehon's arm. 'Yet stay with them while I find Nairb and a solution to this chaos.'

'I cannot,' Lehon frowned. 'I must to the Elder with the seals.'

'Then let us meet in my chambers on the hour of seven,' Regor entreated. 'We shall sup together and talk upon your deeds and mine.'

Lehon nodded agreement and watched the elfin push through the crowd towards the heavy doors of the east wing. 'Each shall have his say!' he heard Regor assure them irritably. 'But each in turn and not before I have spoken to the Lord Wizard myself.' The crowd fell silent and Lehon saw the great doors open to the elfin and then close. He stroked his chin, his placid brow etched with consideration of all the words and deeds that had greeted his return. Then with firm resolve he paced away towards the Loric chambers and the Elder who awaited him within.

—— 2 ——

Nairb frowned and then blinked hard. The surface of the crystal sphere seemed strangely dull. With narrowed eyes he scanned its screen for the colourful display of the time-lights. They were slow to respond, and even when the doves stirred on the sill and flew away on noisy wings Nairb heard no sound, so intent was he upon the crystal and its blur of images. Even when the sun sank in the west he still remained, hands cupped firmly about the mystic sphere until, at last, the time-lights spoke, yet so faint was every pulse of colour that he felt he would expire before their rhythms and their psychic rhymes were done. He grew perplexed, for he could not fathom their strange resistance to his touch.

Just then, a sudden sound from without disturbed his trance. A sound like the slithering of ice. He glanced towards the window . . . was there snow upon the roof-tops? Had winter crept in upon the kingdom by some spell? He stood up and moved to the arched slit to view the courtyard below. There he saw page-boys and servants rushing to and fro, ornate mirrors stacked within their grip. These they placed upon a greater pile of mirrors and hand-glasses which stood at the court-yard's heart.

Bewildered, Nairb inspected the jagged heap, its pyr-amidal structure climbing to the zenith in a criss-cross of angular planes. Rainbow refractions on each fragment caused the chance-made structure to gleam like a prism, seeming to pierce the red disc of the sun. Before the giant prism, the leather-clad ostler and his lad made ready for the shattering of the glass, and Nairb's eyes widened in sudden panic. In an instant he had raised a bone-white forefinger and halted the hammer's destructive arc. In that moment all movement in the courtyard ceased and Nairb breathed a thankful sigh of relief.

The sudden knock upon the door caught him off guard and he dithered momentarily before the window; then, with quick decision he took up the precious sphere and hid it deep within the box of Horatious Thor. The heavy knocking was repeated as Nairb seated himself at the chamber's centre. There he spread out his arms then brought them slowly together again, and as his fingertips met, the perspective of the chamber altered and the room began to shrink. Satisfied at the room's return to normal dimensions, Nairb turned his attention to the door. 'Open to that impatient spirit,' he groaned beneath his breath. At his bidding the door flew open and Nairb beheld the anxious-faced elfin.

'Lord Wizard!' Regor began, striding down the chamber's length.

'What panic?' Nairb asked quietly.

''Tis the King,' Regor frowned. 'I fear . . .'

'Fear?' Nairb raised an eyebrow of concern.

'All is not well,' Regor blurted out. He glanced towards the window and, seeing the ghostly company assembled in the courtyard, grew pale. He turned abruptly to the wizard, but before he could make question Nairb thrust a tapering finger in the direction of the jagged pile of glass below. Regor watched in awe as the structure began to rise, as if borne upon the air itself. Soon it levitated to the full height of the castle-tower, its triangular mass filling the window space at which they stood. At Nairb's quiet command the giant prism began to turn, and then to spin, until it had diminished in size, and together they watched it shrink to a glittering pinpoint as mystic force sped it far away from Rhye's towers. It vanished from sight and Regor turned, his azure eyes meeting the wizard's look of total satisfaction.

As if drawn back from trance Nairb moved away from Regor and the window. 'Now,' he said abruptly, 'what was it caused this madness?'

Regor followed the wizard to the chamber's heart.

'Eider ran through the corridors like a wild-cat!' he began. 'Banished mirrors from his sight . . . from the castle and the kingdom!'

'Tut,' Nairb exclaimed beneath his breath.

''Tis no surprise,' Regor shrugged. 'He kept the tall-glass draped by day and night.'

The wizard said nothing, and Regor frowned. 'What does he see there . . . within the glass?' he quizzed the wise man.

Nairb shook his head and clasped the box of Horatious Thor to him as if it held his most secret thoughts.

Regor drew close. 'Why, in these days of autumn, does Eider seek out spring, believing it stolen?' His elfin face grew strained. 'Speak wizard!' he commanded. 'The King falls into madness, and we into despair.'

At these words, Nairb raised a bony finger to his lips and bade Regor speak no more, yet the elfin clutched the silken sleeve. 'Speak I say! Friend . . . I fear . . .'

'Ah,' Nairb's hazel eyes blinked into the oval face, 'the word returns to us.'

'Not merely a word,' Regor growled. ''Tis the look on every face in Rhye's Halls!' He nodded towards the window, 'I myself came here with a warning: protect the earth-mirror! All are banished, sacred or profane!' As he spoke he scanned the chamber for sight of the crystal sphere.

''Tis safe hid,' Nairb assured him softly as he led him to the door. 'Come, let us to the King and find a meaning for this riddle.'

Soon they were weaving through the dim-lit passage-ways where, amid the wine-red carpets and the heat, they came upon the endless line of time-held servants frozen by Nairb's spell, the banished looking-glasses held firm within their grip. Regor swallowed hard, nervous of the eerie stillness but the wizard led him on.

'To the Monument Hall,' Nairb commanded softly.

'And with all speed!' Regor echoed at his side.

Inside the Monument Hall yet more servants stood

transfixed before the vast wall mirrors, and the wizard breathed relief that his enchantment had spread so quickly and so far. Yet Regor gasped and pointed upwards, tracing the soaring line of the giant step-ladder which stood at the centre of the marble floor. At its pinnacle the aged servant teetered, singing softly to himself as he worked on, oblivious of the silence, untouched by the spell! Nairb and the elfin watched the servant's trembling fingers reach to pluck the first droplet of glass from the giant chandelier, but even as he held it in his grasp the wizard halted him. 'Touch it not,' he breathed command.

The aged servant descended the steps to stand expressionless before the wizard, who drew close to him and whispered into his ear. At sound of the magic word the old manservant scurried about the Hall, repeating the cantrip into every ear. As he did so, each spellbound worker awoke from trance, though none could recall the reason for his presence there.

The wizard gave a satisfied smile and beckoned Regor to follow him into the Throne Room. There Rhye's vast throne resided unharmed beneath the protective wings of the majestic phoenix. Its red eye gleamed still, and the Triad amulets too remained untouched, within the crystal cabinet.

'Praise the Gods no harm be done,' Regor voiced their shared relief.

Nairb nodded agreement. 'Yet still, 'tis time,' he decided. 'We must to the King.'

The elfin shook his head adamantly, 'Not I. He would have nought of me these past days, and I would not provoke.'

Nairb's kindly eyes read sorrow in the elfin face. 'As you wish,' he said softly.

Regor shrugged away all trace of hurt, 'I go to meet the mortal, returned to Rhye this day.'

'Good Lehon,' Nairb smiled fondly. 'When the time of consultations is at an end, I shall speak with you both.'

'There is much to be said,' Regor nodded agreement.

Nairb's voice was soft, 'Until then, the Gods go with you.'

Regor watched the wizard move towards the inner chambers of the royal wing. 'And with you, good man,' he said beneath his breath.

The door closed quietly at his back and the wizard felt the humid air grip his lungs. He blinked, adjusting his eyes to the dim light of candles.

'Lord Wizard!' Eider greeted him from the shadows. 'You honour me. Come, sit before my fire and take some wine.'

Nairb shook his head. 'I must abstain. 'Tis the time of consultations and my mind must be kept clear.' His long face grew momentarily distant, 'Though it would seem that time, and age, have dimmed the Sight . . .' he murmured, as if to himself alone. He watched Eider return the carafe to the hearthstone, noticing his sallow skin, the dark circles about his eyes. Now the delicate jawline was obscured by stubble and the once silken mane of hair was cropped close to the head. Nairb was secretly tracing the fine white line left by the hawk's claw upon his soft cheek, when Eider spoke:

'So . . . what disturbs your meditations?'

Nairb noted the glitter of red fire in Eider's dark eyes. 'Sire, the castle is in uproar at your decree . . .'

Eider gave a flippant laugh, 'That I must take a wife?' He slapped his thigh. 'The old men talk, and leave the rest to youthful vigour!' He drank down the wine nonchalantly.

'The kingdom needs an heir, 'tis true,' Nairb replied quietly.

'And I shall make many!' Eider vowed into Nairb's placid face. 'I shall view all presented with a keen eye, but marry none that does not please me.'

Nairb seated himself at the King's side. 'Then choose well, for the good Lehon returned this day with seals and the likenesses of the fairest maids in all Rhye's lands.'

'Then the nuptual day is close,' Eider mused.

Nairb smiled. 'Even now preparations are being made for the guests' comfort, and for the masked ball to be held in their honour.'

'No masks!' Eider snapped, turning on the gentle wizard. 'Neither in the land, nor in Rhye's Halls! State it plain! No masks to be worn!'

'Majesty, be calm,' Nairb pleaded. 'It shall be done, yet why such innocent sport . . .'

'Do as I bid, that is all!' Eider commanded above Nairb's quiet reasoning.

The wizard read a strange terror in the dark eyes, and knew the time had come to broach the subject. 'This banishment of the mask follows close upon your banishment of the glass,' he ventured.

'An end to all mirrors!' Eider declared downing more wine.

Nairb's eyebrows arched, 'Throughout the kingdom? For all time?'

Eider's sharp eyes flashed, and Nairb raised both hands instinctively as self-defence. 'I ask the question with the best intent,' he said. 'I must know this action has been considered well.'

Eider grew irritable. 'Do not humour me, wizard,' he said. 'I am no child to be reminded of etiquette!'

Nairb's benevolent smile faded. 'Eider, I entreat you, reconsider this decr . . .'

'I have considered well!' Eider snapped and stood to his feet. 'Leave me now, return to your consultations!'

Nairb fixed Eider's glare with his own placid gaze. 'Again, I say, consider well,' he urged gently. 'Consider all that shines and reflects within these walls.'

Eider's teeth were bared yet the wizard pressed his point, 'Consider all those in your keep, whose duty it is to serve or to amuse. How may any of these hope to please their King without the glass and all its uses?'

Eider shrugged at the words of reason and fell silent.

'How many of those who even now travel towards Rhye's gates, may earn a daily crust without the mirror's sheen?'

'No more!' Eider cried above the wizard's persuasive tones. 'The servants shall find new means to meet my needs. The entertainers shall all be gone! This day! Those without the gates be turned away!'

Nairb's eyebrows arched. 'Then you would have nought of Light?' he insisted softly. 'Would deny your subjects sight of the sacred Triad amulets and their aura of Good? Would banish the wisdom of the Eye of Time?'

Eider's implacable gaze flickered as the wizard stretched out his long arms in supplication, 'Sire, all reflect as mirrors do. All give off Light, for the Kingdom's sake! Where can this banishment end?'

At his words, Eider gave a weary groan and clasped both hands to his face in anguish.

Nairb watched him, aghast. 'Eider, surely you had thought of it?' he said, incredulous. 'Surely you did not place yourself before the Kingdom?'

Eider threw back his head in despair. 'Rebuke me not!' he pleaded. 'For the Kingdom's sake alone did I traverse the realm of Dark in sleep.' He thrust a trembling finger at the silent wizard. 'You know it well! Know the suffering I bore there!' He hugged himself for comfort. 'The suffering I bear still . . .' his voice trailed off.

The wizard watched on afraid as his King paced the chamber, lost to torment. The malady lingered . . . 'Sire, 'twas but a fevered sleep, a time-slip that stole you from us.'

Eider shook his head adamantly. 'The medic's draught can make no sleep for me where night's black agent does not follow. Still it stalks me.' He flinched. 'It shifts its shape then grows in such dimensions that this very chamber is consumed by Dark.' Eider was distraught and circled the room like a frightened animal. 'I cry out but have no voice, I try to run but can no longer use my limbs, I feel the dreadful shudder of its approach and know it comes for me . . .' He turned to the wizard, his face riven with terror. 'This shadow that haunts me still . . .' He cast his hands to the heavens. 'Shall I never be rid of it?'

Nairb moved quietly towards him. 'Eider, in all of us there is a thing of fear.'

Eider pulled away to avoid the wizard's comforting touch. 'A thing of fear,' his mouth twisted as he mulled over the words. 'The Feared Thing,' he repeated as if conferring a title. Now he stared ahead of him, his eyes glazed with unspoken visions. 'One day I shall confront it and for one of us it will signal the end.' He rallied excitedly, 'I shall outwit it! Banish the realm of Dark forever!'

In the second that it took Eider to round upon him, the wizard prepared himself and raised both palms as a shield of peace against the hostile spirit before him. 'Sire, the lessons of that realm are here reversed,' Nairb's voice poured forth as a soothing balm, imbued with the tone of ancient authority. 'Therefore, I command you, desist! Shatter not the victory!'

The invocation halted Eider and as his eyes widened with realisation, he opened his mouth to speak but could not. Sudden exhaustion flooded through him and he slumped back into his chair. 'I would have destroyed all things that reflected light!' he cried into his shaking hands.

The wizard tried to comfort him. 'And by that deed in this realm would all our treasures have been taken, our sacred lore defiled.'

At Nairb's gentle rebuke, Eider raised his right hand – it trembled before his face. 'Still Darkness seeks to conquer Light,' he cried. 'And by my own hand!'

Nairb clasped the careworn shoulders. 'There is the lesson learned,' he breathed assurance, yet fell abruptly silent as he beheld the King's outstetched hand. There he saw a scar, the dark remains of a burn mark which zigzagged up the inside of his forearm. Nairb felt the blood drain from his face.

'Seer!' Eider cried, turning to the white-faced wizard. 'Give me vision! Give meaning to this torment!'

The wizard shook his head, unable to summon speech.

Eider's face was wracked with despair. 'Friend, do not desert me now!' he pleaded. 'Will not the vision of the Eye grant me ease?'

Nairb could barely reply. 'Sire, the hand of Dark is close. I dare not risk the sacred sphere.'

'What?' Eider shouted above his grief. 'Does evil taint the pure heart still?' He clasped his arms about his chest and rocked for comfort, 'Have I not served the Kingdom well?'

Nairb trembled at his King's unfolding sorrow.

As quickly, Eider rallied and turned to clutch at the wizard's silken sleeve. 'Help me! Tell me what you have seen in the sphere!' he begged.

Nairb's heart ached for Eider's grief and he closed his eyes, no longer able to bear the sight, yet still he could not close his heart. 'Soon . . .' he said at last. 'Soon we shall consult the sacred sphere.'

Eider sprang to his feet. 'Now!' he urged. 'Before it is too late!'

Nairb raised a hand of calm. 'Hold friend. I must first make all things ready.'

Eider nodded agitatedly and backed away in remembered reverence of the Sight.

Wearied, Nairb turned towards the door. 'On the twelfth hour of the twelfth day of the twelfth month we shall consult the crystal.'

'But to wait so long?' Eider pleaded.

'The pendulum swings not within the sphere, the Eye sees not the setting of our sun, nor rise of moon. Trust in me, the hour is that which Time itself has set aside and you must question not.'

Eider's dark eyes lowered in submission. 'It shall be done.'

Nairb clasped his shoulder. 'Until then, seek out the Elder and do the bidding of the Loric Seals.'

Eider gripped the bony fingers as a gesture of his good faith, then as the wizard stepped out into the gloom, he turned back to the hearth. The fire blazed in the grate and, as he resumed his seat, Eider drew his dagger to

23

him for he had seen it – the barbed shadow cast momentarily by the fireglow. Just a glimpse before it had dissolved into the rippling patterns set in motion by the flames. Eider tightened his grip upon the dagger, knowing the night demon would be alert to his readiness, and that he would find no sleep this night.

Nairb paced the corridor with a heavy heart. How had it been missed? A wound too deep to be received by accident or in duel, yet the medic had said nought of it, and neither had the King. The wizard clenched his fists in silent rage. How could this be? Had the tainted mirrors of the dream-realm drawn blood or white hot wax branded the wielder's hand? He gave a muted cry . . . he had seen it not! The wizard trembled to the core, his thin lips parting in utterance of the vile name. Had that demon-twin triumphed after all . . . through the silent mingling of blood? Worse still, had the victory of Light over Dark been nought but a dream?

Nairb slammed the door of his chamber upon terrible imaginings and hurried to the table at centre of the room. 'Yes,' he muttered calm resolve. The sphere must be risked and Eider put to the test. The thin white hands shook as he took the sacred orb from the box of Horatious Thor and set it at the table's heart. As he took his seat before its mystic aura, his hazel eyes welled up with bitter tears. 'Eider, my dearest friend,' he breathed, 'to test thy shining spirit is no fault.' He shook his head for sorrow, 'Yet to seat a tainted heart before the Eye is sacrilege indeed.' The chair scraped the flagstones as the wizard rose to his feet. 'There must be some other way?' he cried aloud. Yet as he looked upon the ancient sphere, its oscillating time-lights drew him back and he resumed his seat once more. 'Yes,' he conceded at last, 'it shall be done.' The soft voice was lost to silence and tears of crystal purity glistened on the whitened cheeks.

3

In the ice-draught Regor scanned the shadows of the keep then took the steps to the parapet. The ancient stones of Rhye's battlements gleamed blue-white in the moonwash and the elfin drew his cloak tighter about his frame. On reaching the far tower he halted, secretly watching the silent guard knock the bowl of his pipe against the frost-edged wall. Regor moved stealthily in upon him, saw the glowing embers of the pipe fly away into the black of night. He waited, then with one swift motion he sprang forward and grabbed his unsuspecting victim by the throat. 'Soldier, you are dead!' he growled into the dirty ear. 'I am the enemy, my dagger at your heart!'

The guard cried out as Regor flung him against the wall. Dazed, the man snatched for his blade but the elfin's sword was already at his face. 'Again, too late!' Regor spat his contempt.

The terror-struck eyes of the guard widened. 'Lord Regor!' he exclaimed with a sigh of relief.

Regor scanned the empty battlements and nodded to the deserted towers beyond, 'Soldier, a man could ride clear through the gates unseen and unchallenged!'

'My lord, I . . .' the guard began apologetically.

'Where is your company?' Regor demanded. ''Tis regulation, no man stands watch alone.'

'Lord Regor, I am not first but last upon the battlements, I freeze and wait for relief from my vigil.'

'Indeed?' Regor glowered and turning into the bitter night wind he went back the way that he had come, the guard's futile presentation of arms echoing at his back.

The elfin moved through shadows towards the open doorway of the mess-hall. As he drew close the erratic

25

scrape of leather on stone announced the presence of a young soldier, his drunken weave carrying him unsteadily towards the well at the yard's centre. He did not get so far since with the flash of his blade Regor had him in his grip. 'Go to, subaltern!' he growled, and turning the youth about he cast him headlong through the doors and into the smoke-filled mess-hall. The sudden commotion and the appearance of the stone-faced lord had the men on their feet in an instant.

'Captain!' the elfin roared across the debris of the long table. 'Rouse the night-watch! While you sup and snore your comrade freezes on the ramparts!' At his command the men rallied as one body and ran for the door with all the speed they could muster.

When at last the hall had emptied, Regor looked about him. He scowled in disgust at the dirty floor, the fog of pipe smoke and the wine-stained wood of the tables. In sudden fury he dealt the nearest table a heavy blow with his fist, sending dust spiralling up into the rafters. The noise of it ricocheted off the walls and resounded like a war drum as he paced out into the darkness once more. Across the yard he saw the armoury, solid and silent, next to it the barrack block and beyond, his own apartment. He shivered and made for its comforting light.

Once within, Regor felt his spirits rise as he saw the well-banked fire and Lehon sitting before the hearth, his mortal face half etched in the fireglow. The old chair on which he sat creaked a soothing song as he rocked from light to shade in the warm alcove. There too the silver-coated wolfhounds lay outstetched, wire-haired and long of leg. Their vast shadows loomed across the white-washed walls and as Regor approached, their thick tails beat the rush floor in welcome. He ruffled the coarse hair of their heads and grinned into the smiling face of his friend.

Lehon's broad face glowed gold in the firelight and he proffered the jug of mulled wine. 'How is the night?'

he asked as Regor settled down in a chair before the hearth.

'Cold,' the elfin sneered. He took a great gulp of the wine and wiped his mouth with the back of his hand.

''Twill get colder yet,' Lehon assured him. 'Rhye's lands are already gripped by frost.'

'Hecate!' Regor swore and turned a glare upon the mortal. 'Even now the guards are loath to stir without.' He finished his tankard and told of his discoveries. 'I found the battlements unmanned these few short minutes past and had to shift the night-watch from the hearth myself!'

Lehon ceased his rocking and turned steady eyes upon the elfin. 'Just as I found all changed without, so upon return I find all changed within,' he mused.

Regor eyed him quizzically, ''Twas the King bade you go forth?'

'Nay,' Lehon shook his head, ''twas the Elder sent me to the First See and the council held there.'

Regor shrugged irritably, 'Why Eider cannot find himself a wife beats me!'

'Because the King must look to future wielders of Triad Lore in his match,' Lehon reprimanded the sour-faced elfin.

Regor sneered, then cast the mortal a broad grin. 'Tell me, how fair are the wenches you spied out?'

Lehon shook his head and laughed. 'I saw only the likenesses of the maids and brought them back for the Elder's perusal. 'Tis he who will advise the King.'

'There is much need of that!' Regor said with a scowl. He leaned closer to the mortal and frowned, 'Yet tell me of the lands – you say they are much changed?'

'To Gaunt's lands and beyond. Elfin, it would grieve your heart to see it so.' Lehon's green eyes grew sad.

'Yet speak of all you saw,' Regor insisted.

Lehon gave a weary sigh, 'There was little more than flat and frozen earth in parts . . . that and the lines of travellers.'

Regor frowned and he bade the mortal tell him more.

27

'Many landsmen have left their homesteads, seeking warmer winds and fertile soil,' Lehon explained as he silently filled his pipe. Then taken by sudden mirth he turned back to the elfin, 'I did see mountebanks, though, and players too. Their wagon was both dwelling and stage and on it they performed such comic scenes . . .' He shook his head, amazed, 'Some so tragic . . . the like I never saw.'

Regor gave a sigh. 'Then thankful am I,' he said, pouring more wine for them both.

'Aye,' Lehon agreed, striking a spark from the tinder-box. 'That fresh entertainment comes this way will surely please Eider.'

'And, pray, distract him from battle-lore!' the elfin exclaimed.

Lehon questioned him with a frown and Regor felt obliged to explain. 'Eider says he would relearn the vital skills, lest some enemy usurp the throne.' He drank deeply of the cup once more. 'Though to what end save nightly duels and loss of friendship.'

Lehon lit his pipe and pointed at the elfin with the stem. ''Tis clear to me you grieve, friend. Come, tell all that has passed during my leave.'

'Aye, I grieve,' Regor admitted, 'as does all of Rhye's court.' His azure eyes searched the guttering flames for long moments. ''Twas a night like this one, and returning from an errand I spied the mess-hall doors cast wide apart.' Regor held the mortal's gaze within his own. 'The place was packed with men, guzzling and swearing, shouting the odds. In their midst I saw the flash of steel and as I pushed through the crowd I heard the clash of blades. At the sight of the King my blood ran cold, for in his eye was the look of the hunter.' The elfin shuddered and drew closer to the fire for warmth. 'The youth he fought – one of the King's company – was gallant. He observed every noble rule of swordskill, yet the King baited him cruelly, treating courtly style with disdain and raising brute strength above the code of combat.'

Lehon saw the muscles in Regor's face tighten with each recollection of the scene.

'The crowd bawled their rough allegiances, and Jules, the youth, did rally, going at the King like a battering ram, forced for his life to forego etiquette.' Regor's knuckles turned white about his tankard. 'Eider's reply was swift. I saw the gold-haired youth fall to his knees and rushed forward, for there was murder in the King's eyes.' He snatched his hand into a fist. 'Eider raised his sword against me and I reached for my dagger, but then thought twice and took two paces in retreat. "How dare you intrude on royal combat," was what he said.' Regor frowned into Lehon's look of disbelief. ' "Where the noble art is debased I dare intrude," says I.' The elfin's scowl vanished as the latch of the door rattled and the younger of the hounds stirred from the hearth.

Regor and the mortal felt the cold of night steal in as the door eased open and Hariss came quickly into the room's warmth. 'Sol, my fine laddie,' he grinned, patting the hound as it gave him welcome.

Regor proffered the warmed jug. 'The night watch is set?' he asked of the shivering captain.

'Aye,' Hariss nodded, blowing upon his hands, 'though the night is cruel.'

'Cruel or not, watch must be kept,' Regor said stiffly.

Hariss nodded, and silenced by the elfin's tone he sat himself down to partake of the mulled brew.

'What happened then?' Lehon asked quietly drawing Regor back to the tale.

The elfin settled himself down before the flames. 'Eider paced forward, his sword marking my heart, but I marked him step for step in retreat. "You take the coward's stance," he swore at me. "Against the artless blade I take no stance at all," says I.' Regor shook his head sadly, unable to continue the tale.

Lehon looked to Hariss but the honest captain's face only creased with remorse. 'The King's wrath grew,' he began, his sombre tone chilling Lehon's blood. 'He gestured unseelie insult at Lord Regor and the company

29

about fell silent. Yet the King laughed out loud into Lord Regor's face.'

''Twas provocation!' Regor protested. 'Honour forced me to unsheath the blade.'

'You fought the King?' Lehon started worriedly.

'Nay,' Hariss assured, 'I stepped between and bade them both desist.'

'Aye, and then was challenged in your turn!' Regor said scornfully and turned back to the mortal. 'Eider commanded us to fight on . . . set us up for the duel. Fighting cocks for the King's cruel pleasure!' He spat into the fire. 'Hariss will tell you what happened next.'

In the dreadful silence, Lehon looked to Hariss and the solemn-faced captain tore open his shirt. Lehon gasped as he beheld the deep red weal that marked Hariss's golden skin.

'Not until blood was let did Eider raise the cup of royal assent,' Hariss said coolly.

'How long before only death will suffice?' Regor shook his fist emphatically.

Lehon felt the warm blood drain from his face. 'Truly the bitter chill of dark days scrapes at the heart of Rhye,' he said quietly as they all fell silent and sought answer to secret sorrows within the rippling flames of the fire.

'Some terrible change has overcome our King,' Hariss muttered at last. 'Yet none can find its source.'

Lehon stroked his chin thoughtfully. ''Tis clear that fevered sleep has left a restlessness upon him.'

'Aye,' Regor shrugged, 'and some other thing.'

Lehon frowned into the elfin's face as he continued with his observations. 'The King would not have mirrors in his sight.'

'Ah, the mirrors,' Lehon exclaimed with realisation. 'I saw them cast out, set in a pile at the centre of the courtyard.' He looked to them both in puzzlement. 'They will be destroyed?'

Regor shook his head. 'The wizard sets all things right and talks with Eider even now upon the deed.' He drew closer to Lehon and whispered, 'As guardians of seelie lore we can have no part in the destruction of all that reflects light.'

Hariss frowned. 'Yet why should the King cover the glass?'

Regor shrugged. 'No one knows, but he insisted on it by both day and night.'

'The question is not why, but what does Eider see within?' Lehon pronounced with a wry look at the elfin.

'Something untoward,' Regor concluded with a sniff. 'Something that leads him into actions that are out of step!'

'And what of the spring-woke glade,' Hariss declared, changing the subject.

Lehon scratched his head, confused.

''Tis a place Eider beheld a distance off, one day upon the hunt,' Regor explained quickly.

'In all that frosty 'scape no other saw it, I swear,' Harris assured.

'There have been frosts?' Lehon cross-questioned the captain.

'Aye, yet no matter how cold, the King rides out daily in search of that woodland apparition. Its sight and sound haunts him still.'

'In truth he is exhausted,' Regor concluded. 'If he does not wander abroad in search of spring, he makes the challenge, if not with one of us, then with his own shadow!'

Hariss gave a short laugh, 'You do not know that is true.' He thought for a moment. 'Yet how soon before it is?' he finished wryly.

''Tis yet one more remnant of the fever-sleep,' the elfin ventured worriedly.

The mortal leaned closer. 'Do I understand you well, my friends?' he said quietly. 'You think there is a madness in him?'

Hariss gripped Lehon's arm. 'Be wary how you speak it, friend,' he warned.

Lehon looked into their concerned faces and knew there was both truth and treason in his words.

31

At that moment the dogs stirred from their dozing and the threesome watched as the animals whined and padded the rush floor towards the door. There they halted, listening intently, their large eyes fixed and distant.

The moon hung full and white, suffusing the courtyard with silver ghost light and inky shade. Beneath the arch of the outer doorway, Eider halted, his dark eyes meeting the moon's gentle face. He had draped the colours of the Cloak of Light close to his frame for warmth and had turned its jet black lining to the night sky. Glossy folds cascaded from his taut shoulders, concealing his form within the shadows. He breathed the chill air, and heard the winds moan and flurry about Rhye's towers. Silently he led Zephyr out across the moon-bleached stones of the courtyard and walked her on towards the gatehouse. In the half-light the watchman stirred and the King ordered him to leave the main gate and throw open the portal at its side. The man did as he was bid, silenced by the touch of his lips upon the seal of Eider's ring.

Thus did Rhye's King gallop away into the cruel night, Zephyr's ivory form flashing like lightning across the wind-blown earth, and as the.four winds buffeted the glass, Hariss turned back to the fire. 'Nothing stirs save the watchman at the gate,' he said, calling the dogs back to the hearth.

4

Morning mist hung upon the walls of the castle-town like a damp shroud, its fragile yet impenetrable gauze dripping from the stones and obscuring everything from sight. Hariss rubbed his frozen fingers, the leather of his tunic creaking as he pressed closer to the crenellated wall. How long the night's vigil had seemed, how like an age had been the hour before the rising of the sun. He watched the semi-circle of its watery disc cast a faint golden line across the horizon and prayed that its rising would bring a new warmth to the place.

Today, Rhye's lands needed just such a radiance. Today, the chancellors, lords and elders of the Seven Sees would convene within Rhye's hallowed halls and the foundation for Eider's dynasty would be set in time and place. Hariss's face beamed his inner joy, though his eyes smarted with the cold. He shook his head. This premature autumn would soon be harsh winter. He narrowed his eyes abruptly and scanned the shifting mists . . . was that movement he had glimpsed afar off? He watched on, the steadfast eyes recognising the swaying motion of a rider momentarily etched against the fog and then consumed by it.

Harris strained his ears, catching the fitful scrape of bridle and stirrup. In an instant the guard was alerted and soon Hariss and the gateman stood eager, yet wary, at the portal. Slowly, the mist gave up its imprisoned traveller as first the sturdy forelegs of a horse came into view, then the black-draped figure of a rider, stooped low and barely clinging to the equine neck. Hariss saw the pure white head of the mare and as she whinnied low in greeting he needed no further sign. 'The King!'

he cried, racing out to meet him. "Tis King Eider at the gate!'

The watchman hauled back the great iron bolts and the gates swung apart. Hariss was the first at Zephyr's side and grasping Eider's bedraggled form, he helped him from the saddle.

'Sire, you are frozen to the bone,' Hariss held him firm.

Eider's face was stiff with terror. 'That thing of fear did stalk me this long night past, pursued me to the very edge of daylight!' He clawed at the captain's arm. 'Friend, it was close. I felt the touch of its wet hand and thought myself lost.'

Hariss tried to reassure. 'Sire, you are safe within Rhye's walls and nought can harm you here.'

Eider's black eyes flickered bewilderment. 'And the bower . . . I saw its spring woke trees. I saw it clear.' He gasped as the bitter wind snatched his breath away.

'The night was heavy with frost. Come within, there is a chill upon you.' Hariss nodded to the farrier's boy, 'Quickly, we must get the King to warmth and the medic.'

At his words, Eider rallied and waved his hand dismissively. 'I am weary, nothing more. Tend my noble mare, she brought me safely back . . .'

The lad rushed to do as Eider had bid him and Hariss aided his King's tentative steps across the cobbled yard. 'Sire, 'twas a danger to be abroad on such a night,' he chided quietly.

'Get me to a fire,' Eider growled low reply. 'I freeze upon these ice-cold stones!'

Hariss led his King into the shadow of the portico, then up the deep cut stairs of the inner chambers and along the winding corridors of the east wing. Once within, their clothing steamed as frost crystals melted in the warm atmosphere. At the low door to the royal apartments they halted and Hariss turned the iron ring of the handle, yet as they pushed across the threshold, Eider raised a hand, forbidding the captain admittance.

Hariss bowed politely, feeling at once the full force of the draught as the door was slammed firmly shut in his face.

Pacing back the way he had come, Hariss saw the first shimmer of sunlight ripple across the latticed glass of the tall window. He leaned against its stone-arched frame to look outside and saw the cobblestones glisten as the sun's warmth melted the last remnants of frost. He saw too the gates now wide apart and, just beyond them, the bustle of activity. Rhye's folk had brought their stalls up early from the market-place in the hope of selling wares to the eminent entourage expected here this day, or else had come to sight the maidens to be presented at court.

From his vantage point, Hariss could see the joyful chaos as far as the main street and the castle-town gates; they too stood wide open and he glimpsed a mass of dark edge through their frame. It lingered within the great shadow of the keep and Hariss frowned, awaiting its progress into the town square. Soon it rumbled forward into the watery sunlight and he gave a sigh of relief, it was no more than a wagon, garish of colour and top heavy. The horse that pulled it was nought but skin and bone and the wagoner who led it was drab and draped, a wide-brimmed hat shading his face against the weather. Hariss's brow creased slightly. What strange contrast the man and his beast made against the gaudy cart which gleamed with tongues of red and orange flame painted bold across its timber sides. He watched the yellow trim, and the red and purple spindles of its wheels rotate; saw the blood-red canopy lurch from side to side as the wagon halted. In the blink of an eye the travellers' caravan and its occupants were besieged by intrigued townsfolk and Hariss's pulse raced with curiosity in his turn. Thus he left the window and ran the corridor's length down to the outer courtyard, there to view the strangers for himself.

Regor raised his cup in a silent toast and caught the eye

of Lehon who, seated at the farther end of the Hall, did likewise, their smiles appraising the beauty of the Monument Hall and of the Throne Room beyond. The place was bedecked in the colours of autumn bloom and leafage and the lights of myriad lanterns were reflected over and over again in the ornate wall mirrors. The crystal chandelier echoed their shimmer in its slender droplets and the glossy marble floor reflected a twin world in its sheen.

Along the row of balconies courtly ladies were seated, their gowns of taffeta glittered with sequins and gems in the burnished light and they fanned themselves as their attentive lords proffered sweet delicacies. Meanwhile, high in the musicians gallery the quartet plucked gently on finely tuned instruments and below, Harlequin danced with Columbine for the delight of the gathered courtiers.

When at last the high-pitched fanfare resounded from without, the dancers stopped their minuet, and all eyes turned from them to the grand staircase and then to the ivory and gold-leaf doors above. They dazzled as they swung apart and when the three most awaited personages filled their gape, the company below released one unified gasp of disbelief. They did not gasp at the sight of the Elder, the ancient stave of wisdom in his grip, and the pure white hair that cascaded down his rose-red gown. Nor did they gasp at the curl-haired Nairb, draped in the sacred robes of Horatious Thor, the fragile orb of seelie lore held firm within his grip. It was at sight of their King that they all gasped, for they could not believe their eyes. His breeches were of leather, his tunic of braided velvet and both were jackdaw black. The lining of his cape was vivid magenta and the knee-length riding boots were edged with silver studs. At his shoulder an ornate clasp held in its grip a cascade of peacock feathers which floated in vain display, framing Eider's head and face. Gone the long black tresses of youth, the shining silk of his hair was now cropped close to his head. Now the coal-black eyes lay deep set in the square face, and the fine scar of the hawk's claw was clearly drawn, stark and white across the sallow cheek.

The lightest touch on Lehon's shoulder made him start. It was Regor, now close at his side. "Tis all wrong!' the elfin fumed. 'Should not the King wear white to greet Rhye's lords and elders?'

Lehon could not recall, and frowned, returning his bewildered gaze to the unfolding scene.

The three eminent figures slowly descended the steps into the Hall and moved on towards the Throne Room and the Royal Seat. Lehon and Regor followed in the wake of the curious courtiers, and once within saw the majestic throne and the gleaming red eye of the royal phoenix high above. Page-boys scurried to ensconce their King within the marble throne, while Nairb gently placed the fragile sphere on a plinth next to the seat of All-Power. He took his place at the King's right hand, while the Elder of the Seventh See took his place at the left. With a slow and deliberate nod, the command was given for the ritual to commence.

So they poured in through the open doors of the Monument Hall, down the stairs and across the marble floor, on through the arch of the Throne Room doors and across the chequered tiles towards Rhye's throne. First came the Lord of the Sixth See and his Elder who brought forth exotic birds to adorn Rhye's palace and its gardens. The colourful entourage moved towards Eider as a tide of summer sunshine, their voluminous robes edged with gold. They presented him with the most beautiful of their hills and meadows, a maiden of twenty summers, draped in the daffodil yellow of her clan. Her chestnut hair was adorned with primroses, but though her beauty was alluring, she could not hold Eider's interest long and when the sudden fanfare announced the Lord of the Fifth See, the King's eyes were diverted.

Now green of every hue flooded the vast Hall and in the midst stood the Lord and his Elder in drapes of moss green. He laid tributes of healing herbs before the King as the aged Elder led forth a girl of fourteen summers. Her leaf-green dress crossed at her small breasts and her copper hair was braided and twined with celandines. But though her smile captivated him and drew forth smiles from his lips, Eider's dark eyes lowered, and with a curtsey she was led away.

The ancient Elder looked to the sombre-faced King. Which of these would His Majesty choose? But Eider shook his head discreetly and the stave was lowered, thus signalling the resumption of the presentation.

At the door of the Hall stood the dark blue uniforms of the Lord of the Fourth See and his two sons. They carried fruit and wine as tribute from their lands, and from their midst the Elder brought forth their chosen maid. Her chiffon gown was of every shade of blue and wafted on the warm air, casting sweet perfume where she walked. Her brown hair held a coronet of silver interlaced with forget-me-nots and Eider's gaze never left her as she drew close. Rhye's Elder turned to him. Would His Majesty now make his choice? But Eider only stifled a yawn and bid the ritual continue.

Now through the open doors a cascade of mauve and purple burst forth as the Lord of the Third See led two maidens to stand before the King. The two were twins and so alike that Eider spent long moments comparing the beauty of one with the other. His heart raced at their uncanny sameness, their auburn hair, the intricate weave of their silks of mauve. They laid before him bowers of lavender and the scent delighted him, yet at that moment a flurry of pink and pale blue drew his attention back to the doorway and he watched as the Lord of the Second See made entrance with his clan. They bore bolts of silk and bright feathers to please their King, while their Elder presented him with their chosen one. The sky blue of her eyes reflected Rhye's splendour of glass and gold, and the finely stitched velvet of her robes was the colour of fuschias. She lay a posy of violets upon the cushion of his footstool and Eider marvelled at their fragile beauty. Nevertheless, his interest waned and with a nod of thanks he turned away.

Lord Gaunt of the First See and his Elder moved forward, draped in silk of tangerine and red, the heraldic colours of their clan. With offerings of wheat and corn they proudly bid King Eider look upon the fairest of their lands. The maid was seventeen, her hair of fine spun gold and her eyes, clear grey, held Eider's for long moments. Yet his gaze finally flickered and he bade the maiden take her place among the rest. He scanned the Hall awaiting more, but alas, all had been presented and his heart grew heavy. He looked again upon the shimmering colours of the spectrum displayed for his delight in a profusion of silks and velvets, flowers and ornaments, tributes and decorations, and sighed wearily.

Rhye's Elder turned to look at him: the King had now to make his choice. Eider could only shake his head finding himself unable to speak. As the Elder turned back to the expectant gathering the anxious-faced wizard drew close to his King.

'What troubles your Majesty?' Nairb coaxed.

Eider looked into the confused faces of the seven Elders, then into the placid face of Nairb. 'I cannot decide,' he confided at last.

'No need for haste,' Nairb said calmly. He beckoned Rhye's Elder to him. 'The King is quite amazed at the beauty of Rhye's maidens and bids the court wait on his decision. Meanwhile, let the musicians play and the gathering take its ease.'

So they led the courtly dance in strict formation: the lords and ladies of the seelie line of Eyre, their handsome sons and beautiful daughters; the young gallants of the royal guard and the stout advisers to the court with their wives. In their wake, and with a keen eye on decorum, the guests followed on: the lords and ladies of Rhye's Six Sees, their rugged sons and dutiful daughters, their upright captains and lieutenants, their staunch advisers and their rounded wives.

With heavy eyes, the King watched all pass by as first

Rhye's Elder then the wizard tried to rally his spirits. But even when the chosen maidens danced before him to the lilting notes of the mandolin, he made no stir, he did not even smile.

'Sire,' pleaded Nairb at last, 'what is it ails you so?'

''Tis a farce,' Eider scowled and waved his hand dismissively. 'I can choose none of these.'

'But choose you must, my King,' said the Elder. ''Tis written.'

'Written?' Eider glared at him. 'Where is it written?'

'Why Sire, in the Book,' the Elder replied, as if the King knew and had no need to question.

Eider sneered and turned his attention to the stairs and the heavy doors which had now swung open. Nairb heard his sudden gasp and turned to focus on the doorway, seeing in its gape a berobed figure, chestnut hair cascading about the contours of a white mask. The wizard's heart froze in his chest and he could not move to prevent Eider from leaping to his feet, sword drawn.

Regor clasped Lehon's arm as he watched the King push through the dancing crowd. 'Who becomes Eider's target now?' he frowned, rising to his feet, sword-hilt grasped firmly in his fist. Lehon followed the elfin as he edged round the nervous crowd towards the staircase, and the cause of Eider's sudden anger.

'Lord Regor,' asked one pale adviser, 'what threat befalls us?'

'What is the King thinking of?' another asked discreetly.

'Is he drunk?' he heard another whisper.

'No, he is mad!' leered a red-faced serving wench.

Regor tightened with annoyance and his glare sent the girl scurrying back to the kitchen as the elfin lord paced on in Eider's wake.

'Hold!' he heard the King cry above the dwindling music. Eider had confronted the masked stranger at the bottom of the staircase and now held him at sword point. 'So, Bloodseed, you come at last?' His sword toyed only inches from the stranger's heart. 'Defend yourself,

Ruthra, for none here will fall for your deceit,' he growled.

The stranger said nothing and nearby courtiers pressed themselves against the ornate walls, well out of harm's way.

'Sire . . .' the muffled voice protested but Eider prepared the blade and whipped its lethal steel through the air about the stranger's form, severing a lock of chestnut hair either side of the mask. As the silken hair fell to the floor, the stranger backed away, knowing his life was next to be forfeited. Clearly provoked, Eider pressed in upon him, eager for blood.

'Stop! Stop at once! Sire, I beg you!' The voice of reason met Eider's ears as Lord Gaunt came forward to intervene, followed by a higher pitched voice mingled with tears and sobs.

'Oh mercy, Sire, 'tis Evan my third son! 'Tis Evan come to give you greeting.' The lady of the Third See ran towards them, yet was halted by her husband, Lord Constante.

'Beg him not, wife. 'Tis an insult on our house.'

Eider fumed at them and turned to where their trembling son stood, his back against the slammed door, the white mask hanging limply in his hand.

'The King is mad,' Regor heard someone whisper.

'Quite insane,' he heard a second comment. The elfin's heart raced as he moved towards Eider who now stood before all transfixed by shock and remorse.

'Lord Constante,' Regor said, taking command of the situation, 'there is no insult here, other than that brought upon the King by your son.'

The courtiers murmured as the elfin lord continued in Eider's defence, 'The King gave decree that no masks be worn upon this day.'

The Lord of the Third See drew back and with a low bow he addressed apology to his monarch. 'Sire, Evan has travelled far to be here and knew nought of the ban.'

Suddenly Eider rallied. 'If he knew or not, the insult

remains and your son being a gentleman shall buy back the honour of your house in duel.' His eyes were bright with anger.

Regor turned on Eider, his mouth agape, yet before he could speak the wizard had made his way to the King's side and had gestured to the elfin to be silent.

'Sire,' Nairb suggested softly, ''twould be wise to forgive so small a misdemeanour.'

'Would it, indeed?' Eider snarled, slashing at thin air with the blade. Nairb's calm hazel eyes never left his and despite Eider's menacing sword display, the wizard never flinched. Eider glared his defiance and turned from him to rivet Evan with the deadly glare of the hunter.

At that moment, the trumpeters' shrill harmonies filled the Hall and with the entry of two royal guards, the King, his wizard and all at court moved aside to grant admittance. It was then with silent bows that the Lord of the Third See withdrew from confrontation, then that Regor and Lehon closed ranks in protection of their King.

— 5 —

At the door there stood a dark and strong-limbed man. His drapes were of black satin, edged with the deepest purple. His long white hair and beard were streaked with woodland green, and in his grip he held a gleaming staff of thorn. The court drew back as his glittering eyes met the King's, for this was the Maquis Caulide, he, the poorest, most vindictive of seelie lords upon whom no one ever called. He, the lord of hedgerows and wastes, whose briar borders flanked Rhye's lands; he, the Elder of the Edge, of the twilight Halls of Driad, and the dusky line of Calabash.

Eider frowned at recognition of his unwanted guest, for talk of this sombre lord and his wanton tribe had filled many a night at the banquet table. For though the much maligned Maquis had never erred too far from seelie ways, none could say he never would.

'The Maquis Caulide brings greetings from his Halls and tributes from his people.' The loud voice boomed across the silent expanse.

Eider nodded royal recognition of his presence and flanked by Regor and Lehon he went back to the throne and took his seat.

The Seventh Elder turned calm eyes upon the uninvited guest. 'Rhye's King accepts your greetings and your gifts. Pray, enter Maquis and take your ease.'

Eider and all his gathered court watched the brusque Maquis clap his gloved hands, and as he descended the marble stairs into the Hall, a crowd of autumn-clad attendants poured after him. The first of them bore baskets of wild fruits, herbs and nuts, others scattered the smooth floor with bracken and wild flowers.

'Weeds?' the courtiers whispered one to another, but

43

the stern-faced Maquis passed close by and no more was said.

Eider graciously accepted all that was set before him until at last the Maquis raised his staff of thorn. 'Now, the greatest gift of all!' he declared, in a voice that could summon storm. 'The most beautiful of all Rhye's maidens I give to you. My daughter, Baobhanshee.'

At his words, boy attendants flooded into the Hall carrying Baobhanshee upon a heather draped litter. The company gasped as one when they beheld her, for her curious beauty was a sight uncommon in Rhye's halls. Her robes were of black velvet overlaid with mauve gauze and given shape by bells and clasps of silver, while her wrists, neck and fingers too were ringed with silver ornament. Small of stature, she was fine-boned, with high cheekbones and a petulant mouth. Her lips and nails were painted mulberry and her ink-black eyes glittered, reflecting the glowing lanterns of the Hall. Her skin was of the tincture of olives and her long black hair flowed to the hem of her robes and bore streaks of mauve from widow's peak to the very ends. Her pointed ears matched her small, pointed teeth and she cast Eider a wanton smile as she rose from her litter.

Eider was captivated. He glimpsed her small feet and heard the chime of countless tiny bells which were clasped about her ankles. His ears tingled with their magic sound and his eyes were dazzled by her strange allure. He saw in her wild beauty the enchantment of woodland and forest, and felt his heart race in his breast. Unable to avert his eyes from her penetrating gaze, he watched her approach and as she stood before the throne her father, the Maquis, flanked her with his satin cloak.

'Sire,' the Maquis bowed. 'She is called Baobhanshee, yet call her Shee for 'tis the sound of the wild wind through the trees and will always remind her of her home.'

Eider's skin grew ice-cold as he looked into the menacing face of the Maquis, then as he turned his eyes back to Baobhanshee he smiled and his heart smouldered with fiery desire.

Knowing his task completed, the Maquis stepped aside and cast dark glances at the assembled maidens who had gathered together in whispers, their fair cheeks flushed with anger, their rose-coloured mouths turned down in distaste at Baobhanshee's presence.

Eider watched her thin lips part as she proffered him the silver cup held in her palms. She made not a sound and Eider smiled as he spoke her name. 'Is this the tribute, Shee?' he asked.

She nodded and he looked into the vessel, seeing his own dark eyes gazing back from the tiny pool of pure dew held therein. 'Why, 'tis beautiful,' he said tenderly, and as he spoke Baobhanshee raised the cup above her head. Eider laughed at her sport and watched as she tilted the cup, but as the water cascaded from the rim he drew back, momentarily offended by the prank. The contents, however, did not fall as splashing liquid, but bounced down the marble steps as a shower of diamonds. Eider laughed aloud at her magic and Baobhanshee giggled her delight at his pleasure.

Soon their mirth had set the entire court alive with laughter as they tried to help their King retrieve the scattered gems and return them to the safety of the cup. While they were thus preoccupied Baobhanshee's laughter ceased, and mesmerised, she padded to where the sacred orb of pure crystal stood in reverence on its plinth beside the throne. The intensity of Baobhanshee's gaze raised the sphere aloft and none saw it hover to the bowl of her outstretched hands as she carried it towards Eider. She held the sphere above her head and with a high-pitched laugh declared, 'A million more bright gems be yours, my King!'

A terrible silence swept the Hall and Eider looked up to see the crystal orb levitating within Baobhanshee's palms and held high above her head. She took a breath, her lips pursed with determination, but with one deft

45

step the wizard seized the orb and clasped it safely to his breast.

'The Gods be praised,' the Seventh Elder shuddered, though the tragedy had been averted.

As he retrieved the sphere, Nairb saw Baobhanshee's berry-black eyes flash, saw her bare her pointed teeth and as he felt the blood drain from his veins, he knew her look to be a threat. He turned panic-stricken eyes upon the King, but Eider was enthralled and had seen nothing of her spite.

'Sire, beware,' Nairb gave quiet warning.

Before he had uttered the words, Baobhanshee began to cry and the tears that ran down her cheeks were black. The Elder gasped, but Eider drew her to him to comfort her. 'The innocent sought only to please me, nothing more.' As he took her in his arms, he turned to the Seventh Elder, his face lined with resolve. 'This one I choose . . . Baobhanshee for my bride!'

At his words the court erupted in a tirade of anger, the lords of every See cursed beneath their breath and their maidens wept a sea of bitter tears.

Rhye's Elders paced towards the throne. ''Tis witchcraft!' they adjudged. 'She is evil, a wanton and a meddler!' they agreed. 'Nought but the unseelie plays with the sacred sphere as if it were a bauble,' they decided.

'Silence!' Eider cried, halting their approach and casting an implacable look at the Seventh Elder. 'Fetch me the Cup, the Bell and the Book, the Candle and the Rings. This night I take my mate!'

At the King's words the trumpets filled the Hall with their noise, drowning out the sound of tears and dispute as Eider moved away towards the royal apartments to prepare.

His task complete, the Maquis wrapped his cloak about and drew his entourage to him, while in the chaos Regor and Lehon flanked the wizard and the holy orb, protecting seelie lore from further unruly tampering.

So the ceremonial artefacts were brought and the velvet-coloured table set with all, as Rhye's court and every invited guest gathered to witness the nuptual rites. Some were prudent and agreed with their King's choice, while others hoped against hope that somehow the Elders could change his mind. In their midst, Regor and Lehon looked on, careful of their uninvited guest, the Maquis, shaking their heads at his daring and the mischief of his wild offspring. Meanwhile, Nairb and the Seventh Elder paced the marble floor, the wise men admonishing them to persuade the King against what was certain folly.

"Tis too late!' Nairb insisted into their wrinkled faces. 'Eider shall have his chosen. Both heart and mind are set on her.'

'Pah!' the Seventh Elder glared. 'If 'tis so then she must be watched by night and day lest her meddling lead Eider astray from Triad lore.'

'The goodness of his heart shall prevail,' Nairb declared calmly. 'Trust. Have faith in him, as do the Gods.'

The Seventh Elder threw up his hands in despair and led his six brethren to their alcove behind the throne. Nairb watched them go, then catching the eye of the elfin, he nodded and together with Lehon they drew aside, but their whisperings were lost in the cacophony of sound as musicians greeted the entrance of the King.

As he moved from the door of the royal apartments, Eider held out his hand to Baobhanshee. The Maquis bid her go to him and as she stepped forth, low whispering spread round the Hall.

'She can be no match for him! A hedgerow wanton? A meddler?'

Regor nudged the mortal. 'Eider brings calamity to Rhye's Halls in this deed!' he scowled.

Lord Gaunt who stood close by, turned patient eyes upon them. 'There is yet the Cup,' he whispered, nodding towards the Seventh Elder and the table set before him. 'The girl must first pass that test.'

Lehon frowned, not understanding the meaning.

'If her heart be not true, she cannot be Rhye's Queen,' the aged Lord explained.

'But how may the Cup help?' Lehon quizzed.

'They must partake of it and no drop be spilt in the drinking,' Lord Gaunt gave reply.

'Yet she held the sacred orb, and could not the strangeness of her power also control the Cup?' Regor asked worriedly.

Gaunt was adamant. 'Nay, elfin. The sphere was not in use and so its force was weakened. The Cup of Truth can never be ill-used.'

'Still, be wary, I say,' Regor concluded uneasily and Lehon silently agreed, clutching their sword-hilts as they watched Baobhanshee take Eider's hand in her own.

Together the couple moved towards the Seventh Elder who spread out his arms to encompass the round table, its velvet coverlet spread with the fruits and flowers of Baobhanshee's clan. At its centre the Cup of Truth stood full to the brim, there too the Bell of Knowledge, the white Candle of Purity and the great Book of Seelie Lore. Upon its glossy black cover lay the three sacred Rings, the first of ebony, the second of ivory and the third of gold.

As they drew close to the table, the Elder lit the Candle and rang the Bell. Baobhanshee's eyes flashed at its sound and as the Elder raised the Cup, Eider guided her to her knees upon the cushioned floor. The gathered company watched intently as the Elder raised the Candle. 'Purity be yours,' he said as he passed the slender white taper to the King. As Baobhanshee took it from Eider's grasp the fragile flame flickered wildly and the courtiers held their breath awaiting her failure. But the flame did not die, and Eider smiled into Shee's happy face as the Elder returned the Candle to the table's centre. Likewise, he gave to Eider the Bell. 'Ring the bell, so all may hear the sound of your truthful heart,' he commanded. Eider did as he was bid with the certainty of faith in the lore and Baobhanshee delighted in the sound it made. Taking it from him, she made its clear chimes echo throughout the Hall and pouted, displeased, when Eider directed her to give it back to the Elder.

Now the Elder stood before them with the gold Cup and though the ruby wine lapped at its edge, its contents never left the bowl. 'Raise the Cup and spill no drop, lest the drum of life do stop!' he decreed. Eider took the vessel from him, steady of hand and eye. Carefully, he sipped from its contents and proffered it to the waiting Baobhanshee.

The hushed crowd watched on, keen-eyed, waiting for the tell-tale droplet on mouth or gown, the droplet that would betray the impure heart. Baobhanshee drank from the Cup, unshaken, and the two passed the golden chalice between them, again and again, until the sweet brew was gone.

As the Cup was returned to the Elder, the courtiers clapped their hands, though this, their ritual acceptance of Baobhanshee, was cool and half hearted. The Elder turned, beckoning the wizard to bring forth the heavy Book of the Lore and the three Rings resting upon its smooth sheen. Nairb bowed reverently and carried the black bound volume to where the King and his bride knelt. He looked to Eider whose dark eyes were wide with joy, and then to Baobhanshee whose olive cheeks were rose-blushed in the heat. Yet as the Elder spoke his words of seelie blessing, Nairb's heart leapt, for he saw a tiny red droplet trickle down Baobhanshee's breast. He gasped for air, his lungs drum-tight but could do nought but watch it vanish into the shadowed valley of her cleavage. Nairb faltered, unable to believe his eyes, unable to cry out.

The Elder's voice droned on in the distance as the wizard tried in vain to rally, to cry out, to stop the ritual, to protest, but not one sound escaped his dry lips. He struggled against the silence he knew to be imposed on him by some strange spell, yet could do nought but watch the ebony ring placed on the little finger of Eider's left hand, and after it, the ring of ivory placed on the same finger of his right. He saw the gold ring taken up, and panic-stricken gasped anew for the air needed to cry out, but the glint of Baobhanshee's berry-black eye silenced him, and he could neither move nor speak as the golden band was placed on Baobhanshee's finger.

'Eider, my King,' Nairb's voice was barely audible as the trumpeters drowned his desperate plea and Baobhanshee took Eider in her immovable embrace. Over his shoulder, her stone-faced glare met the wizard's look of loss, and as her tiny teeth flashed in triumph, the wizard slumped in a state of collapse. Oblivious, the Elder gave the signal and Eider raised his bride from the cushion. Now the elders of the Seven Sees chanted their ancient blessings on the pair and in the midst of singing and prayers, flowers and incense, Regor and Lehon struggled to help the white-faced wizard to the open window.

'Stop the ritual. Hold the King from folly!' Nairb pleaded breathlessly into the elfin's confused face.

'Friend, we cannot,' Lehon mouthed against the cacophony of trumpets and bells.

''Tis done. The King is wed!' Regor shouted into the waxen face.

The clocks in the Hall and upon Rhye's tower chimed twelve and all three looked helplessly to where the Elder took his place at head of the royal procession. To the sound of fanfares and the noisy tolling of bells, the wedding party set forth and with slow and regal pace it wound its way to the royal apartments and the bed-chamber prepared for the marriage rites. There, from midnight to midday Eider and his bride would consummate their marriage, there too, the elders of the Seven Sees, their lanterns shining bright, would keep their vigil, to witness all as Ancient Lore decreed.

─── 6 ───

There were those who said that they had glimpsed him on lonely coastal roads, others who swore he had chased them along woodland pathways, reviling them in a voice thick with scorn. Wilful offspring were frighted with stories of him, thereafter to haunt the sleep of innocence. Yet what were tales and what was true blurred over the years in the telling; but when his name was mentioned it was always in whispers and always drew forth fear and superstition alike.

This was the day for the telling of tales and gossip, a day that played host to newcomers drawn to the castle-town by the King's impending union, and attracted by the air of liberality fostered since his joyful accession. Ale flowed as freely as coins on the card tables, and the streets and alleyways were crowded with people meandering in lazy rhythm towards tavern and fair. There were rich pickings for quick and skilful fingers and in the long shadows between the dwellings, a group of street children huddled about a spike-haired youth as he divided the spoils of their morning's work.

When first they heard the eerie notes of discord on the air none stirred to look, until the conflict of sounds grew too loud and shrill upon the ear. Soon, in the half-light the perpetrator of disharmony materialised. Small of stature he was, swathed in hessian robes that once had been deepest purple but which time had faded to a mottled weave of violet hues. The pale skin stretched tight over his protruding bones was sign of an ascetic life, whilst the bowed head emphasised the large cranium, covered in coarse grey stubble. His slender and bloodless fingers ran the length of a reed pipe and dissonant notes issued forth.

The urchins eyed him and then each other, their solemn faces breaking into smug grins at the thought of a moment's sport and easy pickings. The nod was given and the spike-haired youth rushed headlong at the stranger, wheeling him about until he was giddy. Then the nimble fingers snatched at the worthless pipe, and stole it from its unsuspecting owner. The thief brandished it aloft with a shout of triumph but it was a moment short-lived and one to be regretted. No sooner had the crime been committed than the gaunt stranger fastened the lad within the extended folds of his robes, muffling his cries for help in slow suffocation. The boy's companions fled.

When at last the hessian shroud was unravelled the boy fell to his knees, faint with terror and lack of air. The rush of blood to his face brought with it the sense of renewed panic as the lad looked up into wide and penetrating eyes. They were the blue of robin's eggs and when he met their intense gaze it was as if he were drawn into a fathomless sky. Though his throat was dry, the boy released a hoarse scream and the stranger thrust his face towards him.

At the centre of the creased forehead a mystic sign was traced, a third eye. Its kohl-lined lid swept from one corner to its opposite and finished in an elegant plume and within the fine-etched socket a circle of silver encased the iris. As the pipe was retrieved from the boy's grip, the eye fixed the lad with a nightmare intensity. In that moment the youth glimpsed the mangled hands, they bore but three fingers on each and he gasped, knowing the stranger's identity for sure. Suddenly the lad was fleeing the alleyway and as the shrill notes of the pipe drifted on in pursuit, he gave voice to his realisation:

'Be gone! 'Tis Mad Darius – 'tis the Ranter!'

The allegation was damning enough for the ale-fired townsfolk to seize the stranger and proclaim him the cause of every malady, the fount of every stroke of ill luck. There were calls for a flogging or his speedy dispatch, but those who clung to sobriety and reason said it was for the King to decide the Ranter's fate, lest some ill-considered act bring unseelie calamity down on them all. It was thus agreed that the King would make the judgement.

Eider's step was marked by agitation as he paced the stone corridors and took the steps down to the courtyard. As the great doors opened so the noise of the crowd greeted him, yet as he went out into the glaring light of mid-morn the townsfolk who had swept within, unheeding of the protesting gateman, retreated and bowed their heads in respect of their monarch.

Eider beckoned to the captain of the guard. 'What commotion calls me from my bed?' he complained in whispers.

The captain bowed, 'Sire, the townsfolk seek judgement in some matter.'

Eider stiffened with anger. 'I am abed with Rhye's new queen and you disturb me thus?'

The captain fidgeted. 'Majesty, they say they bring a demon before you. A threat to Triad Lore.'

Eider flinched at the word. 'Demon?' he raised a nervous brow. Turning to the crowd he demanded, 'Where is this demon?'

As the Ranter was manhandled forward, he wrenched himself free of his captors and turned on them, wielding his pipe as a lethal blade, his robes swirling about him as he spun in frenzied dance. Shrieks resounded as the crowd scattered and the royal guards moved in to protect their King.

''Tis one in league with Dark!' a drunken voice shouted as soldiers closed in on the stranger.

As Eider took one tentative step towards him, the Ranter's blue eyes grew brighter and as the King circled him, Darius leered menacingly. Eider stepped back, noting the emaciated form and threadbare robes, the staring eyes and the mystic sign drawn at the centre of the wide forehead. At the sight of it he faltered, then, seeking to recover himself, waved a dismissive hand. 'You are all too full of ale. This is no demon only some old fool who frightens with his countenance,' he said brusquely and turned to the guards. 'Bid the Elders hear the accusation, then deal with him.'

'Sire, 'tis you should judge him!' came an adamant cry. ''Twas his unseelie hand left my Jonty lame!'

'Aye . . . and he brought Abel's babe a twisted foot!' shouted another.

All at once the crowd jostled forward eager to air their fears.

'His curses frighted my calving herd and saw three dead born!' one landsman accused.

'Caro, the blacksmith, be dumbstruck and taken wi' fits these two nights past!' another cried.

'Hold!' Eider raised his hands against their clamour. 'You blame this man for all your ills?'

Dunsan, the thatcher, ventured to speak. 'Sire, I am an honest man,' he said, removing his hat and bowing reverently. 'Yet I tell you 'tis no normal soul before you 'ere.' As he spoke the stranger wheeled about and fixed the good man with his penetrating gaze. Dunsan fell silent and shrank back.

Eider waved the guards aside. 'Not normal?' he quizzed, viewing the stranger as some rare exhibit. He looked closer at the gaunt face and his voice dropped to a whisper. 'What do you call yourself?'

The stranger stared back with a look of mountain cold. 'Truth,' he answered in an unworldly tone. Eider drew away from him, unnerved.

'Majesty, be wary,' Dunsan advised him softly. 'For 'tis Mad Darius – the Ranter he be!'

The spoken title stretched taut every nerve in Eider's body. 'Ranter?' he repeated mechanically, then as if woken from trance, he turned on the stranger. 'A madman?'

Darius looked at him with narrow eyes. 'Are we not both mad?' he challenged.

The crowd fell silent at the Ranter's calm reply.

54

Eider pointed an emphatic forefinger. 'Have a care, Darius, your words may cost you dear!'

The piercing blue eyes did not waver as Darius raised the pipe to his lips and trilled a melody. A melody as old as the ages, though none could hum it. Familiar as a minstrel's song, yet none could recall the words, and though Eider looked upon its player for the first time, he knew him well from times past, from tales . . . from sleep?

'What brings you here?' he demanded, seeking to put name to a half-remembered moment.

The Ranter took the stem of the pipe from his lips. 'I bring answers to the dreams that haunt you,' he said, adding quietly. 'I know well the fear that stalks you.' Now whispers erupted from the waiting crowd for at his words the King's face grew pale.

Had this Ranter knowledge of the Feared Thing that dwelt often at Eider's shoulder? Or was he no more than a madman whose random speech gave meaning to a chaotic mind? Eider masked his agitation with a broad grin. 'So, Darius, you are a Seer?' he baited.

The Ranter took his pipe and pointed to the mystic sign traced on his forehead, ''Tis the Eye of All-Knowing . . . it sees what you cannot.'

Eider measured his words. 'And of course you would tell all for silver?' The grin faded to a sneer.

The Ranter was impassive. ''Tis my fate to tell, and yours to listen.'

Eider was clearly angered by the response. 'You issue your King with a command?' he snapped.

The Ranter's slender fingers slid back and forth along the silent pipe as if in time to some imagined melody. ''Tis no command,' his voice was steady, ''tis prophecy.'

The word 'prophecy' sobered many and unnerved all present, for tales of Darius abounded with his visions. Visions of things to come, and with them the certainty of their coming to pass.

Eider smiled though his voice betrayed concern. 'That

the King of Rhye should believe the ramblings of a madman?'

The Ranter was implacable. 'Believe or not, 'tis your fate I speak.'

Eider snatched his hand into a fist and shook it at Darius. 'Insolent dog, you speak thus to the wielder of Triad Lore? The chosen one? I who freed Rhye from eternal Dark?'

'And will return it thus,' the Ranter finished.

Eider bared his teeth. 'Were you not mad, I would have you flogged for the insult!' he warned.

The Ranter shook his head adamantly. ''Tis no insult, but true vision!'

Eider snarled. 'A visionary?' he flourished an impatient hand. 'Friend Darius, you are yourself a vision,' he provoked, and as those gathered laughed at his jest he added sarcastically, 'of ugliness and villainy!' The ensuing laughter grew louder still and Eider delighted in the power of ridicule. He pressed a hand upon the Ranter's bony shoulder. 'Pray, Seer, tell us this vision, that we may all prepare for its arrival.'

The Ranter gazed hard into the dark eyes. ''Tis a vision meant for no one but yourself,' he said solemnly.

The comment twisted Eider's heart and his mouth twitched as he attempted bravado. 'Then truly I am blessed by the Gods!' he cried to the watching crowd of guards and townsfolk. But laughter ceased abruptly as the Ranter spoke on oblivious of their amusement.

'Dark times will pass for all,' he said, scanning every face in the crowd. He turned back to Eider. 'Soon these folk will shun you as the fount of all strife.'

Eider gave a cursory laugh. 'The people pledge allegiance to the Triad wielder, for nought can taint him or his realm.'

The Ranter traced his own jawline with the pipe. 'That protected by ivory shall claim bloody victory!'

With that pronouncement Eider's face drained of colour, he trembled visibly and his heart raced. In his mind's eye he saw again the cold unremitting cruelty of

Ruthra's mask, felt the suffocating heat of his demon presence. He cried out, 'Never!' and snatched at the Ranter's robes. He shook the man violently. 'I shall defy Fate, and so shall my offspring!'

The Ranter gazed immovably into the frightened black eyes. 'You shall have no issue in this realm,' he said, seeing the King's face tremble as one caught in a spasm of fever or sudden pain. 'And Fate,' Darius continued, 'will leave its laughter lines upon your ageing face!'

The anger in Eider erupted and he struck the Ranter hard across the face. 'Be damned!' he swore, the sudden blow knocking Darius to the ground. 'Rhye's King defies the vision of a canting prophet, and strikes the first blow against unkind Fate!'

The Ranter raised a hand to staunch the bloody trickle from his mouth. 'No King can match the hand of Fate,' he spoke it clear. 'For 'tis close! And soon 'twill strike your tower.'

One of the crowd sprang forward to aim a hefty kick at Darius, and fired by the action his fellows fell in upon the helpless man. They spat on him and kicked him, calling for an end to him there and then. Eider watched their cruelties impassively until at last his anxious captain drew close. 'Majesty,' he urged, 'surely we cannot allow . . . ?'

Eider's hesitation seemed endless but then, as if brought back suddenly to the reality of the situation, he signalled the guards to break up the fray. As the crowd was dispersed Eider looked again upon the Ranter. The bloody face stared back at him in cool defiance as Darius held the pipe in his bruised hands and blew upon it. The chaos of sound that poured forth set the town's dogs howling, cracked the window glass and pained the senses, for these were unseelie sounds, sounds that frighted babes and men alike.

Eider clapped his hands to his ears. 'Get him gone!' he cried, and watched on as the Ranter was dragged from the clutches of the crowd. Eider glared into the captain's face. 'See the old fool far beyond the gates,' he said, but then his mouth narrowed in spite. 'Be sure he remembers never to pass this way again!' The command given, Eider turned on his heels, the shrill notes of disharmony still ringing in his ears. They were to stay with him in the long days to come.

That evening before the tall window Baobhanshee was absorbed in the task of combing her raven hair. In the haloed light of a dozen flickering candles, her olive skin glistened like a spring woken leaf and her long tresses shone smooth and glossy black. Within the window's reflection she watched in secret as Eider paced the length of the chamber like a man possessed. When at last he paused to down the contents of his goblet, Baobhanshee followed him, marking his footfall so perfectly that he released a gasp of surprise when her slim hands slid from behind to blindfold him. Eider clasped her wrists and turned to meet the childlike gaze, a weary smile etching his pale face. She looked up at him and her wild black eyes consumed him like some potent brew.

Eider pressed the inside of her wrists to his lips. 'Forgive me, lady,' he whispered, folding his arms about her to hold her close. 'All is change, and I am out of step with time.' He shook his head in self-reprimand.

That his thoughts were not of her displeased Baobhanshee and she pouted. She snatched up a lock of Eider's hair in her tiny fist and twisted it cruelly. Soon, before the blazing hearth, Baobhanshee soothed his sorrow with waves of soft kisses, healed his torment with the ecstacy of her passions, and for a while it was enough and he slept.

He slept a sleep so dark and deep that he dreamt he would wake no more. Too soon the reedy warble of the Ranter's pipe drifted to him from the recesses of the unconscious and the madman's prophecy echoed on and on. And in his dream, Eider saw a terrible thing of Dark, a wedge of blackness that moved towards him, growing in dimension until it engulfed him and he woke in sweat-drenched terror.

In the grate the sunken coals flickered like molten jewels and Baobhanshee cradled him in her arms as he retold his incoherent dream. She listened in silence, watched him tremble with every moment relived, saw him raise his hand as a claw in vivid depiction of his fear.

Baobhanshee pressed her cold fingers to his brow to staunch the flow of visions. He rallied against the nightmare of his imagination. Here all was safe, protected by Triad power, protected from every vestige of unseelie force, and as Baobhanshee wrapped her legs about him, Eider moved into her, desperate for the sleep of spent desire to erase his dark terror, desperate for the dawn to break.

—— 7 ——

Morning announced itself with Regor's jaunty step as he
entered the ante-chamber with news that all was ready
for the Hunt and that the company waited on the King's
arrival.

Hoar-frost coated the hedgerows as they rode out,
Eider seated straight-backed upon the white mare,
Hariss and Lehon flanking him. Ahead, Regor and the
huntsmen cantered on into the mist, their lean-limbed
hounds scattering rotten leaves in their wake.

Eider saw his breath spiral white against the dank air.
He marvelled at the red sun rising in a blazing arc against
the horizon, yet could feel no warmth upon his face.
Now the burnished colours of autumn sank to sombre
brown, and thorns wrapped their barbs about blackened
boughs. Eider inhaled the musky scent of earth and the
frost-laced air. How he mourned the loss of colour from
the landscape, how he longed to draw back winter's
heavy veil and seed new life.

Soon the fiery orb of the sun was high in the sky, its
meagre fire slowly eating away the ice-chill and dappling
the contours watery gold and sepia. Patiently, the company moved on, from coarse cropped meadow to gorse-
clad heath, the horses snorting in the midday warmth.
Soon Hartsmere was in sight, deep and sapphire blue,
a still pool where wild fowl built their nests among the
reeds at its edge and a solitary willow hung its tresses in
sorrow. There was a sense of deep melancholy about
this place, and as Eider breathed in the moorland perfumes, he watched the shimmering water dance with a
myriad ripples as the sudden draught skimmed its surface. He inclined his head quizzically, for with the breeze
came a sound more pleasant to the senses than sight or

scent. The purity of the music made his heart leap and turning in the saddle he halted the company and gestured towards the mere, smooth as glass beneath the winter sky.

'Mark you!' Eider bid them. 'Listen well. There comes the sweetest melody upon the air.'

The company listened as they were bid, yet heard no sound save the lap of water and the stirrings of the fitful breeze.

Eider scanned the landscape, seeking out the origin of the enchanting refrain. ''Tis a flute!' he insisted, adding in a voice laced with sudden awe, 'its pitch and melody more beautiful than the lark!'

The huntsmen gazed at him perplexed and Regor turned away, embarrassed.

At length Eider shook his head, the flutesong lost to the ebbing winds. 'You heard it not?' he asked of them.

'Nay, Sire. We heard nought but wind and waterflow,' they all agreed, each looking to the other in concealed mirth at their King's strange mood.

As the party trotted on towards the pool, Eider's gaze was drawn beyond the waterline to where a wedge of shadow seemed to recede then sparkle with the sudden motion of the wind. He stood in the stirrups, yes, those were trees that he beheld, their tossing boughs beckoning to him until all at once he could smell their foliage and glimpse their colours bright as spring.

''Tis a circle of trees!' he announced with a smile and pointed far ahead.

The riders strained their eyes to see the apparition, making no sense of the King's excited speech.

Eider spread his arms. 'See, the trees are fully clothed. 'Tis a wood of evergreen!' he grinned, elated at the prospect.

Regor reined in his horse alongside him. 'Friend,' he whispered, uncomfortably, 'I see nought but grass and the hillside beyond.'

Again Eider raised himself in the stirrups, his eyes

61

searching out the waving boughs, his ears straining for the plaintive song of the flute.

The awkward silence was suddenly broken, for having traced the scent of the quarry, the wolfhounds began to bark frantically and the shrill blast of the clarion announced the first sighting of the wild boar.

Eider turned to see the huntsmen racing on towards the lines of gorse spreading beyond the mere to the sparsely covered hillside. They moved as one straight and solid formation, beating down fern and briar until they were within range of the tangled lower slopes. There they veered to right and left to form a circle of nets and staves. Now they moved with silent caution amid the brakes and savage bramble, careful not to disturb the beast before the trap be ready. At last, the ambush set front and rear, they raised their hands as signal of their readiness and Hariss motioned to the royal party to be alert. With Lehon and Regor on either flank, Eider pressed Zephyr on into the streaming sunlight as it washed light then dark over the coarse grassland in between.

As the King approached, the huntsmen began their slow, deliberate advance, beating at the thickets with their staves, nets poised. Now the air was filled with the baying of the hounds, the scattering of frightened birds and the muffled rhythm of the drum.

Eider felt a rush of blood to his face and urged Zephyr on, eager to catch a glimpse of the beast, eager to be the first to take the quarry. The huntsmen continued their steady drive forward, their voices raised in warlike chants as they flattened every knotty web with boot and stave. Without warning the beast sprang from its hide, a terrible high-pitched squeal alerting all to its anger as it bolted towards its trackers. A curious piebald of grey and black, the narrow body and thin legs belied the raw power of the boar as it hurtled at the huntsmen. At the sight of it several faltered, tossing their nets in panic and failing to halt the beast. Maddened, the creature darted back and forth then criss-crossed the tangled arena, scattering all in its path.

Crouched low in the saddle, Eider watched the mêlée, his fingers tightening about the lance as he steadied Zephyr for the advance. He clenched his teeth determinedly as the boar charged from the battered briars, thorns and burrs still clinging to its coarse back.

'Arm yourself!' Lehon cried as the wide green nets were flung again in a desperate attempt to capture the beast. Only two found their mark yet the huntsmen seized their chance, hauling at the nets, trapping the frantic quarry and halting it abruptly. The fine woven network of strong gut held fast the straining sinews and bones and though it twisted and squealed, the boar could do no more than rage as it enravelled itself still deeper within the nets.

Eider leapt from his horse, aligning his lance as he moved in steady paces towards the squirming animal. There was something about the sight of its bristled hair standing upright along the beast's spine, something in the blazing eye that chilled Eider to the marrow. In the filtered light, the lethal ivory tusks glinted like cruel scimitars and Eider was stirred to reckless violence.

Suddenly this was no wild beast that confronted him but a shape-shifter that threatened him alone. The dark assailant of his nightmare, or else some unseelie ally. Eider felt a sudden weight upon his chest and began to sweat. Was not Ruthra protected by that very same substance that now threatened him like a dagger? A creature so evil, had within it the power to choose whatever guise it wished, animal or man. The Ranter had sown fear in him and it had grown into madness. No longer did he see a trapped and shrieking beast, but Dark revealing itself to him alone. He must destroy it. Unheeding of the cries of his men, Eider raced forward, fear and hatred blinding him to reality as he lunged at the floundering animal with his lance. The impact resounded as a dull thud, cleaving muscle and bone but failing to kill the boar outright. Eider snatched back the weapon and made to strike again but the animal, mortally wounded, tore at the restraining nets in a desperate bid to escape. Eider hesitated, seeing blood gush from the deep wound as the animal writhed on the wet earth, then alert once more, he moved in to finish it off.

He did not hear the warnings of his aides, nor the frantic yelping of the dogs. He did not feel the sun on his face, nor the sweat trickle in his palm. He could feel only the insistent tug of the past, hear only the Ranter's terrible prophecy.

'Sire, have a care!' Hariss yelled as his monarch advanced heedless of their fears.

'I shall claim victory over you!' Eider vowed beneath his breath, but before he could deliver the fatal blow, the animal, crazed by the agony of the wound, had turned its final surge of fury into awesome strength and tore through the enfolding nets as if they were fine gauze.

Eider stared aghast, unable to move to safety as the maddened beast hurtled towards him, head down, tusks extended, eager for blood. Yet the daggers of ivory did not make contact with the terror-struck King but found instead the valiant Hariss, who, sensing Eider's vulnerability, had flung himself in the path of the animal, taking the full force of the lethal tusks. Rage unquenched, the boar bucked and gored the brave captain until Regor and two huntsmen raced forward and fell upon it, plunging swords and staves into the creature's straining body. Eider watched, dumbstruck, as the boar writhed and twitched in its final death throe.

The elfin fell to his knees beside Hariss and wept unashamedly. His effort had been in vain for the brave man had breathed his last. Eider touched Regor's shoulder in a gesture of consolation. ''Tis done. This victory has claimed triumph over the Ranter's curse,' he said confidently.

Regor shrugged away from him. 'Victory?' he said bitterly. 'An act of madness has brought us tragedy.' He gestured contempt towards the slain animal. ''Tis the beast has had victory this day, not we.'

Stung by the elfin's words, Eider's face tightened visibly and he went to where the boar lay oozing crimson. Straddling the animal, Eider gripped the sharp tusk in his fist and snatching at his dagger he gouged out the ivory at its root, speckling face and hands with blood as he twisted it free. This done, he stood in triumph above the beast, the tusk held aloft, his steely eyes intent upon its white sheen. In that moment he glanced at the lined faces of his companions who had watched his brutal actions in disbelief. Eider laughed at their silent outrage, bidding the huntsmen shift the carcass as he moved aside.

He extended the bloody token to Regor. ''Twas no beast,' he grinned with certainty, 'but the masked enchanter!'

Regor turned his head away in disgust and Eider, suddenly struck by stark reality, looked down at the bloodless face of the faithful Hariss. Crouching beside him, Eider brushed the fair hair and gently drew down the shutters of the grey eyes.

'Friend,' Eider whispered, his voice laced with remorse, 'I never meant this to happen.'

Regor pushed him away and taking off his cloak he draped it over the lifeless captain and gestured for the others to follow suit. In white-faced rage he turned to Eider. 'Your Majesty would be advised to return to Rhyc with his fine trophy!' he sneered.

Eider stood to his feet and did not pursue the threat. There would be a time more fitting to settle quarrels. Mounting Zephyr and accompanied by three of his retinue, he galloped towards the castle-town. At his back only the yelp of the hounds broke the silence as they fell upon bone and offal thrown into their midst. In sorrow, Lehon helped the men to wrap Hariss in their cloaks and secure him to his horse's saddle. Then, remounting, he led them off in the tracks of the monarch, leaving Regor alone to cleanse his skin of the blood of the beast.

The long trek back to Rhye was made in doleful silence, every head hung low in sadness, every heart brimful with grief at the passing of a friend. Onward the party rode, through fields marbled with frost and rotting crops, beneath the watchful gaze of dark hills where trees stood in stark relief against the empty sky. Now death and winter were one, and its ice-laced breath blew snow flurries about the leafless boughs.

Eider rode on ahead quite alone, isolated from comfort, his shoulders bowed beneath the burden of guilt. He glanced at the sunless sky and pulled his cloak tight about him, but the terrible cold of sorrow could not be assuaged. The death of Hariss filled him with a pain so deep, so all-consuming, that he felt his heart would break with the agony of grief. As he spurred Zephyr on, he thought again of the fatal scene, heard again the Ranter's words, saw again the folly of his deeds. A tear glistened in his eye as he dwelt on old remembrances, the laughter filled days of the past, and the bonds formed between those who had striven with him to free Rhye from tyranny. He thought too of the selfless acts of valour, and now of the sacrifice of honest men like Hariss. Eider felt his sorrow break from him, felt anger and anguish rise in his breast as he kicked hard at the stirrups and sped Zephyr on towards the castle-town.

By the time he approached the perimeter gates, Eider was lost to torment. The Fool in him had triumphed again, he had fallen victim to a moment's madness, an act of recklessness that had led him only to . . .

'Calamity!'

The cry snatched Eider back from thought as Zephyr reared up, startled by the cry of stern Judgement and the wave of raucous laughter that followed it. As he settled the nervous mare Eider glimpsed the edge of a painted wheel, the flurry of a canvas and then, borne on the wind, the haunting melody. It weaved about him like a spell, and he moved forward into the narrow street in search of its source. He listened intently and nodded, it was the plaintive song of a gypsy violin, but the notes drifted to him from every direction at once and soon he was so bewildered he had to pull Zephyr to a halt. Then the solitary violin played no more and Eider turned about in desperation.

Just ahead the townsfolk were gathered about a brightly painted wagon, and upon it, garishly clad travellers performed a drama. Eider moved Zephyr closer to view their rough crafted tableau: a pot-bellied fellow cowered beneath a flapping canopy upon which a shoddy depiction of the heavens had been scrawled in blue with tiny gold stars. Behind him, 'Judgement' appeared in sombre robes, holding aloft a crudely fashioned arrow of silver with which he menaced his grovelling victim.

'The wrath of Jupiter shall strike!' 'Judgement' declared in a theatrical voice of doom, and with bold gesture thrust the glinting prop as a lightning shaft, jabbing his victim's well-rounded buttocks. The crowd cheered and laughed as one, and raised their fists urging 'Judgement' be dispensed upon the wretch. In an instant, tragedy was turned into farce as the intended recipient side-stepped every thrust of the arrow, denying his fellow player the moment of triumph. But retribution was close on his heels and punishment soon meted out as the quick foot of 'Judgement' unceremoniously tripped its posturing victim and sent him sprawling headlong to the dusty boards.

As if on cue a tiny squirrel-monkey darted from its safe hiding-place beneath the wagon, clutching a paper wreath. This he dropped carelessly on to the head of the dazed actor, darting clear as 'Judgement' stepped forth once more. 'See here the triumph of Fate. The act of celestial Judgement!' the berobed figure announced solemnly to a cacophony of cat-calls and some applause, a barrage of well-ripened fruit and some coins.

Yet there was one amongst the onlookers who was not amused, who neither jeered nor applauded the

67

scene. The tableau had struck a deeper chord in Eider's soul. For him it was no mere play, but a pointed reminder of the Ranter's prophecy. 'The hand of Fate shall strike your towers,' he murmured to himself, and the spark it struck within him burst forth as a terrible anger. These were no mere travellers, but an unseelie troupe, in league with ·Darius! This was no innocent play, but a satire, staged to fright him with the madman's visions! Anger turned to rage and pointing immovably at the players, he summoned a handful of soldiers to his aid. 'Rid me of these loathsome wasters!' he commanded.

The soldiers of his retinue were quick to obey, and elbowed roughly through the crowd. Drawing their swords they slashed at the gaudy backcloth and toppled the garish wagon. Eider heard a woman's scream and saw the players manhandled towards the outer gates protesting their innocence. He saw the anger on the faces of the crowd, and heard the jeers that greeted the soldiers' actions. With a sneer Eider turned Zephyr about and spurred her on to the castle, convinced he had written a new conclusion to the fateful scene, and beaten the madman at his own game!

Eider and his retinue wound their way towards the great castle, and the folk of Rhye, having heard the fracas and of the death of the good Captain Hariss, huddled about the main gate whispering rumour as Eider and his small party passed through.

Beneath the shadow of the sturdy walls Eider drew Zephyr to a halt, his body taut with frustrated anger, but before he could dismount a terrible crack resounded and from the cloudless blue heavens a jagged finger of lightning issued forth to strike the western turret tower and shatter its top. A section of the tower collapsed, flinging a sentry headlong to his death and burying several others beneath falling masonry. Zephyr reared, almost unseating her rider, but Eider managed to manoeuvre her to safety amid the spiralling dust and the ensuing chaos. He looked anxiously about to see soldiers and servants clambering over the rubble, digging with their bare hands in search of friends and survivors.

Eider glanced at the sky, it was not stormy as expected but exuded a calm blueness, the colour of robins' eggs. He smacked fist against palm. Fate had dealt this blow in spite of him and now this day had twice seen its victory. Eider rallied, urging reason above irrationality. It was all coincidence, not Fate, he told himself, and if it were not . . . then he would find the perpetrator of this curse and show no mercy.

'Quick, get the King to safety!' the captain of his retinue cried, snatching Zephyr's reins and leading Eider away. In the confusion, none saw the fleet-footed squirrel monkey clamber over the debris, a mangled wreath of paper poppies held fast in its claw.

8

The mists cleared, and through the fine sheen came a line of landsmen marching up the pitted road. Their faces were white and drawn, their bodies thin and bedraggled, their picks and axes rusted by time and weather. The headman said nothing as he led them past the silent rider, and on, up the hill. The horseman watched them go, then turned to look over the land.

He saw the first snow flurries coat the scorched furrows, white on black. There were no field fires here, the burning had been done long ago. Here there was only charred earth and broken fencing. He watched the whirling snow powder every contour of the land, and shivered. Winter had surely come to Rhye and with it sorrow and starvation for its people.

The rider urged his mount down the stony track past the old tavern. A place once warm and full of storytellers, it stood empty now, its windows shattered, its roof caved in. Across the pathway stood the grazing field where livestock had once thrived and reared their young. Now it held nought but their dried bones and nurtured only briar and carrion crow. In the distance a bonfire spat heat against the cold wind. Along the way he had seen many such fires where broken timbers and even furniture were burned to keep people warm, keep them alive. He pushed on towards its heat.

The women wrapped in their shawls made no sound as he approached, nor did they offer meagre hospitality, only drew their little ones closer to the flames, watching the fire's throbbing heart as if for a sign. The rider drank from his waterskein, cleaning mouth and throat of dust and smoke, then like the dispossessed souls among whom he stood, he too watched the churling flames. How their dazzling heat reminded him of Eider, burning at the heart, raging with a strange passion. He, like all, had heard the Elders tale of how well the Duchess of Dark had bedded Eider on their wedding night. The rider shook his head. That marriage was an act of reckless will, and had become the shackle by which the King was held to Baobhanshee's side. The insatiable Queen pampered his every excess, nurtured his unruly ways, fuelled his love of warcraft. Now the duelling blades were always stained with blood and the shrill cry of the hunter's horn more common in the land than birdsong. The pure heart was in bondage to the baneful Baobhanshee and at that thought the rider spat into the flames. There he saw again the wild boar, the broken thicket, the hoof, the tusk, the blood . . . he closed his eyes and the death-grey face of Hariss rose up from darkness to greet him. When he opened his eyes the women were casting more wood on to the flaring heap.

How these troubled days reflected Rhye's troubled court and how like these cold outcasts were the lords, the wizard and the Elders of Rhye too long ignored, too long abused by Eider and his meddling Queen. Had Baobhanshee, or even the strange Maquis, brought this chaos to King and Kingdom? Or had the Ranter made it so? That Ranter and his wretched prophecy . . .

The harsh winds gusted and the rider clutched at his flapping cloak. He spat again into the fire. 'Prophecies . . . nought but words!' he shouted into the blast. He turned his elfin scowl upon the frozen land, words could never do such harm. 'Nay,' he agreed with his own thoughts. He shook his head and turned his mount eastward. Yet in that moment he had gleaned a sudden truth and he held fast the reins. 'Nay, 'tis not the words . . .' he murmured against the bitter wind. 'But that the folk believe them brings it all to pass!'

With fresh vigour he pushed his weary horse on into

the whirling snowstorm. Now he had seen the land as Lehon had said it was, and worse. He would return and tell the wizard his truth. Together they would persuade the King to summon Darius and make him change the prophecy! 'Yes!' he cried, and with an inner smile the elfin pushed on into the howling wind and was lost to the drifting snowfall.

When only the delicate stars of snowflakes made design upon the crystal screen, the wizard turned sadly from the sphere. 'Too late, my elfin friend,' he whispered, the crescent face streaked with tears. ''Tis all too late.'

Along the road to Rhye, Regor passed endless lines of bedraggled landsmen. Yet as he drew close to the castle-town he frowned, for the gates were cast wide apart and in their gape an old cart creaked, blocking the road, its back axle broken and trapped between the worn cobblestones. The guards swore, pushing and heaving in their efforts to get it moved, while the gangs of footsore travellers passed them by on their route to the market-place. Regor rode in their company towards the square where Rhye's own townsfolk poured from the tavern doors or lounged about the streets the worse for ale. No longer did they make or sell their wares, but put their trust in fate-games, busying themselves with cards or rolling dice upon the dusty steps of run-down dwellings.

The elfin's senses registered distaste, seeing many a newly arrived landsman duped out of the little he owned in a game of chance. Yet still they came and turning back to the gates, he saw the endless line of their kins-men queueing to be admitted. They were coming to Rhye's heart for comfort and for shelter, for help from their benevolent King, but finding no kindness to be had.

He must to the wizard, to the Elders with his truth, then the proper order would be restored. As he pushed on to the inner gates Regor passed a garish wagon and a gathering of drunken townsfolk drawn about it.

'Cock-a-doodle-do! Cock-a-doodle-do!' He heard the

high-pitched cry and his pointed ears ached at the sound of the drum. He scowled at the rough troupe who, as part of their artless mime, hung a harlequin by one foot from a scaffold as he rode by. Regor spat at them and rode on into the vast courtyard of the castle, yet as he entered so he saw Lehon riding towards him through the dust veil.

'Elfin, you return,' the mortal greeted him, smiling.

'And you depart,' Regor frowned, noting that Lehon was prepared for travel.

'I ride with my men to bring Darius before the King,' he explained.

'Then my truth has come to roost!' Regor laughed, but as quickly he was serious again. 'Friend, I rode through Rhye's lands and saw it was all as you told me.'

Lehon heaved a heavy sigh. 'It must surely be much worse by now'

Regor nodded. ''Tis so, now the landsmen gather at Rhye's gates and ask for help.' He held out a pleading hand to Lehon. 'Friend, the King must hear them, and act on their behalf.'

''Tis the reason we go forth, and with Darius return,' Lehon offered.

Regor gave a short laugh. 'Eider will make the old charlatan change his words and all will be made right.'

'Nay,' Lehon grimaced. 'He'll not have a second chance.'

Regor looked at the mortal, confused.

'The King brings the meddler to trial,' Lehon stated simply.

'Trial?' Regor said, incredulous. 'Darius is nought but an old fool. Only make him take back his nonsense and all the wrongs be righted!'

'Regor, 'tis not so simple,' Lehon frowned. 'The Ranter's words are seen as a spell, even the King believes it so.'

Regor shook his head. 'Eider is influenced by Dark . . .'

73

Lehon glared at him and glanced about for fear of being overheard.

'You said it yourself!' the elfin insisted in a whisper. 'Since Boabhanshee came Eider has grown worse.'

'Quiet!' Lehon warned. 'There are those would put a lord to death for words so out of place!'

'I speak true!' Regor scowled as he clasped the mortal's sleeve. 'Friend, wait on this. Stay until I speak with Nairb, for I know how Rhye's release from this malady may be gained.'

With a shrug, Lehon conceded. 'But I must be gone by dusk if I'm to bring Darius back by dawn.'

Regor agreed and as Lehon turned his mount back to the garrison, the elfin rode across the courtyard and on to the door of the lower apartments.

The delicate chimes of the clock struck three and Nairb watched with patient eyes as page-boys removed the Triad amulets from their crystal cabinet. The first bore the Great Sword as tall as he, the second held aloft the velvet red cushion upon which the Gauntlet was set, and the third carried the Cloak of Light draped across his small arms. The wizard led them past the mirrors of the Monument Hall and out along the red carpets of the corridor, then east to the privacy of the royal apartments. Once there they waited while Nairb knocked upon the low door.

The aged servant bade them enter, and the wizard heard Baobhanshee giggle, saw Eider turn from her to greet him with heavy-lidded eyes. He smiled sleepily as he saw the Triad amulets, and Nairb breathed relief that this day Eider wore the white silk befitting a King of Triad Lore. Yet as he donned the sash of crimson the wizard averted his gaze as Eider's face met his.

When the Triad amulets were offered to him, Baobhanshee came forward, filling her dancing eyes with their bright beauty. Her long fingers stroked the gleaming blade of the sword. She trembled with delight, her black eyes flashed and Eider moved close to her, his smile matching hers in a lustful glance.

Now the wizard's heart sank as Baobhanshee moved off to the bedchamber, knowing that Eider was compelled to follow. Thus Nairb turned from them and stepped out into the corridor. Affairs of state must wait, as must all things, while Eider fed his Queen's desires. The wizard bit his lip, should he find Lehon and stop the search for Darius? He paced to the window arch. The afternoon sun was weak and snow flurries dashed against the glass. How quickly winter had reached Rhye's towers.

Footsteps echoed at his back and he turned expectantly.

'Nairb, good friend!' Regor grinned into the wizard's ashen face.

Nairb clasped Regor to him and the elfin smile vanished as he sensed the urgency in the wizard's grip. But Regor's heart was full of hope and would not be suppressed. 'I have it, wizard,' he said as their faces met. 'I know the way to ward off Dark!' But even as he said it, he saw no light of joy kindled in the wizard's eyes. 'We must to Eider, he should call for Darius, make the old meddler recant his spell!'

'Eider is abed with his Queen,' Nairb replied dejectedly.

'Do you not see?' Regor ran on in the wake of his enthusiasm. ''Tis because folk believe Darius's words that all this came to pass! There be no truth in them. Only change those words and Rhye will thrive again!'

'Regor . . .' Nairb began, his voice almost lost to grief. ''Tis all too late. Rhye is lost already and we with it.'

'No!' Regor growled defiantly. ''Tis not so!'

'Eider has summoned Darius. He is to be judged,' Nairb said with a heavy sigh.

Regor brightened. 'Then 'tis fair. The madman shall recant, change the spell and all be well,' he grinned.

Nairb shook his head. 'Laugh not at the madman, for he is a prophet and his words cannot be changed.'

'Nay,' Regor protested. 'I shall never believe it so.'

Nairb's white face met the elfin's with a look of cold intent. 'Eider shall judge the Ranter . . . and on the twelfth hour of the twelfth day shall come to me to look into the sacred sphere.'

Regor fell silent, Nairb's words had the ring of truth, of resignation to a fate unknown to him. He gripped the wizard's arm. 'You know already what will be,' he cried. 'You know, don't you?'

Nairb opened his mouth but the answer never came for the hollow ring of a cracked bell floated through the open window. Together they turned, looking down into the courtyard below and saw the shaven-headed Darius returned to Rhye's Hall at no one's bidding but his own.

'Go to,' Nairb whispered into the elfin's pointed ear. 'Bring him in. I shall to Eider and make all ready.'

Regor nodded and they went in opposite directions, the cracked bell marking both time and pace.

Nairb hurried back the way he had come and bade the servant call the King from Baobhanshee's arms. As he walked into the antechamber Eider looked aghast to see the wizard returned so soon, but then the blood-chilling clang of Darius's bell drew him to the window. His anger was instant and as his eyes met the wizard's, Eider snatched up his silken shirt and made for the door. On their way out into the corridor he growled command and the castle was suddenly alive with activity.

The Elders were brought from their spells and meditations, the lords and advisers from their chamber meeting, the captains from their swordplay, even the hounds roused from sleep and set up a barking and howling that none had ever heard within Rhye's castle walls. The guards took to their posts and the drummers made preparation should some royal judgement be made upon the madman. For Darius would indeed be judged and imprisoned, or else banished, for the chaos he had brought to Rhye's lands.

Nairb watched the comings and goings until at last, with the gathering of the townsfolk and landsmen in the courtyard, and the crowd of Rhye's courtiers and statesmen filling the ground floor of the east wing and Monument Hall, Darius was brought before the solemn-faced King.

9

At the heart of the Throne Room Eider stood dressed in the dazzling white of seelie lore and in full Triad regalia, the Gauntlet clasped tight about his right hand, the shimmering Cloak of Light draped from his straight shoulders and at his side the majestic Sword of All-Power. He waited, silent and erect in the midst of anxious-faced statesmen and elders, he, the powerful wielder of Triad Lore, the untainted ruler of Rhye.

The guards pushed Darius forward and as Eider looked upon him, the bright blue eyes of the Ranter glinted in deepest contempt of him.

'So, Darius, you blight Rhye's Halls once more?' Eider snapped, assuming authority over the figure before him.

Darius said nothing, his bruised face stark against the now simple black of his robes.

'Welcome return,' Eider smiled sardonically.

Darius was impassive. 'A return,' he replied.

The muscles in Eider's face tightened and, noticing his changed demeanour, the elfin alerted Lehon. 'The old man is too reckless,' he whispered into the mortal's ear. 'Can he not see he courts danger?'

Lehon motioned silence and watched Eider take the first of the steps toward the Ranter.

'I had you summoned . . .' Eider began.

'I came willingly,' Darius corrected, softly.

The remark prompted a darkening of the King's face and Regor shook his head in silent disapproval of the Ranter's provocation.

Eider straightened his shoulders. 'You are here to admit the falsity of your prophecy.'

Darius spoke without emotion. 'I am here that you might destroy that prophecy.'

Eider's eyes were bright with fury. 'And why should I?' he baited, the leathered hand straining in a fist at his side.

The kohl-black eye on the forehead of Darius riveted him. 'To avoid your ultimate fate.' The old man's eyes glazed as if charged with Sight and he cast his arms out wide. 'Soon endless night will fall, summoned by your own hand!' he cried aloud.

Eider made to grab the man, to silence him there and then but the wizard restrained him. 'Sire, deal with this in private,' Nairb urged gently.

Eider shrugged him off. 'No! Let all hear the charlatan.' He gave a hollow laugh and turned back to Darius. 'We would all learn of this ultimate fate. Come, tell it!'

Darius met Eider's glare with cool defiance. 'The wielder comes. Born of flame. Gold of mane.'

The gathering gasped in unison, fearing the words spoken and for the life of the man who had dared to utter them. The elfin closed his eyes, unable to understand the suicidal actions of the man, let alone his strange pronouncements.

Eider's face had paled, the Ranter's words waking old nightmares hidden deep within him. 'A new wielder indeed?' he threw back his head in laughter, then flourished an impatient hand. 'Then show him to me! Where is this wielder?' he demanded.

Darius looked at him direct. 'Within you,' he said simply.

Eider laughed louder still, yet his body grew taut. 'Clever answer!' he sneered, drawing close to the Ranter in silent threat. 'But a false one!' He pointed an emphatic forefinger. 'Was it not you said I would seed no issue in this realm?' he challenged.

Darius bowed his head sorrowfully. 'Nor shall you.'

'Pah!' Eider fumed. 'First you make fantasies, then you lie!'

Darius did not speak.

'Cur!' Eider spat, circling the Ranter, his face etched with a terrible rage. 'What price to make you speak the truth?' he growled.

'The truth is freely given,' Darius replied calmly.

'What price your life, old man?' Eider whispered into Darius's ear.

The Ranter looked him in the face. 'A kingdom lost,' he said flatly.

The anger in Eider erupted and he twisted the Ranter's collar. ''Tis treason you utter and by the Gods you will suffer for it!'

Darius tried to speak. 'We both shall suffer for our words,' he choked, as Eider's grip tightened about his throat.

Suddenly aware of his loss of composure, Eider pushed Darius away. 'You think you fright me with your words and signs, your painted face and notes of discord?' he smirked, in a show of ridicule to deflect his mounting distress. 'Where is your demon pipe to play this new tune upon? And what's this? A rusted bell with which to frighten fools?' He tugged at the belt of rope.

'The bell tolls your passing,' Darius replied, unshaken.

The onlookers caught their breath. This comment surely sealed the madman's fate.

Regor snatched at Lehon's sleeve. ''Tis out of hand, we must do something,' he urged, but the mortal's face bore the same look of helplessness as his own and before either could act, Eider had pressed home the point.

'My death knell?' he grinned broadly and drew Darius to him. 'Come closer, I would hear its call.'

Darius took only one step closer to the King but Eider alone observed the moment as the Ranter held up the bell and passed his mangled hand across its pitted surface as if drawing back a veil. In that moment, a strange transformation took place and terror gripped Eider by the throat, for the dull and mottled surface of the bell became a convex mirror in which he saw himself clearly reflected. It was an image that filled him with horror, for he saw the dull eyes, the lines of age, tight and multiple about their sockets. He saw the hollow cheeks and yellowed skin, the gaping mouth and the greyness of beard and hair. He saw himself in a future, which he knew to be close. The images passed before his gaze as slowly as an old man's heartbeat, like unspeakable horror that twisted in his chest like a knife, that stilled the very blood in him. A shadow stood at his shoulder. It was too close. It was not yet time.

'Enough!' Eider cried out, knocking the bell from Darius's hand. It landed with a flat, prophetic clang. 'What spell is this you weave?' The veins in Eider's temple bulged with fear.

Darius's voice was almost a plea. ''Tis no spell, 'tis the torment of your soul!'

''Tis the work of the unseelie!' Eider shouted above the Ranter's patient voice.

'Indeed, 'tis so,' Darius agreed.

At his words Eider rounded on him. 'Hark!' he commanded the gathering. 'He is convicted by his own admission!'

Regor stepped towards the Ranter. 'Darius, recant, or face the consequence!' he urged.

Darius shook his head. 'I cannot recant what is true.'

The townsfolk and landsmen who had forced their way into the lower apartments had swelled in number until they began to jostle one another for space, and impatience and irritation competed for the upper hand. It took but one careless suggestion, one call for vengeance, one man to break rank and spark the riotous surge forward towards the bolted doors. The barrier to the upper levels was successfully breached and trampled underfoot as the crowd raced up every staircase and thundered down every corridor, sweeping guards off their feet, upturning chairs and setting tapestries billowing. On and on they ran in the wake of their own hysteria, desperate to bear witness to the unfolding spectacle and hear the pronouncement of Triad judgement. Only when they reached the Monument Hall did they halt and bow their heads in respect of kingship, only then did the gruff voices still as all strained to hear Eider's punishment of the shriven-headed Darius.

'Your words are false from beginning to end!' he shouted into the Ranter's impassive face and spread his arms towards the hate-filled crowd now clamouring at the door. 'See for yourself. The people know you as the fount of woe, not I.'

Darius turned a steady look upon his accusers. 'They know only fear and that there is madness in this place.'

Eider's look was deadly. 'Then it is a madness I shall purge!' he vowed, shaking his fist.

Darius's gaze was unflinching. 'Only fire can grant absolution.'

Eider started uncomfortably, but then a slow, savage grin crept across his face. 'So be it!' He beckoned to the guards. 'Take him! Burn him!' he ordered. 'Put evil to the torch, let it be done this day!'

Darius did not struggle as his hands were bound, nor tremble as the crowds without bellowed gratitude for their King's command. Yet even as they celebrated and the drums resounded through the Hall and corridor, the court and all its lords, advisers and Elders stood rooted, fearstruck by the King's unseelie decree.

Regor sprang to the Ranter's defence. 'Take the man's life?' he cried aloud.

'And by fire?' the Elder exclaimed in his turn.

'First tell us the crime!' the court demanded as one body.

'Sorcery!' Eider snarled, pointing at Darius. 'He is in league with Dark.'

'But these are mere words,' the wizard cried, aghast.

'You cannot prove the old man's guilt,' Regor challenged and only Lehon could restrain him from pacing the chequered floor.

It was Nairb who moved towards their King, his crescent face drawn and white with fear. At the sight of him Eider stepped back and raised his hand as a shield. 'Come no closer, wizard,' he warned. 'Meddle not in this.'

'Eider, you cannot use Triad power to condemn a man to unseelie fire,' Nairb's voice was calm, yet insistent.

Eider's face darkened. ''Tis you says that, not the lore!' he glowered.

The wizard's hazel eyes fixed him with a chilling cold. 'Be wary,' he countered. 'This is folly!' Before his words were uttered a sudden and powerful surge sent the gathered courtiers sprawling as Rhye's people burst into the Monument Hall. The Seventh Elder raised his rowan staff for order, but the riot had begun and they seized Darius from the guards to drag him from the place of judgement to the place of execution.

'Mother of Hecaté! Protect the man!' Regor yelled into the mortal's ear and together they ran in the wake of the mob, swords and daggers drawn in unison.

Nairb turned this way and that, helpless to stop the fray, desperate for his King to speak, to halt the baneful deed. But Eider did not move, or speak, only watched on as the Hall was overrun, his faithful lords outnumbered and the Ranter taken from their midst.

Regor and Lehon ran with the chanting crowd out into the heavy grey of midday. 'Release the man!' the elfin cried, throwing himself into the fray. Lehon held one of the mob at sword point and the townsfolk that surrounded Darius drew back. Yet the hefty landsmen who held the Ranter did not yield and against their hunger-dulled eyes and silent resistance Regor's blade was impotent. 'What justice from burning a fool?' he cried in frustrated rage as he and Lehon were pushed aside and the crowd hauled their captive away.

10

How quickly men can work when fear is their taskmaster, for no sooner had the punishment been spoken than folk had brought forth wood and things combustible, had built a pyre between the inner and outer gates, had tasted vengeance in their mouth and now craved blood.

As they dragged him towards his death, Darius turned back to glance at the elfin and though he did not speak, the serene blue of his eyes pierced Regor to the heart. Regor stood transfixed, unable to land a blow, useless to protect, to stop the aged limbs being stretched across the wooden frame, the unbreakable bonds being twisted and tied at wrist and ankle. He trembled to his very core as the frame was raised by the strongest and Darius carried helpless to the waiting pyre.

Lehon gripped the elfin's shoulder. 'Seelie ways are not my own, but in this may be Rhye's cure,' he offered with a sigh of resignation.

'Fool!' Regor scowled into his face. ''Tis all unseelie! There can be no cure where pure blood is spilled!'

'Then the consequence must be the cure,' Lehon insisted with strange certainty.

Regor opened his mouth to reply but the deafening boom of combustion stopped his speech and he turned his face to the blistering heat of the pyre. 'No!' he cried long and loud, until his heart ached.

Within, Eider had turned his back on chaos and walked away to the great doors and his private chambers. In his wake, the wizard turned too and though the Elder tried to stop him, Nairb followed his King into the ice-cold silence of the Throne Room. Halfway across its chequered floor Eider stopped, aware of Nairb's presence. 'Go from me,' he commanded, not turning to face his wizard.

'I shall not,' Nairb said quietly. 'To leave you is to leave Rhye to its death.'

Eider turned on him, his face flushed with anger. 'You think you hold Rhye's fate in your hand?' he sneered.

'I hold it in my heart,' Nairb said softly.

'None holds Rhye's fate but me!' Eider glared, moving to the great windows.

Nairb followed still, looking out upon the courtyard and the cobbled ground beyond where Rhye's people were gathered about the pyre.

'In the name of the Gods, stop this!' Nairb pleaded as he drew close to Eider. 'Stop this violence before it is too late.'

The hollow thunder of ignition followed his words and the amber flare of fire rippled upwards behind the glass.

'Ignis,' Eider breathed as if it were a secret pleasure.

Nairb looked at him, panic-stricken. His King's face was impassive, the pointed teeth bared in a cruel smile. A shudder crept through the wizard's heart as he saw the swirling flames reflected in Eider's dark orbs.

''Tis done!' Eider said with cold certainty. 'The death of the madman brings folly to an end!'

Nairb felt the breath stopped in his throat, felt his eyes brim with tears as Eider strode off to the royal apartments and slammed the low door shut at his back. The wizard shivered, knowing that Rhye's fate was lost to Dark. He turned from the distorted glass of the window and walked to where the empty throne awaited.

Above the throne, the carved wingspan of the royal phoenix remained, outspread in welcome. The wizard cried out in anguish and fell to his knees upon the marble floor, his own bony arms spread out in bird-like fashion. For long moments he watched the gleaming red eye of the sacred bird, then he lay himself down, arms still outstretched, his forehead pressed to white marble. As the robes of Horatious Thor cascaded to the chequer-board floor, the wizard began his mystic chant, and the ancient mantras of seelie lore were brought to life, despite the bitter cold.

In the silence that followed, Lehon watched the dying embers which glowed as nuggets of gold in the consuming grey of the late afternoon. The pall of Darius's death pyre hung like a dark veil about his charred remains, and its blackness embraced the sky turning it to deadly green, the colour predicting heavy storm. The mortal waited for the first fitful gust of wind to toss his hair, the first drop of rain to splash his skin, yet there came nought but thunder. It rumbled afar off, and the menfolk, their fears played out, turned from the smouldering pyre. Regor did not move for like Lehon he watched still the embers and longed for the deed to be undone by some spell. Lehon clasped him in brotherly embrace. 'Come, elfin, 'tis all done,' he said. 'Come from here. Winter storms are violent and distant thunder warns me of the coming wrath.'

With heavy hearts they turned from the ash-caked scene of misdeed, desperate to cleanse themselves of the taint of woodsmoke, the bitter taste of guilt, but the sudden thundercrack struck fear in them and they halted abruptly. The earth shuddered violently beneath their feet yet the storm voice had yielded no viperish tongue of lightning against the dark sky. Lehon looked about him, confused. He scanned the rain-charged clouds for sign of the fork but saw only the churning heavens. A new tremor rippled underfoot and it was then he realised that the earth itself had begun to break open.

Regor caught the mortal's arm, aghast. Solid cobblestones were being wrenched apart and the age-old foundations of the outer courtyard strained to fracture point, started to crack, then slowly to craze as from the base of the pyre a mighty tectonic force erupted.

The creaking was dry as aged boughs, the cracking was of splintering wood, the rumble was not thunder, but an agonised moan as the earth gave birth to knuckles of old bark, then a roughly jointed wrist and as it thrust towards the zenith all recognised it as a thick, knarled fist of wood. As it grew, so the forearm emerged, twisting upwards, fibrous and weather-grooved, the hand of a living-dying tree clenched in terrible rage. It heaved, it seethed, it split and cracked clear of the ruptured earth in which it stood rooted, until its height was that of Rhye's outer wall.

Those who had not fled at sight of it, stood terror-stricken within its gruesome shadow, saw the fingers slowly spread, extending the calloused palm towards the storm-riven sky. A giant hand it was, of scarred wood, a dying tree begging alms.

'Calamity!' Regor muttered, white-faced at the sight.

Lehon crossed himself yet could not avert his mortal eyes. Now lightning sprang from the knotted fingers of wood, tracing jagged weals across the black sky and those who stood the closest and could not stir, were struck dead. It was then that Lehon caught the sound of cartwheels on the smoke-laced air, glimpsed the garish wagon and heard the wild cry ring out like a death knell:

''Tis the hand of un-plenty. The Dearth Hand is risen!'

Eider looked out from the narrow window of the bed-chamber, unsure if the new day had dawned for the sky remained heavy and dark. No birdsong filled the air, no braying of livestock or movement of townsfolk. Only the moaning of wind, the creaking of massive boughs and the steady scrape of the rowan staff as the Elder led Nairb out towards the vast and ugly growth that stood just beyond the inner gate. Eider looked upon its fibrous mass, seeing in its bulbous joints the resemblance to an aged hand. He saw Nairb and the Elder halt within its gruesome shadow, saw them look up into its begging palm and strained his ears to catch a sound of their discussion, yet heard nought.

'My son,' said the Elder, sadly, ''tis the Dearth Hand, symbol of foreboding, of seven lean years of strife and woe come to our lands.'

'Nature has turned against us,' Narib said solemnly. ''Tis retribution for the burning.'

The Elder shook his head. ''Tis more than that. 'Tis the consequence of misdeed and misrule. 'Tis sign of the wielder's fall from grace.'

Nairb hung his head, unable to deny the Elder's words.

Within the chamber Eider shivered and snatched the curtain shut. ''Tis nothing,' he growled. ''Tis some grotesque tree obscures the light. Some meaningless spell wrought by Darius.' He turned back to his bed and the warmth of Baobhanshee's body.

Through the long dark days and nights, rain the colour of Baobhanshee's tears fell. Rain that drenched all things yet made nothing grow. With it there came black winds, that tossed the withering foliage of the land, rattled at the windows, gusted through the corridors and halls, and found a way into the channels of mens' hearts, carving a sorrow so deep that none could bring himself to stir, not even to cry his woe.

With every passing day Rhye's good earth grew hard as iron, and everything that could be burned was set alight to give men warmth, yet no fire they built gave off heat or comfort, and so the people of Rhye, and even their King, starved and froze beside their ice-cold hearths.

Again and again Rhye's most desperate came to plead with their King. ''Tis the tree!' they cried, and soon Eider had to agree. At his instigation the men set to with axes and saws, but their blades made no mark upon its knarled surface. So the living-dying Dearth Hand remained, a constant reminder to Eider of how his lands dwindled and with it his people.

One day, in the shadow of the deformed Hand, Lehon halted his small company of soldiers and turned to Regor. 'This has become the symbol of all Rhye's woe.'

'Aye,' the elfin agreed mournfully.

Lehon's green eyes narrowed. 'Friend, I am fearful.

No longer do the people journey here to find help, though their need must be dire. We must to them with blankets and provisions from the castle store.'

Regor clasped the mortal's hand. 'The landsmen know you as their own and will bless your compassion, good Lehon.' The azure eyes met the mortal's in a look of determination. 'Be assured, I shall to Nairb and together we will rally Eider,' he gave an uncertain laugh. 'We shall all be together on the land before these seven days are passed!'

Lehon's mouth flickered in a sad smile. 'Nay, Eider shall never leave his Halls. He crouches before a heatless fire, clutching the Triad amulets for fear the hand of Dark may take them away.' He frowned into the elfin's sorrowful face. 'Regor, our friend has fallen into madness. Now only we can give Rhye's folk relief.'

As the mortal turned to lead his brave battalion onward through the gates, Regor stood in the stirrups. 'Within seven days!' he called out and Lehon raised a hand of farewell. When the heavy outer gates closed again, the elfin turned his worried gaze upon the sinister tree. 'The Dearth Hand.' He shuddered. It stood as a memorial to Darius and to the dying Kingdom of Rhye. A symbol of the King's right hand, the impotence of the Triad wielder. The elfin heaved a sigh, the corruption of the pure heart had brought winter to the land. Eider had fallen into dark insanity and now the people knew him to be the source of all their sorrow.

. . . And there were whisperings in Rhye's Halls, whisperings that seeped through the walls like the iron-cold frost, that crept through the winding corridors and lurked in every shadow . . .

'The King is a wanton his Queen is a whore witless and a fool he is careless of lore contrary and tainted since Baobhanshee's rule cruel and unkind hapless and blind the thin worm of Darkness grows fat on his mind now for all wrong he is where once for all right drunken and greedy and lightless as night as sun without ray he is seven

shades grey vain and unruly selfish and sad heartless unfeeling violent and . . . mad.'

'Listen!' Eider commanded nothingness as the red wood of the chamber doors flew open and he ran out into the corridor. The echo of the doors resounded about the crouching shadows and Eider pressed his hands to his ears in pain and panic. 'I hear it, I hear it still!' he cried out.

'The earth shall shake, its crust will break in two . . .'

'Listen. Listen!' Eider pleaded, hurtling along the silent corridor as a man possessed.

'Listen . . . listen . . . listen to the . . .'

'Madman!' Eider staggered as he hid his face. Yet still he could not escape the chorus of omen and accusation that echoed from the whispering walls.

'Endless night will fall, summoned by your own hand . . .'

'Silence!' Eider ordered darkness. He fell back against the wall, trembling to the very core as he removed his hands from his ears. The silence lasted as long as it took him to breathe a sigh of relief, as long as it took him to blink. First, there came the serene notes of a flute, next the discords of a pipe, the dull clang of a bell, then laughter, screams and the clanking and chiming of every time-piece in the castle! The cacophony of sound set his teeth on edge . . . *one* . . . *two* . . . the echoing chimes resounded and Eider wheeled about. 'Midday or midnight?' he screamed at the invisible source of his discomfort, unable to determine which clocks struck, or where . . . *three* . . . *four!* Gripped now by a terror bordering on hysteria he ran for the intersection. 'Wizard!' he shouted above the din, clawing at tapestries as he rounded the corner and raced along the long flagstone corridor ahead.

Like a wild cat he chased on, calling out the wizard's name as he disturbed the steady flames of the torches and stirred up spirals of dust . . . *five* . . . *six*. Suddenly he was within sight of the ancient chamber of Horatious

Thor, and as the now distant clocks chimed on, he twisted the ornate handle of the door.

'Riddle-me-Ree. Riddle-me-Rye,' Baobhanshee sang as she rolled upon the velvet smooth carpet, her pointed teeth gleaming with cruel delight as she twisted Tiffan's tail. The cat spat at her and ran for the safety of the divan. Baobhanshee yawned, her dark eyes heavy with boredom. She reached for the tray of sweets and deliberated long upon her pleasure until, unable to make a choice, she devoured one and then all. The diversion used up she tossed her hair, eyeing the overturned chessboard, and the doors left wide open in Eider's madness to be gone.

'And to where?' Baobhanshee sighed with a 'tut' of displeasure. He had left her again, and had taken with him the shimmering cloak. Now there was no warmth to comfort her and the night would be chill and interminably long. She stamped her little foot. She shivered and moved closer to the hearth, to where the heatless flames licked the grate. In vain she held up her hands to warmth but felt nothing, not even the smallest cinder burnt her skin.

She pouted and turning to the bed, tugged hard at the silken sheets, giggling as she wrapped them around her nakedness, round and round. She fingered her long tresses, pushing them up in seductive fashion, but then the hair-clasp fell to the floor and rolled away. She darted after it, but could find no trace of it. She knelt on all-fours, her deft little fingers searching the carpet with the speed of light, her endless hair cascading down her back and shoulders. She looked under every table and cabinet, under every drape and divan until the only place left unchecked was the royal bed itself.

She peered beneath it, and with eager fingers traced the polished wood of the floor until, at last, in the darkest recess, her touch responded to its find. Once it was within her grasp she frowned, for it felt too smooth and was so warm against her palm. As she pulled it out into the light she gasped, for in her hand was no golden hair-clasp but a slender shard of glass. Exactly the size of her hand it was, and shaped like a stiletto dagger. Fascinated, she gently fondled the object's smoothed end, where she fancied the hilt and pommel might be. Mesmerised by the strangeness of her find she held up the shard, seeing the tiny red gems that decorated the inside of the jagged shaft, watching their rubescence dazzle and grow brighter in the firelight.

Baobhanshee purred delight. How beautiful it was. How warm and comforting it felt in her grip. She held it to her breast, unable to resist its heat-pulse. How like her Lord's heart-beat it was. How like the tingle of his body heat. She moaned as it made her cold skin flush. Groaned as it made her blood race like fire through her veins. She pressed it to her lips in innocent anticipation. In the shard there was beauty enough to feed Baobhanshee's vanity, power enough to assuage her fever-lust, evil enough to ensure her survival.

11

As the door flew open, Nairb stepped into the seelie ring and turned, holding both hands up as a shield. Thus he halted Time and rooted the fevered King upon the threshold. 'You are come at last,' he said patiently. He looked at the motionless figure held fast within the malady of deep despair. The ebony eyes were lifeless, yet their irises gleamed cruel red. The pale face was veiled by the growth of beard and defiled by the lines of sudden ageing. Nairb's heart ached, for alas it seemed even the Cloak of Light could not protect him from the sorrow of time's passing. The sacred raiment hung from his shoulders now like limp gauze, drained of its colour and warmth. The Great Sword, so long kept from daylight, so long embraced in fear, was sheathed and useless at his side. The Gauntlet, granter of his sudden entrance to this sacred chamber, still clung to his right hand, still shone, yet with a strange, uncanny light.

Heavy of heart, Nairb lit the incense sticks and then the three sacred candles. Moving from them he whispered the mantra of seelie protection and carefully opened the box of Horatious Thor. From the depths of it he took the crystal sphere, and placed it gently upon the plinth at the circle's heart. As he watched it, it seemed to hover there, white and ghostly silver, like the sphere of the moon. He turned back to the time-held King. 'Beginnan,' he commanded, and as the distant clocks struck twelve Eider blinked his eyes.

He breathed in the sweet perfumes of incense, saw Nairb before him standing within the mystic circle and draped in the ancient robes of Horatious Thor. At the heart of the traced circle, the pure white sphere hung, delicate as a crystalline bubble. To right and left of the wizard, tall white candles burned, a third stood between himself and the circle. Eider stepped towards it and taking the Triad blade from its scabbard, he raised it high in seelie reverence.

'Intrata,' Nairb said softly, granting Eider admittance to the mystic ring.

At Eider's sudden presence, the crystal sphere was shot through with violent and vivid colour which oscillated in manic display, and cast a vibrant shower of spangles across the chamber walls. Nairb watched Eider take his stance, though his brow creased to see him lean upon the sword's hilt for support. ''Tis the hour of twelve,' Eider said arrogantly, his eyes full to the brim with the reflected colours of the crystal.

'The appointed time,' Nairb agreed. He took the silken tallith that draped his arm and kissed it, then he lay it about Eider's shoulders. 'Look into the sphere,' he prompted. 'For with the passing of the time-mists our fate becomes clear.' Thus he focused Eider's full attention on the crystal, while the seelie mantra for the Sight drifted from his own thin lips. Soon the ebb and flow of the wizard's words imposed some invisible force upon the colour-haze that emanated from the orb, and their vibrant display weaved a bright cocoon about Eider's frame until it seemed he stood within the sphere itself. His eyes were dazzled, his senses confused but held fast in the sphere's mesmeric grip. He clung to the Great Sword as he would to a solid and reassuring stave and as the swirling colours made his pulse race, his head began to spin. Yet soon the oscillations ceased and mist, like cloud-spun gossamer, spread across the surface of the sphere.

Nairb saw Eider's tense limbs relax and knew the time was close.

'The mists clear,' Eider said, his voice weak with exhaustion.

Nairb nodded but before he had time to take breath the sphere turned a vile green, as green as the sylvan heart of the forest. What Eider saw within the crystal the wizard knew not, yet saw the King's skin tinge with the same ghastly hue, saw his lips part over the ivory grille of his fangs, saw his eyes glisten like green moons in liquid silver. A sudden rasp of hatred and Eider spat venom at the sphere, prompting a dramatic change of colour within the orb. It blinded Nairb momentarily, but soon through the hectic red light he saw Eider once more. His stance had not changed and his face once again was set as the crystal displayed his life's chaos and the woe he had yet withstood. Suddenly his skin flushed red and his body twitched in spasm.

'Evil . . . I deny you!' he growled, his threat echoing round the sacred chamber. 'Evil . . .' he began again. 'Evil . . . I,' he half vowed, his voice changing to a drone of deepest tone. 'Evil . . .' the phantom voice rippled in his throat like a dirge. 'Evil . . .' it groaned like a curse.

Nairb's heart ached and he wanted to dart clear as a sudden unexpected spark sprang from Eider's lips. It flamed as it flew between them yet with fearless heart the wizard held his ground, his holy presence extinguishing the firebrand within the hallowed circle. As the winged flame died, Eider turned to face him, his eyes protruding from their sockets, red as coals. His tongue oozed from his mouth like a molten serpent as he spewed up a stream of caustic white-heat. It turned red as it cooled and Nairb gasped at its vile sight, his heart beating steadfastly as he gave firm command.

'Ignis . . . vaneece!' And the disgorged succubus vanished into the vacuum of the mystic ring.

At the sudden loss of heat, Eider shuddered in violent pain as if his inner soul were lost. He leaned heavily upon the Triad Sword and clutched at his right arm, desperate to erase the burning shackle of the viper's scar, but it held fast. It was then that his skin turned grey with cold, and Nairb shivered with him as the chamber cooled. Eider groaned helplessly and in that moment the crystal sphere turned serene white. Nairb's thin lips quirked in a smile, but it was short-lived for as suddenly the orb was eclipsed by a menacing disc of Dark. Both watched the silver corona sparkle and saw ancient words take shape against the blackness.

'Dyed yfel!' Eider read aloud but did not understand.

The wizard knew the words well and before they had been spoken the rhythmic knock-knocking of a cracked bell resounded round the walls of the chamber. In the blink of an eye, the sphere itself was ablaze and Nairb raised his arms, useless to stop it. His heart flew to his mouth but even as the sardonic smile flickered across Eider's face, a pall of smoke blinded the crystal eye and the room was cast into deepest shadow.

Now they watched together, Eider taut with fresh agonies, the wizard's pulse racing with anticipation. Had not Eider's baneful infection now been purged? Had not the corm of Dark that dwelt within him now been exorcised and Eider's heart rekindled in purity? If it had, then new vision was to come, the vision of wholeness so longed for would surely grant the wielder of the Triad joy and strength of spirit returned. If not . . . yet the thought perished as Nairb's crescent face lit up with the shimmer of gold and he looked to Eider. The King's face shone with the same light, and the crystal itself hung gold as the harvest moon. The wizard closed his eyes in a silent prayer of thanksgiving for he knew that Eider would now see the fount of Triad power and as reward for tribulation, would see himself invested by the Gods as wielder in true unison at last with the sacred amulets.

But the wizard's eyes were closed and he saw not the horror of Eider's gaze, the baring of the pointed teeth, the painful tightening of his limbs. For within the sphere Eider beheld more than the fount of Triad power, more than a vision of seelie unity with ancient amulets . . . he beheld their wielder, and it was not he! 'Karatak!' he snarled as he watched the berobed form, saw the long hair of burnished gold and auburn cascade the strong back. 'Ruthra!' he cried the name out loud, feeling the sting of a terrible defeat.

Nairb opened his eyes, for the words were out of step!

He too saw the berobed figure, his face turned into the glass, saw the hair of gold, and opened his mouth to speak . . .

'Deceiver!' Eider cried accusation into Nairb's passive face. 'Fate shall not repay me thus!' he vowed, snatching at the Great Sword.

At that moment, the doors to the chamber were cast open. 'Lord Wizard, the King runs amok . . .' Regor began but did not finish, silenced by the chaos, by the strange amber light of the orb, by the motionless wizard and the raising of the Triad blade against seelie lore.

'Hold!' Nairb and the elfin cried as one, but in the time it took for the blade to fall they saw it fall a thousand times, so powerless were they to prevent the violent shattering of crystal by hard steel . . . And it was the foulest deed imaginable, for it was the defilement of Ancient Lore. It was the desecration of Triad power. It was the violation of seelie rites. It was the betrayal of trust. It was the blind destruction of the crystal heart. It was the reckless defiance of the Gods. And in return the Gods cast him out, cast him into silence . . . and the terrible Dark.

—— 12 ——

Eider saw the crystal shatter, heard the wailing of the four winds, then the flapping of the cloak about his head as he fell. At least he seemed to fall, or did he soar? The life within him dimmed and Eider sped on, or did he slowly slip away? He wanted to cry out, but had no voice, wanted to weep but had forgotten how, wanted to transcend the frontiers between waking and sleeping. But what if this were not sleep? What if it were some dark, interminable voyage without end? Would he ever wake again?

He felt no pain harsher than the sting of bitter cold and then the freezing of his fingers to the Great Sword's hilt. Unbalanced by its sudden dead weight he lurched, and then plummeted. There followed the inner shock of impact and the crunch of something like ice beneath his feet. He blinked hard, his eyes straining to gather what meagre light they could until amid the noise of the gusting wind, a sickly green orb of sulphur light was freed from the cloud pall. 'Luna or sol?' Eider gasped not knowing if he floundered by day or by night.

Where was he? In forest or fathomless chasm? He could make out no thing of recognisable shape or texture, could find neither tree nor landmark familiar to him. He could hear nought but the moaning wind and the frantic beating of his heart against his chest. If this were Rhye then it was held fast beneath the curse of deepest winter. Yet where was the castle, and his faithful aides? Where were those he loved? If it were not Rhye . . . . Eider could barely swallow with the thought. If it were not Rhye, this was a place so heavy with horror that he dare not look behind him for fear of what he might encounter. Would he at last confront the Feared Thing? Was the trap sprung, and he caught in it?

Now the rancid light struck panic in him, a panic that multiplied a thousand times to sheer terror as with one high-pitched screech and the manic flapping of wing-skin, a flock of vampire bats sprang from the iron-cold dark. Their claws scraped his flesh and their leather skin smothered his body as he became the axis of their flight. Eider raised arms and hands to protect his face, reeling violently to be free of their clammy touch, their sharp teeth and giddy chaos, until at last they flew from him, their hectic spiral casting them out across the face of the sullied orb.

Rigid with fright, Eider gazed up at the eerie light. It was not the serene white face of the moon which he beheld but some dark imposter and as he looked upon the ghastly glow he struggled with half-remembered images. Where was the moon's white face, the goddess of the night so beloved by the wizard, the benevolent radiance that they had often looked upon together? Wizard. The word summoned Nairb's gentle features in his mind's eye. It was then that Eider recalled the act most foul, the terrible misdeed that had brought this about. Yet where was Nairb? And where his elfin comrade? Had recklessness condemned all to this unseelie place?

Eider fell against fibrous roots, exhausted and afraid, yet his touch set off a slithering of wetness and the dead bough was suddenly alive with newt's tongue and snake's skin. Eider recoiled but with the slipping of his foot he realised that the half-lit floor of the wild place glistened with venom, churned with the bile of the mandrake. His cry of terror came back to him not as an echo but as a wolf's cry and he felt the blood-call entrap him in a menacing circle as the night-dog's brethren gave reply. Eider stumbled on barely able to see his hand in front of him, knowing not where he trod nor what horror lay in wait. He must find a way out, a way back, must make reparation, must stop the nightmare, must break the spell.

The fitful scattering of fragments, of silent flakes of blackness through the sentinel trees startled him. They touched his skin, ice-cold and he watched the intricate jewels of frost fall as snow. Yet the crystals did not melt, neither were they white. They were black, black as jet, black as Baobhanshee's tears on his hands. The knot that she had tied in his heart twisted tight at the thought of her, knowing she was lost to him, just as the castle and the Kingdom of Rhye were lost. His heart burst with anguish and he wept, for his folly, for all that he had squandered; he wept for his plight. What was he now, a solitary spore tossed upon the night wind? A speck of dust on an insect's leg? Whatever had befallen him, whatever fate the Gods had decreed, whatever the horrors to come, he would face them alone, and the certainty of it filled him with a fear that made him retch until his ribs ached.

Now in the never-ending monochrome of twilight he saw his body draped in the suffused white of seelie lore and moved through the encroaching darkness like a wraith, clutching himself for comfort and for warmth against the stinging cold. He longed for dawn, but knew that it would not come. He hoped for rest, but knew that none would be found.

He felt his eyelids grow heavy and tried to rally as they shuttered his eyes. He would not submit, would not let go the thread that held him safe from nothingness. But it was only sleep into which he fell. A deep slumber induced by a gentle ticking rhythm that rose up from the shadowed ground, to soothe him, to reassure him. Time passed. A second – a year? It was something in the sudden change of pitch and speed of that innocent sound that forced Eider to awake. He tried to focus in the dim light and started as he heard a high-pitched whistling akin to that made by air blown through the nostrils. He felt the tingle of fine hair rush over his arms and legs. He blinked hard in the poisonous light, catching the reflection of something bulbous and hard cased. He strained to see, then gagged upon his fear. About him, above him and upon him crawled a legion of sagging abdomens, an army of identical hair-coated heads, a tangle of long legs and sticky strands of webbing. As soon as he saw them he felt them dart closer. Soon they would nip his flesh, would eat and suck him dry of blood. He yelled out, set to take flight but their spiders' nets held him fast until with a madman's strength he wrenched himself free, floundering as he wielded the leaden blade that had become his burden. He slashed the web strands, severed the spindle legs and split the bulging egg sacks until at last they fell from him, the hooked mouths agape as he shouted and stamped in their midst. But the hollow he thrashed in was a colony and as the dark masses regrouped Eider staggered away, tearing aside the layers of webbing that stuck to his hands and face, knowing that the creatures hung from him as he stumbled on.

He ran until the sweat trickled down his neck and backbone, ran until his breath came in tortured gasps and an iron band of pain tightened about his chest. He knew that he must at all costs keep moving, for there was something more to be encountered, something he could not see and yet knew himself to be its prey. And so he raced on through the black of the snow, knowing the Feared Thing was near, feeling it draw closer. He felt it now as so often he had felt it before. It hovered both above him and about, yet was always close upon his heels. He sensed its shadow spreading over him, its wet hand about to clutch his shoulder, felt the heat of its breath upon his neck. He ran from it as he had always done.

Ran until he had forgotten the flock of bats and the hungry tribe of spiders, and until he grew accustomed to the grim light. He ran until the landscape was no longer new to him, until he could not remember why he did so. Yet he could never run far enough. At last he stopped, for the breath in him had stilled. Now the weight upon his chest was unbearable, the heavy air unbreathable. He clutched at his tight throat. He must find something to breathe but his body stiffened abruptly – the Feared Thing stalked him still. Perhaps if he did not move and made no sound it would leave him be? Perhaps if he crouched very low against the ground? His trembling fingers fumbled with the clasp, perhaps if he reversed the Cloak, became a dark thing too, a shadow, he would not be found? The Feared Thing drew close, and stopped . . . it knew these tactics well. It could afford to wait.

Now Eider crept upon the ground, moving on all fours like a beast. Through endless night he scrambled on, but the Feared Thing was never far away, rustling through the trees like the black wind. In his exhaustion Eider fell amid the tangle of nettle and briar. He rocked himself for comfort's sake, and sobbed for happiness lost. He ached for the return of light but knew it would not come and when at last the pure heart broke, the scream that was born echoed the luna day all darkness long. A cry more woeful than that of the starving beast, it frighted the carrion crow and silenced the wolf until, through the timeless dark, a slender shimmer of silver gave reply.

— 13 —

A shooting star it was, half seen, half hidden, arcing the jet sky and falling to the ground. A dazzle amid the blackness, a glimmer lost among trees. The scream died, for his eyes had glimpsed the gentle glow as it lit up the tree towers in the distance. Light! So long awaited, now it had come and again his aged pulse raced as he gave chase. He scrambled like a wild thing through the night-day, scraping the black-spiked bark, withstanding the hemlock's toxic breath, trampling the hectic root-red to reach the place where starfire had fallen.

He came to where the pale light seemed to hover and crouched low among the dense undergrowth, his black eyes full of the ethereal glow, his battered spirit strangely eased by the perfect circle of the lush green bower. His heart raced at the sight so longed for and he opened his mouth to shout aloud his joy. Yet he could make no sound higher than a growl that rattled in his throat and crept from the rail of his teeth. His keen eyes narrowed as they caught a rhythmic movement deep within the bower – an odd dispersion of light, as if colour had itself formed clouds. Eider was unnerved and looked about . . . if he had seen this glimmer-glade, the Feared Thing could not be far behind. More afraid of his pursuer than the star-fall, he scrambled through the tall bracken and into light, protectively enclosing brightness behind blackened boughs and heavy vines.

Now the brilliance of the light stung his eyes and he blinked hard, seeing the silver mist rise where dark and damp collided with warmth and light. From the ghostly vapour the colourful clouds spiralled upwards and Eider watched mesmerised by their dancing rhythms, bewildered by the delicacy of shade and hue. His senses had begun to tingle and a gasp of awe caught in his throat, as within their silent display he recognised the shape of bright wings and slender antennae. 'Butterflies,' he whispered, yet heard nought but a low reverberation in his chest. He moved towards them, trying to weep then trying to laugh as he followed the flight of a million tremulous wings. Of every design and shade they flurried upwards in the spiral of life from chrysalis to air, encouraged by warmth and starlight. Eider's face creased in smiles at their splendour and he stood erect at last, running like a child among them, head thrown back, arms outstretched as he awaited their velvet touch and begged their beauty alight upon him. Yet soon he halted for notes of enchantment floated upon the air, sounds both unknown to him and familiar. Sounds like a harp, and then a flute, yet created by a gentle voice. Sounds to which he felt himself begin to sway and towards which he knew the dancing butterflies were lured. He had heard no song like this before yet knew it to be of the Ages. As the butterflies responded to the mesmeric aura, so now Eider responded to the lilting melody, drawn to his full height, and following on to the heart of the bower. He breathed deep the sweetness of the wet grass. Then, as if his presence brought about some magic there, the evergreen was splashed with vivid colour and the blossoming of every seasons' flowers erupted, casting their alluring perfume upon the air. Delicate blossom of cherry and plum weaved amid white apple and Eider's heart leapt as the ephemeral creatures of the colour-clouds lingered there, taking the gift of nectar from the blossoms. Poppies spread through the bracken in garish profusion and the delicate creatures of the air nestled inside them on black velvet beds or mated among the petal layers of chrysanthemum.

Eider's senses were running riot, his heartbeat quickening as his feet carried him on across the luscious carpet of moss and lily of the valley. He heard the music still and fancied he had heard its haunting melody before, upon a hillside, a moor, or was it yet . . . 'Hartsmere'.

The mangled word fell from his trembling lips and he heard his own voice for the first time in all the long dark night. As the hypnotic strains of song floated to him on a new tide of blossom mist, the sadness in him soothed. He passed on to where roses grew, some red and rounded heads winding a path to their deep sweet hearts, some white and seven-petalled beauties offering stamen and sweet dew. Eider thought then on the seven planets by which he had found his fate and the Seven Sees of the Kingdom fate had given then so cruelly snatched away. His heart grew heavy but the call of the curious melody drew him forth and no rose thorn pricked him as he moved blithely on to the luminous heart of the bower.

When the melody ceased Eider halted . . . which way to go? A heavier aroma met his nostrils and throat, and he parted the evergreen. In the time that it took him to blink even to gasp delight, he was enwrapt, for here was a forest of tall lilies, virgin white, laden with buds and with nectar. The butterfly clouds engulfed him anew, weaving and diving in chaotic flurries, seeking food of the stamens and rest in the hollows. Eider felt himself swoon, intoxicated by the scented mist. The lilies stood like slender white sentinels guarding a circular pool of silver which lay at the heart of the bower. Yet Eider's gaze was riveted not by the flowers, nor the pool, but by the maid seated on an opal rock at the water's edge. Her robe was lunar white, embroidered with strange glyphs, her hair was of fine golden thread and at centre of her forehead a bright star glimmered. Eider dared not stir, dared not disturb the beauty of her song and when she looked up from her task, he braced himself, dreading that her eyes might alight on him. But it seemed she saw him not and as she raised the heavy jug to her lap, Eider watched the pure water slide from its dark mouth. He was uncertain if the contents flowed into the pool or out, for the silver surface did not shift or ripple. His puzzlement found rhythm in her curious song and hearing it once more he knew it well. It was the song he had heard that day beside the mere, the music that had drifted to him from . . . 'Hartswood'. He said it aloud, forgetting his need to hide.

The maiden dropped the jug and leapt to her feet, watching the shade in which he stood, yet seeing nothing of him.

''Tis Hartswood,' he heard her say, her large eyes flashing silver. 'Who comes here?' she demanded.

'I . . . I am . . .' Eider began his speech, but his voice was no more than a growl in his throat. As he stepped out into the brightness he heard her gentle voice trapped fast in fear of him, saw her graceful form retreat. He started abruptly . . . what had frighted her? Was it him? Or was it the Feared Thing at his back? He glanced over his shoulder seeing only the wild profusion of Nature about the magical bower. What had become of the Feared Thing? What had become of him throughout the long dark night? He turned to look upon the maiden once more and though her face registered revulsion at his presence, he saw that she held out her delicate hand to him in welcome. The closer he drew the more beauty he saw in her and all the while her eyes fixed him, at once blue then lilac, their colours shifting as in a crystal orb. They held Eider spellbound, reminding him of . . . He felt a spark of knowledge rooted deep, a truth given to him in dream, a gift from Nature's heart. 'Waisel,' he said, knowing no meaning for the word.

He saw the maiden's brow crease, for she could make no sense of the sound he uttered, and he watched her crouch at the water's edge once more. Would she sit patiently? Await his approach as one waits for a feral creature to eat from one's hand? Would he eat from her hand? He saw her look into the calm water and smile. What was it kept her by that smooth pool? He moved closer.

The water lay like a flat silver sphere among the tubular stems of lilies and green moss. It lay like glass . . . like a mirror. Eider shuddered, thinking of the dream realm, of a mirror's lies, of Ruthra. If he drew too close would he see his demon twin again? Yet he could do no more than move closer still, as curious as he was afraid. Now the pool looked like a circle of pure crystal and despair welled up from his heart as he was reminded once more of that long lost and hateful deed. He glanced at the maiden's face again, and could see from its sadness that she read his thoughts. He shook his head for shame, conscious of his ugliness and the state of his tainted spirit in this place.

The maiden beckoned him to the water's edge: would she have him drink or look? There was something in her eyes that bred new trust in him and Eider took the final steps towards the pool. As soon as his eyes met the mirror-sheen they grew heavy with tears. His silk-black mane was gone and his cropped head turned grey, his wan face veiled with the fine lines of age, and yet the marks he bore spoke of no mere span of years, but of endless time. He stretched a knarled hand towards the water, his body a-tremble for the worst sight of all almost stilled his heart. The Cloak about his skeletal shoulders hung by the faintest threads, its colours dead, its tracery long lost. The great Triad sword was nought now but a blade of corrupt steel, its gemstone hilt a leaden weight. The Gauntlet, though it still clung to his hand, was rusted, its leather mildewed by the damp. Eider could no longer bear the vision and he fell to his knees beside the water's edge. 'Rhye?' The word fell as a question from his tear-stained lips as he looked deep into the pool.

. . . *There stood the ruined castle-keep, blackened and bereft, yet within its grim shadow a pulse of life stirred. A lone stallion reared and clambered from the rubble. On its back a rider, cloaked against the bitter blast, raised a banner against the churning sky. Upon the ice draught the ragged phoenix insignia flew in a last stand of defiance. But the rider could only hang his head in sorrow as the night black steed carried him away, far from the shattered tower and the walls of mourning, far away across the hills that rolled down into emerald valleys, where eagles circled in the warm air, where razor-edged mountains pierced the flat blue sky and temperate plains melted in rivers of crystal, lapping at the edges of Time. He saw it all in one time-slowed moment, saw fertile earth cast up its shoots, saw buds born and flowers bloom in gaudy array – and all in the blink of an eye. He smelled Nature's perfumed breath, the tang of brine and then the terrible stench of burning. And about him the wild cried out and the wind roared like a beast a-prowl. There were voices too, waves of distorted sound and gritty debris that scratched his face.*

He rode on, treading in the footsteps of the dawn-bringer until it was forever Now and the land was nought but flat empty waste and the air was thick and arid. The angry sun blistered his skin and the sky began to race, its clouds scattered and stretched like rippling silk. In their wake all time and experience was revealed and lost in rapid succession, until all was gone, gone forever.

He no longer had a destination, held no recollection of the past, only clung to vague, fragmented images that flew, and echoed, then sank away. He felt a sense of loss and then a deep sorrow and though he knew not why, still his heart was broken by nameless grief. In his grip the sturdy rowan stave displayed aloft the flag of lost hope and as he rode the Plains of Time the shimmering light glowed saffron over the land and he slipped into the spaces between past, present, and future, between movement and stasis. A time of suspension where the landscape remains forever unchanged, and the bone-white trackway neither diminishes nor comes to an end. He, the axis around which all experience revolved, he the eye of the storm and when the time-held fragments sped to him he could do no more than watch them go by for he had forgotten all meanings, could make only random connections. Sounds flew about him at high frequency, sharp shadows fell from the sunless sky and the first drop of rain splashed his face. Cold, diagonal rain, that slaked his thirst, that saturated and renewed him. Then rain became a storm, and storm a flood, and the flood produced a river, and he crossed it, crossing the border-line between Now and Then.

He traversed the lowland plains of twilight seeking questions for his answers, but found instead the hill of the One-Tree. Beneath its outstretched boughs a wagon burned like an angry beacon beneath the thundery sky. He pressed his mount on towards the amber flare. There was nought left but wefts of smouldering canvas and the buckled ribs of its framework. He paced his steed on past its charred timbers and the fire-curled edges of tarot cards scattered amid the ash. On top of the crest he halted, for he beheld a vision: a solitary homestead of coarse grey stone was set beneath the black and brooding hillside. The dwelling stood derelict, its usefulness long past, yet as he coaxed his horse down the slope towards it, he fancied he saw smoke spiral from the squat chimney, and the fragile trumpets of bindweed blow about its lintel.

A seed of joy germinated in his heart as he drew close to the homestead, then dismounted and walked up the narrow pathway to the house of stone. He examined the windows but found them shuttered against him. Yet an ecstasy grew in his heart and he started to push at the strong wood of the door.

As light flooded the square room, so a smile lit up his face, for he knew the place. Here his lost years were held, and lived again in this glorious moment. He knew the simple furniture and spotless floor. Knew the table scrubbed white by loving hands, and the hearthstone where the welcoming fire blazed forever. He knew the time-caught rhythm of the rocking chair that moved with the shudder of an old heartbeat between this world and that. He knew the laughter, heard it again, recalled the tears, and saw them wept. He knew it all, and more.

In the alcove by the fire a grey-haired man drew upon his clay pipe, and rocked from shadow into light. The tobacco smoke drifted from him in ghostly blue layers and his moist eyes were wide, all-seeing. They fixed upon him, and recognition was instant, yet strangely silent.

At that moment he saw her, a young woman standing

*before the fire. She sang to herself, and though he heard
the melody, it came to him distantly and he could not
recall the words. Contented by the sight of her he leaned
upon his rowan staff and gently pushed the door to its
full gape. The woman turned from her task. He saw her
fingers fumble with the collar of her dress, saw her shield
her eyes against the brightness, her face registering disquiet, uncertainty . . . then love.*

'Is it you?' she said, taking one tentative step forward.

*As their eyes met her face lit up with smiles. ''Tis you!
Praise the Gods!' she cried, and spinning about she lifted
a green-eyed child from his play by the hearth. 'Come
Lehon, greet your father's return wi' me.'*

*Her voice echoed round the grey stone walls and as he
crossed the threshold of the place the insistent creak of
the aged chair ceased. Then Time slipped from him and
old age withered him, death fell upon him, and he
crumbled to dust.*

*Then, through the windows and broken rafters the cold
wind moaned its lament, while amid matted roots and
nettle-weeds a stave of rowan lay, solitary marker to the
brave past, and the future lost. Then, as the dust of
centuries scattered on the flagstones, the timeless sun sank
low in the west.*

'Lehon!' Eider groaned as slender fingers brushed the
surface of the pool, and the watery vision faded to the
depths. Eider cried out, 'My mortal friend, I shall see
him nevermore.' And he wept. Wept for everything
wasted, and everything lost. 'And Regor,' he sobbed.
'And Nairb, my true wizard. Where are they lost?' he
pleaded and she soothed him. Eider cowered from her
gentle touch, ashamed to look upon her beauty. He
must hide his ugliness from her. Yet as she raised him
to his feet and bade him follow, he hesitated. She
beckoned to him and he flinched, afraid to trust.

'Have no fear of me,' she whispered, drawing close.
She reached out to him but Eider shied away from her
touch. Still she coaxed. 'I shall not break your spirit,
but shall heal it with my own.'

As the pulsing colours of her eyes met his, he knew she was his only hope, knew that he must trust her or submit to the waiting Dark. So he followed the primrose footprints that she made upon the moss and thankfully partook of all she offered him at the heart of the bower.

Time-passing, she soothed him, tending all that briar and venom had inflicted on his limbs, healing the fine line of the hawk's claw, the unseelie brand upon his forearm, until the sound of her melody healed all that Dark had wrought in his heart and Eider's spirit was filled with her music, his eyes with the unending enchantment of her bower. Hour by hour she sat contented at his side within the arm of the linden tree, and he would look into her lovely face, a question on his lips, yet he said no word, should his feral voice fright her away. But soon, when the dragonflies waltzed in elegant display and the shimmer of the pool reflected upon his face, he found a sense of calm within and the question was asked.

'Lady, how came you here?'

The maiden smiled at sound of his voice, for it was soft and courtly. She raised her head to give reply, a string of snowdrops adorning her slender neck. 'As a child, the Elder hid me here in Hartswood.' Her voice was like the gentle ripple of a woodland stream.

'Hide beauty away? To live alone?' Eider replied sadly.

'To live,' the maiden replied simply. 'The Elder feared for my life.' Her lilac eyes lowered in melancholy. 'Since I came here all time has stopped for me.'

'But . . .' Eider began, recalling the star-flare that had led him to this secret place. 'You have been only . . .'

Her delicate fingers brushed his lips. 'Quiet, my gentle Eider, not all questions have answers.'

'My name!' Eider gasped not having heard it spoken for so long. 'How can you know my name?'

The maiden smiled as she touched his cheek. 'Yours is the face I saw within the pool. That sound belongs with its beauty.'

111

'Beauty?' Eider pulled away from her. 'There is no beauty in sound or sight of me! Be wary, I am cast out!'

'Speak it not!' The maid insisted. 'My only purpose is your sweet repose. My gift for you, the secrets of the Lore.'

The words crept softly into Eider's memory, once he had longed for the secret knowledge of Elders . . . of wizards. 'And you shall have it,' the maid smiled triumphantly, having heard his thoughts.

'You are a mystic?' Eider ventured shyly.

The tiny pearls of her teeth shone in knowing laughter. 'I am Lumin, banisher of dark ignorance!'

'Lumin . . .' Eider echoed her, then frowned. 'You are of light, yet darkness does not harm you?'

Her lilac eyes watched him intently. 'Trust that in this place Dark cannot impinge on us. The screen is delicate as crystal but protects as steel.' Her heavy eyelids lowered and there was sadness in her voice. 'Yet when the allotted time is at an end, Dark shall swallow me, as it swallows all.'

'And me?' Eider pressed the question, though afraid of the answer.

Lumin clasped his hands in hers. 'You shall be safe. For just as Dark dwells in the realm of Light, so here in Dark's lair a little light survives, and the knowledge I hold gives all to you.' She turned from him, her delicate hands placing two cards upon the moss. Their size and design drew him close and he saw that they were of the mystic pack of seers. He trembled as some distant fear coursed through his veins, but he could not avert his eyes. The first card he knew was the card of Hope and in its character's likeness he saw Lumin's face. The waters she poured out, the same mystic hue and the same bright star was drawn upon her placid forehead.

Lumin spoke softly. 'I am the flower of the field and the lily of the valleys. I am the mother of fair love, of knowledge and of hope.' Gently she turned over the second card. 'And here are you, the Magus or Minstrel. Your dark twin is the deceiver, the one you overcame.'

112

She pointed to the elaborate design of the card, its gold leaf, its flowers. 'Lilies and roses lie at your feet and give sign of solace,' Lumin explained. 'Soon your journey ends.'

Eider's fear melted away and he breathed the perfume of the thornless blooms upon which he knelt. The colours held within Lumin's eyes gleamed crystal vision into his as she whispered, her voice a soothing balm. 'You found my bower at last and brought with you the gift of bitter experience.'

'That is no gift,' Eider frowned perplexed.

''Tis the best that you could bring,' she reassured. 'For we learn by our mistakes, the wounds we bear are healed by Fate.' Carefully she placed a third card beside the others. The card of the Sun shone up at him with a joy of design and colour he had not beheld for so long a time. Eider gazed at the magical garden which lay within protective walls, and drawn there he saw two children dancing on the velvet green, one in shadow, the other in light.

''Tis like this bower,' Eider decided as he looked into Lumin's serene face.

She nodded and golden hair cascaded about her ivory shoulders. 'They are opposites, yet their unity brings wholeness, knowledge and procreation.' Lumin's lilac eyes met his in a steadfast gaze. ''Tis the symbol of our union. Fate dictates our match and I shall sow in you a seed of Light.'

Eider's dark eyes widened for her words drifted into his memory as those he had heard in her song. At sight of her rose-blush his heart leapt, he longed to feel her warmth against his skin, smell the perfume of her hair, hear the wistful melody of her voice. But she turned from him and awkwardness led his eyes back to the lilies and the still pool. At her return she held out her hand to him and there upon her open palm sat a small but perfect prism. 'Here is Sight beyond Sight!' she offered with a smile.

Eider gazed enrapt upon its mirrored planes, its tiny

refractions of light and colour, until he perceived its very core and fancied he saw movement there. Within its arc he saw Rhye's turret tower and the arched window of the wizard's chamber. Gazing within the window's frame he saw the familiar outline of the wizard, and there at his side the awestruck elfin. 'Dear friends,' Eider blurted, his eyes moist with silent tears.

Lumin bid him look on. Now Eider saw a shimmering object drift skyward from the courtyard below. He frowned, unsure. How it gleamed, this strange construction of glittering planes that looked like . . . 'Mirrors,' he whispered, recalling his fear of the glass and his banishment of all that reflected. He saw Nairb stand within the shadowed archway, saw the slender arms raised and the sparkling mass levitate outside the chamber window. It had begun to shrink in dimension until at last Eider recognised it as a tiny prism and watched it vanish to a pinpoint at the wizard's command. As it vanished, a spark of light ignited at its very core and Eider was brought back to the bower and to the perfect prism resting upon Lumin's palm.

'See?' Lumin said softly. ''Tis the mystic light, 'tis the star you saw. When it fell into my bower I knew that you were close.'

As he looked into her eyes, Eider's heart welled up with joy. For iin her he had found the deepest love, a pure love that transcended his physical union with Baobhanshee. Had he ever loved his raven-haired queen at all? In that moment he felt grief for his loss, or his misjudgement. Had his reason been deceived by her dark beauty, had he been spell-cast by her cunning father, the Maquis Caulide? Yet now it mattered little, for the ancient lore had not deserted him. He was not cast out, not lost!

'Not lost . . .' Lumin spoke his thoughts aloud. 'But found.' She smiled into his confused face. 'I loved at sight of you,' she said. 'In my fourteenth summer I came to this place and saw your face within the pool. I shall love no other.'

Eider's heart pounded with joy and sudden emotion and for the first time he understood the hand that Fate had dealt him. In all his memories, none more beautiful than she. None more wise or magical. None more perfected in the rites of seelie lore. Yet at thought of all these things he grew suddenly anxious. His dark wedding day had long since passed and Rhye . . . the knot in his heart grew tighter still.

Lumin drew close at the sight of his sorrow and leaning towards him, she plucked something fine and dry from the weave of his bedraggled cloak. The featherlight stem of rye grass gleamed gold-green as she held it up for him to see. 'Fear not . . .'tis close,' she said as she wound and plaited the single stem until she placed it, a perfect circle, on the palm of his hand. Eider's awestruck gaze met hers and with the healing of the pure heart he placed the ring of rye upon her finger. Her glade-dappled face shone in the soft-hued light as they kissed and camelias blossomed in the shaded hollow of their union.

And so within the glowing temenos they dwelt together in love, and Lumin taught him all she knew, of how to weave seelie music on the lute and the magical uses of its voice; of how to wield the rowan stave and read its marks within the sand. And she gave him simple gifts of paper, stone and wood, yet they were magic tokens of tarot, runes and darkest sticks of yarrow. And, when at last he had mastered the rudiments of seelie lore she draped him in white robes and bestowed on him a single coin of silver, a baton of smooth ivory and a cup of brightest gold. These she placed with his own Great Sword and Eider bowed reverently as she entrusted to him the four elements: water, earth, air, fire.

'Mediator of the elements, make one to agree with another. That which is cold make warm, that which is dry make moist. That which is hard, soften. That which is Dark make Light.'

'I will,' Eider gave his solemn promise.

Lumin took his hand in hers. 'Come, follow me so you may take the wisdom of the Magus on with thee.'

He walked with her the circle of the arbour three times round until they came to rest before a spinning wheel. 'Now listen to this song of mine and learn it well,' she coaxed. 'For like this robe, 'tis woven both for spirit's ease and spirit's flight.' With the first notes of song her wheel began to spin and cast its spindle shadow over him, first light then dark, then light, then dark again. He shivered, he tingled and shook, knowing himself the receiver of ancient knowledge, the carrier of light and shade. In its minutes, its hours or its seconds length he felt a peace he had never known, for now he heard her well and his growing wisdom made all things clear. Yet as he watched her at her spell so too did his heart ache for had she not told him that Dark would consume this oasis of light when her allotted time was spent? Eider frowned resolve, he would memorise her song and sing it for comfort through the long night of Dark. The sudden wind flurry cast a chill in his heart and drew his sad eyes to hers, yet she did not look at him, nor did she move for now the wheel spun of itself. The breeze of its speeding rhythm spiralled newly fallen leaves and caught up her hair in golden tongues, and though her lips did not move Eider heard her speak, her voice like the magical turning of the wheel was all about him.

'Then memorise three names and speak them only in this way. "Wizard. Regal. King".'

Gripped by the power of the wheel, Eider repeated each word and with each utterance the speed of the spinning decreased. In the sudden stillness Lumin's crystal eyes rose to meet his.

'Remember, sweet Eider. Remember well!' she entreated him. 'For though you hold the Triad, it can give no help in the labyrinth of Dark. Only the wisdom of a Magus can aid you there.'

Eider's voice faltered with sorrow. 'I shall forget no word you spoke or sang, forsake no gift you gave to me.' He gave his solemn oath. 'The love I hold for you will not allow it.' He embraced her in sudden panic. 'Yet how long before the Feared Thing takes us? How long do we have left?' he pleaded.

Lumin pressed delicate fingers to his lips, her lilac eyes shining with new visions. He turned with her to the grains of sand spread flat before the shimmering pool. There he watched her draw with the rowan stick and recognised the outline of a triangle, then an intricate and complex maze of lines which multiplied in perfect perspective to the very core. All was order and perfection within and Eider's new sight gave him clearly the route to the silent cell at the pyramidal heart. Now his pulse raced, but the rowan stave paused. Lumin's swan-like neck rippled. 'Seek out the Ancient Youth,' she charged him. 'He gives direction through the chaos.' At these words the straight line at the base of the triangle wavered and the rowan staff struck out into the void that surrounded it. To the left it plunged, and to the right in a frenzy of irrational squiggles and knotted lines that twisted and turned back on themselves to retrace again and again the echo-tangle that formed the unruly labyrinth. The stave was trapped in an endless circling until suddenly it stopped. 'Temenos,' she smiled at him.

Eider understood then that her wand had come to rest at the place in which he now stood. But he could not return her smile, his face having set in fear and awe for in the blink of an eye Lumin had drawn a route for him. Upside down and back to front it was, having beginning at its end and ending at the point of departure, here, inside her magic dome of Light. Yet the higher wisdom that she had conferred upon him told him it was the journey he must make, and the fate awaiting there. His heart brimmed with sudden pride for his knowledge of the Lore was now complete. He could both read and understand the mystic signs, the meaning of her strange map. Yet though he tried, the certainty of seelie lore would not translate to thought or word and he could do no more than meet her gaze in total calm. He

remembered then her fingers touch upon his lips, saw
again the protective gleam in her eye and knew she
would have him keep his secret safe. So he did not speak
it, only felt her comforting warmth as she draped him
with the woven robe that she had made. An outer gar-
ment of mystic blue it was, the sapphire robe of the
initiate. 'No more the confused wanderer of woeful
Dark . . .' she murmured into his ear. 'But Magus, the
living flame of seelie lore.' She saw the shifting colours
of her own eyes reflected in his dark orbs as he gave
ritual reply.

'I am that living flame.'

Lumin clasped his hands in hers. 'Now you shall meet
power with power, on equal terms.' She drew close to
fasten the carved silver clasp at his shoulder. 'Look to
the lining of this robe,' she instructed softly. 'The threads
of the Triad's bright cloak are hidden in its weave.' She
pressed her lips against the gemstone of the Triad sword.
'Guard it well,' she said. 'Use it only when the power
of the Magus fails you, lest the seelie relics be condemned to Dark.'

Eider saw crystal droplets glisten in her eyes and knew
them to be tears, saw her smile of joy flicker to a smile
of sad farewell, and knew the time was come. She kissed
his cheek and led him to the silver pool. Now he dared
look into its shimmering eye and saw reflected there her
perfect countenance and next to it he glimpsed his own.
He frowned, how could it be? No time-lines etched the
flesh, no grey hair threaded through the black, no fear-
dulled eyes met his, only beauty. There was wisdom in
the kohl-black eyes and in the rich mane of jet a slender
streak of red designated him fire-carrier. Now was he as
he once was, and more, returned to youth and vigour.
His spirit healed, reforged by seelie lore, the true heart
mended and embellished by love. His pulse raced with
elation . . . dare he speak it? Dare he vow that he who
once had conquered Dark throughout Rhye would rout
it again now, and for all time? He turned to tell her it
would be so yet in the time it took him to turn he sensed

118

the upward spiral of flight, felt the draught of wings, saw the flash of colour and watched the rainbow feathered bird climb helter-skelter through the tree towers. It blinked its crystal eye and he cried out, 'Lumin!' Her echo-call came back to him and from her golden bill she dropped a gleaming trinket. It fell through space as she sang on, her magic song echoing in the bower as he ran to retrieve the object from the moss. The tiny prism sat upon his palm in geometrical perfection, the ancient route locked within its maze of planes. Eider's throat tightened with joy and sorrow yet the gentle touch of feather down upon his brow drew his gaze to the canopy of leaves. For long moments he traced the gold edge of her wing tip here, or there the irridescent green of her tail, watching through the network of trees until her song grew distant, her colours vanished and he halted. He kissed the solitary feather in his hand, and plaited it into his own silken hair, then with a final look at the prism he hid it deep within the folds of his woven robes.

In that moment he crouched low for all beauty, all life and light was swallowed up by Dark. Eider shuddered with the sense of loss and glanced skyward, hoping against hope that Lumin would return. But she, the star of his hope, Lumin, the bright bird, was gone from him never to return. He breathed long and deep, yet he felt no fear, for though he was alone, he held both purpose and route, had imbibed all a seelie Magus needed to survive. He clenched his teeth . . . he would survive, he would triumph over Dark, would restore light to this accursed place!

'No more the wanderer . . .' he echoed Lumin's words. 'But the living flame of seelie lore.' He wrapped himself in the cloak Lumin had woven for him and was warmed by the memory of her embrace. He could feel the power of Magus burning at the very core of his being, felt it shine through his wide, glittering eyes. Its diamond light illuminated where he trod and he moved upright through the nightscape at last. He blinked, he could now discern colours and textures, suddenly he was aware that he could at last see the world of Dark Nature in which he stood. The route that Lumin had drawn for him was vibrant still in his mind's eye and so, pulling the cloak tight about him, he trod forth with certain hope.

He marvelled at the troughs and hollows of this realm, framed with sentinel trees, more overgrown waste than woodland, more fearful to him than any forest. All about him, trees . . . some ageless torsos stood guard, others twisted to divert his path. Some were fallen and blocked his route, others pointed the way with their fibrous hands.

Eider searched out the ghastly green of the moon that he had so often wept beneath in those terrible night-days before the star-fall. He could no longer find it, but found instead, hanging as if from the churning black of the sky, three giant orbs. Perfect spheres of mauve they were. One hung so low he fancied he could see his own form reflected in its sheen. 'What kind of moon is this?' he breathed. He stretched out a hand, and yes, he could touch it. He felt its waxy texture, glimpsed tendrils and minute hairs, saw the thick green umbilical cord that anchored it, but to what? He shrank back. The orbs he had misguidedly thought strange moons were nothing more than berries. Grown out of all proportion, enormous spheres of plant juices hung in their thick purple and claret skins. He scrutinised their shape, the permutation of leaf and tuberous stalk. 'Belladonna,' he said aloud.

Now he looked anxiously about him, the realisation that these were the mutant offspring of Dark Nature brought home a sudden truth. These were not trees that he walked amongst, but roots, these were not hills and troughs but the texture of black earth. He caught a handful of ice-cold fragments that fell about him in black flurries and examined them afresh. He had once called them snow but saw now that they were not crystal water. ''Tis a mote of vileness . . . a black spore!' He watched the squirming mound melt against the warmth of his palm. 'Black spores of this Dark forest blow, and germinate in the soil ridge,' he whispered in horrified realisation.

Moving on he passed beneath the wide arches of spike-briar, and further still weaved a path between battalions of giant sharp-toothed nettles. How had Dark Nature spread to such vile dimensions? Or was it he who had changed? Had his endless night in the time-fold reduced him to insignificance in this place? He shivered in the down-draught, the black winds' flight casting the frozen spores to earth, then whirling them into clouds, whipping them into a blizzard. Eider wrapped the cloak about him, covering his face as he pushed on through the speeding blast. Soon the spores were thick black underfoot, crusted with grey ice, yet still Eider trudged on, the maze, clear drawn by Lumin's hand, giving him direction to its heart. Right, then left, then left and right again he turned. Onward, then left, then left and right again until the drifting spores were thigh deep.

Exhaustion gripped him, but the heat pulse within provided the strength to carry on. Indeed, he dare not stop for the seeds of Dark clung to him, their clammy insistence was eager, hungry, and he knew they would consume him should he falter or fall. By the pure light of Lumin's love he swore he would not falter. By the pulse of life inside him he vowed he would not fail. He would push on, would reach the centre of the maze. There he would find shelter, there he would hide from the open orifice of all-consuming evil.

A sudden excretion of slime halted him momentarily and he shrank back from a writhing mandrake. It squirmed in the spore drift like a giant snake, its poison oozing forth in a half-frozen and putrid stream. Now as the black winds gained strength, so the drifts flew in heavy torrents and battered against every root and mound. Soon Eider could not see a pace before him but still he followed the map, held fast in his mind's eye. Turning ever right then right, and left then right again until, blinking the clinging spores from his eyelashes, he saw the faintest glimmer.

'Light?' he chanced to speak it. 'Light, light!' he insisted against the monotony of the spore flurries as he urged his weary body on. His teeth chattered as he felt the ice-breath of the Feared Thing seep now through his cloak, felt it suck at limb and bone. Felt its deadly weight press in upon him. His heart raced against the agony, he must escape from the burden of fear, must avoid capture at all costs. And so he ran . . . ran towards the faintest of all glimmers trapped in the hollow beyond. Yet as he ran the undergrowth began to change. Just ahead strange fungi ranged over the entire forest floor and the nearer he got to their ranks, the taller they grew. Before long the forest of roots became a realm of fungi, towering above him in all their gruesome varieties, and the textures of this vile forest were soon lost to the spreading mass that consumed every dead thing and moved in upon the living.

Eider stepped up his pace, he dared not linger here, for greater than this primeval horde of Dark was the demon of his own fear. It churned inside his gut, the terrible feeling of pursuit, of being stalked, hunted down. Though Lumin's teaching had become the fount of calm understanding within him, though it had afforded him the mystic arts and granted the gift of acute intuition, still the shadow of the Feared Thing haunted him. Sometimes it was a distant nagging, or else it was so close that he felt the vibration of its ·heart-beat resound in his own breast. He longed to confront it, yet feared its presence above all things. He longed to conquer it, but the time had not yet come. When it did come he would outwit it, deny it victory, destroy it for all time.

So tightly did he clutch the cloak to him that his knuckles were white. He glanced at them feeling pain; the Gauntlet that clung to his right hand made him frown, for its rusted fingertips were emitting a faint gleam of light. 'How so?' he questioned, holding up his hand for closer inspection, but as the black winds gusted into his face he was forced to avert his eyes and push on into the Dark heart. Soon even the vaulted roof of the tangled canopy bore parasitic clusters of fungal tissue. It had claimed dominion over all that was in its path and soon its spores would create new networks and obliterate the distant sky completely. The floor was dense with their spongy textures and Eider felt the fleshy tissue contract and expand underfoot as he weaved to avoid hollow tentacles coated with green mucilage. The foetid aroma clung to him as he brushed against the slimy fronds.

The air was thin and tasted of decay, of Dark Nature claiming its own, and more. Repulsed, Eider stumbled on through the tuberous ranks, unlocking spore pods which exploded about him in clouds of violent pink, sulphur yellow and cinnabar red. Was this another trap set by the Feared Thing? Was he moving ever closer to its lair? Eider filled his lungs anew. Now the air was impregnated with spore scent, and soon his head was muzzy with the heaviness of the fumes. Wart-roughened tubers stretched out for him in reticulated lines, clasped and entwined him, brought him finally to a standstill. He looked upwards to see the dark brown underbellies of the massive fungal clusters, opened like vast parasols above his head. Higher still the fantastic and various coloured structures stretched on as a vast system of tiers into infinity. Conical and funnelled, dome-like and hoof-shaped. At their bases the lime-encrusted Flowers of Tan spread cushioned-shaped fruits over the mouldering earth and shone with the softness of kid-hide.

The light was more meagre here yet Eider's glittering eyes spied out the low arch of a tunnel which etched its way through the dying forest. With renewed effort he struggled free and stumbled on towards it. Could he really see a faint glimmer at the pathway's end? Could there be some dwelling there? Or was it the luminous eye of the Feared Thing he saw, drawing him on to the heart of its lair? If it was, would he enter?

He followed the route and soon came upon a strange structure of stone. Besieged by rot, its time-battered mortar was permeated by ribbons of fungus. New spores wedged in every crack and crevice and thick stalks protruded from every mortar free hole. Eider had begun to sweat and then to shiver. His throat had tightened and he could barely swallow back his terror. The coriaceous tubers parted one after the other as if his approach had triggered some secret spell and within the menacing Dark an opening appeared, a wedge of grey amid the blackness, as if light were escaping from a chink in the impenetrable wall of Darkness. Eider ran for it. Whatever it was could not be part of the Feared Thing for he was sure that that engendered nought but shadow.

As he drew closer he realised that the filtered light sprang from a low doorway. He entered in. He appeared to be in some kind of tunnel and as he neared the end of the passage so the grey-blue light that had attracted him changed to a tawny glow. As he emerged into the soft halo of colour Eider realised that he had entered a circular chamber of stone. From the centre, where he stood, seven narrow passages radiated like the spokes of a wheel. From the heart, worn stairs rose in a frightening vertical to the top of some distant tower. Eider turned back to see that the forest of fungi had receded as if in retreat from the light.

The walls were decked with sheaves of evergreen and among them wildwood berries gleamed in the golden light. There was a fire dancing on a stone-carved hearth. The mantle bore green apples ripening in the warmth while before the brightly burning roots and logs, a leather armchair was set. It was high backed and battered with age but a more comfortable chair he had not seen for ages past. His bones ached to sit in it, to be comforted before the life-giving flames.

Beside the armchair was set a low octagonal table upon which a tall candle sputtered. It burnished all within its circle of saffron light: a jug of wine, parchments and quills, a jumble of odd toys, a bowl of pine nuts and two cups. Its glow touched one other thing too, a thing Eider could not recognise: a curious mechanism of wood. He scanned the chamber for sign of life. It was completely empty. He could see all, and saw no one. Yet the fire had been lit by someone, the nuts and wine had been laid down by someone. He watched the fire, eager to feel warmth on his ashen face, but the wooden puzzle called to him and he bent to examine the strange object. Its framework was well carved and polished smooth. Held within it though attached in no way that was visible were three small wooden spheres, the size and colour of horse chestnuts. They were waiting it seemed, poised in readiness on the air itself . . . it took the lightest touch, a fingertip to shift the balance, and the motion began, a perpetual motion that Eider began and found he could not halt. His face flushed, his heart raced as he watched it, heard its click-click-clicking echo about the silent room. Soon above the rhythm came the scrape of aged castors and the heavy armchair turned from shadow into light. Eider's blood ran cold for in that moment he came face to face with the tenant of the round tower.

The eyes that met his were large and mahogany. They narrowed in sudden and critical squint, as the fine line of the eyebrows knitted and the cupid's bow lips pursed in annoyance. Eider caught his breath for the face that riveted him with such disdain was that of a young boy. The close-cut hair was dark as molasses and green bracken was weaved among its curls. Eider made to speak but was silenced by the boy's voice.

'What's to do doody?' he demanded, his anarchic joviality belying the sternness of his countenance.

— 15 —

The boy spoke with the strangest of voices; a hybrid, at once solid bass and the shrill pitch of childhood. Its combined tones pained the ears and set the candle a-flutter, yet before Eider could reply the lad stood up. No more than half Eider's height, he was clad from top to toe in a moth-eaten coat, a worn mosaic of once gaudy fabrics, its sleeves flapped beyond his fingertips, its trim concertina'd about his large ill-shaped feet. His skin was grey as fungi, his hair brown as acorn cups. He made a tentative move towards Eider, then sniffed the air as if to determine the intruder's origin. They weighed one another up in confused silence until at last Eider ventured to speak.

'Who are you?'

'Who am I? Who am I?' The boy pointed an accusing finger in his direction. 'What are you?!'

Eider straightened. 'I am of seelie-kind. Eider, King of Rhye.'

'King?' the boy interrupted.

Eider drew breath to calm annoyance. 'I come in search of the Ancient Youth.'

The boy scowled mischievously and scratched his rump. 'A wanderer . . . ? In search of a truth?' he quizzed, a spiteful glint in the keen eye. He turned to the hearth and snatched up the bellows. Soon great warm flames climbed the chimney back and the lad turned a laughing face on his uninvited guest. 'Eider . . . tasty brew!' He gave a sudden frown. 'Got any?'

Eider did not understand and shook his head.

'Yorath!' the lad spat at the grate. He stood on tiptoe and took down a stem-pipe from a niche high in the wide chimney breast. He filled it with herb root and

127

snatching a spill from the hearth stone, he lit the pipe and slumped back into the armchair to enjoy his smoke, as if Eider's arrival and their strange conversation had never occurred.

Unnerved by his sudden 'invisibility', Eider glanced anxiously about him for a sign, anything that might help him to understand the place that he had found. There was little to behold: a pile of battered objects he took to be playthings; some scattered parchments covered with indecipherable scribbles; a pattern of squares scrawled on the dusty flagstones with a piece of slate. There were platters too, some dirty, some clean, some cups and carafes. How had the child come to be here? Was he alone? Eider turned back to the armchair and found the keen eyes fixed firmly on him.

'Blue as sacred fire . . .' The boy said, half to himself as he stretched out to touch Eider's cloak. 'And his sword shall be the gold of solar light.' He whispered, almost as a chant and Eider, following the lad's gaze, looked down at the sword buckled about his waist. His brow knitted, for the sheath that held the blade was no longer a scabbard of worn leather and dulled ivory but shone with the brightness of gold. Yet how? He studied the hilt of the Triad sword, it too gleamed with the same burnished colour. With trembling hands Eider eased out the sullied blade and his heart leapt, for the fraction of it that he saw was unblemished and in the strange light he fancied he saw its sheen changed from silver to bright gold. How had this change occurred? By spell or by chance? Or was it just some trick of the light, some sleight of an unseelie hand? He dare not chance the blade here. Dare not expose it for long in a place so hemmed in by Dark. Quickly, he sheathed the sword from sight and tried to compose himself once more. 'What is the name of this place?' he demanded with proud assurance.

The lad, who had been gazing in wonderment upon the seelie weapon, looked surprised. 'Why, 'tis the broch of Ancient Merle!' he said curtly as if Eider should not need to ask at all.

Eider drew an impatient breath. Lumin's route had led him to the place. 'Then come,' he commanded. 'Take me to him, to the Ancient that I seek.'

The boy leapt from his chair. ''Tis Merle I am! Merrymasker, wood-whittler and teller of wig-wags!'

Eider was dumbfounded. He shook his head, then frowned at the sapling who stood proudly before him. 'You are but a child.'

The lad stamped his foot. 'I am six time-slips! Near seven!' he protested.

'Time-slips?' Eider echoed the boy's odd speech. 'If you are he . . .' he frowned, 'how long have you been here?'

Merle shrugged. 'How long? How short?' he laughed, hauling up the folds of his patchwork coat. He drew long upon the clay pipe. 'I recall a time . . . a rhyme!' he looked at Eider with a quizzical frown. Eider drew close to him, eager for his tale. 'An ending . . .' he began again. 'Or was it a beginning?' The nut brown eyes widened then slanted. 'No matter.'

'No matter?' Eider urged him.

The lad smiled sideways at Eider's anxiety. 'A time of crystal,' he offered, watching as the stranger drew closer still. 'Nay, I recall it not!' He shrugged and Eider cast up his hands in despair. He stared at the boy and the lad glared back but Eider did not speak, determined the young one would be the first to grow weary of the game of silence. He soon did. 'Yorath!' he swore. ''Twas crystal!' The moon-white face flushed with sudden recall. 'An eye of time, smashed long past!'

Eider's face fell from a look of joy to one of sorrow. 'By this hand was the baneful deed done.' He raised his right hand and looked long upon the tainted Gauntlet. But the dark eyes widened at the sight of the diamond gems. Long dim, they now shone blue as sapphires and the cracked and battered leather was again soft and black as velvet.

The boy paced towards him. 'Then it is for you I wait?'

His speech shook Eider from thought and he met the lad's look of certainty. 'This is your only purpose?' he questioned.

The boy stopped short of answer and shoved his hands deep into the pockets of his coat. 'All forgotten!' he frowned, suddenly taken with the shape of his own feet.

'Forgotten?' Eider repeated mechanically, seeing the boy snatch from the pile of toys a cup and ball of dark wood. Over and over again the ball was swung, back and forth on its coarse string until, with one flick of the wrist it came neatly to rest in its cradle.

'I win!' the boy cried and his look of delight carried Eider momentarily back to his own boyhood triumphs, until new urgency surged through him at remembrance of his present plight.

'Come Merle, I beg you, give me aid,' he persuaded softly. 'Time runs too fast, my time is almost done!'

Merle cast him a sly glance, laughter escaping from the wine-red lips as he took to the slate-drawn squares enthralled in a new rhythm, a new game. 'Time!' he said, landing on the first square and beginning his game of hop-scotch. He spun on one leg then hopped over the scrawled design, his rhyme punctuating every stop along the way.

'Time to kill, time to kill, everyone has . . . time to kill,' he turned on one foot. 'Time to watch the hours go by from the hole inside the eye . . . strange how busy . . . stranger still . . .' he stopped to regain his balance, 'how we find the time to . . . kill!' His spin, point and stare into Eider's face made his blood run cold, for in the boy's mind was his finger an arrow, or a dagger? Should he laugh or duck to avoid its sting? The lad grinned into his fearful expression. 'Time shall not kill YOU!' he guffawed, then the laughter vanished as the young face set. 'But the Scath might.'

The word awoke the tremors in Eider's blood pulse, he remembered again the endless dark and repeated,

'The Scath?' In that moment there was sudden silence, for the click-click motion of the spheres had ceased.

'Omega already?!' cried the boy and Eider looked at him, but suddenly Merle was no more than a fleet shadow racing past him, shouting at a gleeful pitch, 'I hide, you seek!'

Eider wheeled about, but the boy had vanished completely. What could he do but follow? He must find the lad and persuade him to tell all. Though how could he unravel the knot of childhood reason? He took up the tall candle and started to search. At first he peered into each of the passageways that led off from the central chamber in which he stood. Then he looked up the sheer staircase. Still there was no sign, yet surely the lad could not have run up the staircase without being heard. Far above, at the top of the stairwell, Eider glimpsed a tiny dome of light and so began his ascent. But though he seemed to climb and climb, and though all below grew smaller and smaller, the pinpoint of light grew no larger. He was soon tired and stopped to gather air; then the distant hum of speech drifted to him from below. Eider was furious! Somehow the boy had tricked him, had concealed himself and watched his every fearful move.

Eider ran back down into the round room, determined he would allow the lad to beguile him no longer. As soon as he had cleared the last step, Eider realised that the room had undergone some change. Now, where sheaves of evergreen and berries had hung, he could find only wheat and root vegetables. The hard green apples that had rested upon the mantle had ripened to russet and gold. The fire too had changed, for now it burned low within the hearth, its ashes yielding up gleaming embers that were red as jewels. He caught the sweet smell of chestnuts roasting in the grate, noticed that the tall candle he held had burnt so low the flame licked his fingers and he dropped it to the flagstones, scattering hot wax.

Eider rubbed his chin thoughtfully, the game had lasted only moments, he was sure. The sudden click-

click-click of the wooden spheres broke the silence and he looked at the octagonal table. Now different objects lay scattered on its surface and about the floor. A small telescope, a wooden quadrant and, he squinted to see, what looked to be a star catalogue. He frowned; what stars were there to be seen in the Shadowland? Who was it saw them? The boy . . . or someone else? He glanced at the old armchair. It faced the fire, as it had the moment he had entered the broch. Then he caught sight of the edge of a patchwork coat. So, his young host hid within the chair's winged shadow? He would extract the lad and call for an end to these games!

Eider leapt at the chair, plunging both hands over its back and into its cushioned depths. He grappled with the patchwork coat but as quickly recoiled for the chair turned abruptly and the wrinkled face of an old man peered up at him in startled amazement.

'What's to do doody?' he said, purple lips delicately lining the toothless mouth. His fine hair was pure white and crowned with autumn leaves of oak and curls of copper bracken.

Eider backed off. The wearer of the patchwork coat was an ageless creature. The frame was still small, the feet still large and the eyes of the boy still gleamed from the lined face, a face with skin the texture and the colour of bark. His demeanour was that of a revered sage and his presence in the armchair transformed it into a sacred throne.

'I said, what's to do?' the voice of bass and falsetto insisted as the aged one rose to his feet.

'What game is this?' Eider answered with a new question. 'Where is the boy? Where is Merle?'

The old mahogany eyes widened with sudden insight and he gave Eider a lopsided smile. 'Two lives have I, though joined in one. The stiller I stand – the faster I run!'

Eider shrugged, embarrassed beneath the old one's gaze and as suddenly felt his senses tingle with fear as the freckled hand proffered him a gift.

'Hour-glass!' the old one wheezed. ''Tis the answer,' he explained to his bewildered guest. 'Hour-glass!' He rocked with self-congratulation as he placed the object down upon the table, soon engrossed in the trickle of sand that he had set in motion.

'But who are you?' Eider persisted, unsure that he was heard at all.

The old one sank back into the armchair as if his soul had returned from astral flight. His face had taken on the serenity of all-knowing and when he spoke again it was with the echo-voice of the cloisters. 'I am the Ancient Merle,' he said, as if he were administering a blessing.

Eider made to speak but stopped himself. He looked again upon the similarities of stature, the patchwork coat, the thin felt boots covering ill-shaped feet. He recalled the quirky grin and the last word uttered by the boy before he had disappeared. ' "Omega" – the last . . . the end.' He turned the thought over in his mind and the words of the riddle became the answer to his question. 'The Ancient Youth,' he acknowledged at last. 'Two lives joined in one!'

His sudden insight filled him with a sense of wonder and then of calm, though he did not ask the questions tumbling in his mind and he looked to the Ancient to quiz him further. But there was by now something in the sage-like concentration, a sense of greatness that Eider recognised and understood. This was an audience with one of special grace and in the kindly face he saw the wisdom of the Ages. Before such a presence Eider's curiosity was tempered by humility and he gave a respectful bow.

'At last you found your way,' the old man breathed, looking not at Eider but upon the flickering fire. 'From my tower I charted your course. Watched you triumph, saw you falter.' He shook his head sadly. 'Watched and waited. Waited long.'

Eider quietly pressed the question. 'How long?'

The Ancient Merle shrugged his narrow shoulders. 'How long? How short? Times past, or to come?'

Eider took a step closer and stretched out a hand. 'What is to come? What shall I do to set things right?'

The old man nodded gravely. 'Do as the Gods command.'

Eider lowered his eyes, dejected. 'Then my life I forfeit for transgression of the Lore.'

Merle gave a knowing look. 'Die a thousand times, still you could not change your destiny.'

'Destiny?' Eider stated and questioned at once. He paced forward to the dying flames, an anxious penitent. 'I thought my destiny was in saving the Kingdom. In restoring light and hope where dark prevailed. Yet . . .' He raised his sword hand. 'With this hand I destroyed all I valued most.' He grimaced with self-loathing yet as both he and the Ancient looked upon it, the gems of the Gauntlet gleamed sapphire in the fireglow.

The Ancient shook his head. 'My son, you are no destroyer of Light.'

Eider trembled as he recounted the nightmare and the Ancient Merle listened patiently, measured reckless action against baneful deed, misjudgement against heroic triumph, cowardice against compassion, kindness against cruelty. When Eider's voice finally trailed off into a sob of despair, the old one closed his eyes, uttering no judgement.

Eider fell to his knees and clasped the veined hand. 'Wise one, what has happened to me?' he pleaded, distraught. 'Why has Rhye's most faithful son tainted Ancient Lore, defiled the sacred Triad?'

Merle touched the ink black hair as if in blessing. 'Child of the line of Eyre, your blood flows from the noble source of Rhion. 'Tis the fate of his line tears your heart in two.' The old hands brushed Eider's troubled brow. 'Your soul is caught between the poles of black and white as once his was. One forever struggling to overcome the other.'

Eider remembered then the ancient fireside tale told

134

to children, a tale long past telling. 'Yet surely it is right to combat evil?' he questioned the serene face of all-knowledge.

The old man sighed the heavy sigh of experience. 'The power for good or ill lies in all hearts. Yet we all hide from our darkest selves, seek always to conquer, never to embrace.'

Eider was aghast. 'Embrace Dark?'

Merle closed his hand over Eider's fist. 'Only in reconciliation will your true peace be found.'

Eider sat back on his heels, unable to assimilate the Ancient's reasoning. He shook his head. 'I can forge no bond with Dark. Rhye's King must forever defend the pure heart, champion white over black.'

The old man released a sigh of deepest sorrow. 'My son, seek not the impossible, for you are but an instrument of the Gods. A wielder of the Lore no more, the constant prey of instincts both glorious and base.'

The Ancient's calm certainty transfixed Eider and he listened intently.

'Only fulfil the duty laid on you,' he continued. 'From Lumin, your luna queen was gained the gift of light and spiritual energy. Now, if heart and soul are willing you shall honour the dictates of the Lore and the power of the Triad shall be reforged for another's use.'

At his words Eider stiffened. 'Another?' he said, his voice laced with hurt.

Merle clasped his gauntlet-covered hand. 'Eider, 'tis vanity fails you. My son, you are but the smallest link in a timeless chain.'

Eider lowered his eyes in sudden shame and the Ancient Merle clasped him by the shoulders in a grip more firm than the old one's frail body suggested possible.

'For Lumin's sake you are reprieved by Fate. Go forth from here, prove yourself worthy of the title Triad Wielder.'

Eider nodded proudly. ''Tis all my heart desires.'

'Then seek out the path,' the old man stated it clear.

Eider inclined his head. 'The path?'

The Ancient Merle smiled benignly. 'That which leads to the sacred fire. The mystic centre which is your quest's end.'

Eider caught his breath. 'The end of the quest?' he mused. 'Then the winning of the Triad, and of Rhye itself, was not the goal destined for me?'

The old man shook his head. 'We are all pieces in the game. Some of us briefly transcend insignificance . . . yours, my son, is the sacrifice.' He looked at Eider with an unwavering gaze. 'The act that will bring about the reconciliation of opposites.'

Eider's dark orbs swam with bitter tears. 'But what of Rhye?' he said desperately. 'What of those I loved and have lost?'

The Ancient Merle offered him the hand of comfort. 'Rhye's time is gone,' he said prophetically. 'But there shall be a new time, a time darker and more desperate than this. And there will be one such as you, one who will in turn defend the Lore and bring light to the world of men.'

Eider stared into the fathomless eyes, understanding at last the pattern in whose weave he was but a slender thread.

'The Lore is handed on through Time,' Merle reassured. 'And for you, as for those before and after you, there can be no choice.'

Eider gripped the ancient hands in his. 'Wise one, I am afraid. We draw too close; I am yet unworthy of the Ancient Lore.'

Merle breathed calm upon him. 'You shall learn all you need to aid you in the task. Lumin has sown the seed of immortality and with it the mystic gifts of the Magus. Now the realm of sensation is overcome and intellect shall win the game.'

'An ancient game?' Eider pondered, then frowned. 'What must I do?'

The old brow creased in concentration. 'Take the core of light to the barrow grave of Kings. There the Phoenix

136

Fire shall purge the pure heart of all ill . . . then will
you find healing. There the seed of hope shall be given
life and the process of destiny worked out in the world.'

Eider's brow was furrowed deep with puzzlement and
he turned to question the old man but the sage turned
abruptly as if awakened from a trance. He pointed to
the table and as Eider followed the line of the bony
finger he saw the last grains of sand trickle into the base
of the hour-glass. The sudden silence startled him and
he glanced at the wooden spheres; their clicking rhythm
had ended too. When he looked back to the chair it was
empty. His audience with the Ancient was at an end.
Eider closed his eyes for sorrow but in the closing and
opening of his heavy lids, Omega had given way to
Alpha-time. Now the fire roared in the grate and the
boy's laughing face beamed up at him from the shadow
of the armchair.

'Since you could not find me, seelie King, I win!' he
grinned.

Eider smiled with calm understanding, and with a
nod conceded the boy's victory over his own less agile
reasoning. He watched the lad jump from the wide chair
and seat himself cross-legged before the fire, then, careful not to burn his fingers, he teased the charred chestnuts from the hearth. He offered a full platter of them
to Eider and they sat together peeling the brittle shells
and devouring the sweet kernels. Then the boy offered
woodland fruits and poured golden liquid from the jug.

Eider received all with a silent smile and a nod of
thanks, sniffing the more curious victuals and recognising
among them the waxy fruit of Round Morel and the
nutty taste of Penny-Bun. But there was also, in the
midst of edible delights, the wart-covered red cap of Fly
Agaric. It glistened invitingly and as the boy snatched it
up Eider took it from him. He twisted it between thumb
and forefinger as he pronounced it poisonous. Merle
frowned and with a snarl cast the fungus to the back of
the grate. Eider noted the glint in the bright eyes as they
watched it burn but said no more of it. Thereafter, they

often sat together over their meal of berries and roots, then, after all else, their pipes would be lit and Eider would drink the golden cider brew while the boy played at his dice and jacks.

—— 16 ——

So time passed by in the sheltered broch and it seemed to Eider he did no more than eat, drink and take his ease. When the hourglass trickled night to day he would sit at the Ancient's feet and listen as a child would to his words, extracting truths and meanings from their tangle. Gently the old one drove the shadow of fear away and called up a new dawn in Eider's heart. Then with the dazzling of bright flames would come the boy with his endless chatter, his games, his riddles and his weather spells. Soon between the two of them Eider lost the ability to discern where reality ended and fantasy began, and often, when times of quiet meditation were upon him, he would be convinced that there was no distinction at all and that nothing was impossible.

On one occasion before the roaring fire, Eider sat with the boy over their usual game of chequers. Young Merle was winning as he always did, but this time, instead of delighting in the game, the lad seemed irritated and on edge. Suddenly he jumped to his feet and began to rummage among a stack of broken objects piled up against the wall beside the hearth. Eider laughed quietly to himself, hearing the boy swear and curse as he tossed parchments and strings, and articles of every shape and size to the flagstones. Eventually, he returned to the table with a broad grin.

'I kept this for you,' he said, pressing something cold and smooth into Eider's hand.

Eider frowned, finding in his grip a piece of white and brittle bone. He looked at it confounded and bemused. He held it up in the firelight, his frown deepening as he saw its carved grooves and the strangely identical mechanisms cut at both ends. The thing was like a bone but also like a key. 'What is it?' he asked.

'I don't know!' the boy glared at him across the board.

Eider felt embarrassed. 'Thank you,' he said. The boy had seemed slighted by his dubious acceptance of the treasured gift. It was Eider's move and he took it confidently.

The lad drew back. 'You win!' he cried aloud, and together they inspected the pieces in amazed disbelief. Suddenly the small fingers drummed the board's edge and every square changed colour, white becoming black, and black becoming white. Eider laughed with delight at the magical trick but then was more surprised for the black square the boy touched became a minute square of white silk. Young Merle frowned with concentration and took it up. He draped it over Eider's hand as a large silken kerchief. Eider watched all with quiet intensity. Then the lad did it again. This time raising a square of black silk to drape over Eider's hand as before. As their eyes met the boy took the shard of bone from Eider's grip and wrapped it up in the silks.

'Remember me,' he said, handing the silken package back to him.

Eider inspected the strange gift. 'I shall treasure it,' he promised, but when he looked up the boy and his chequers were gone. The hour-glass stood upon the table now and Eider turned to the hearth where the dying embers barely gave out light or heat. 'Omega,' he breathed and moved towards the old chair finding the Ancient Merle asleep in its embrace. He stroked the blue-veined hand and waited for the creased lids to flicker open. When they did, Eider smiled.

'You have a question?' stated the old man.

'I do,' said Eider quietly.

'Ask it,' said the Ancient Merle and Eider did as he was bid.

'When first I came to this place, that thing I fear most was named. The Feared Thing that stalks me, that stills my heart and stops my breath. What is it?'

The old sage had opened his great black book but glanced up intent on Eider's speech.

'You . . .' Eider corrected himself. 'The Ancient Youth called it "Scath".' He frowned at the aged one. 'Yet since that hour no more has been said of it.'

'The Scath is not the creature you fear. It is all you fear the most.' The old one gave reply.

Eider rubbed his chin. The answer seemed clear enough but implied more than it said.

The Ancient Merle continued, 'My son, it is all that you feel, all that you fear, all that you think stands at your shoulder, or at your back. It is all that races with your heart-beat, all that stops your breath in the dark.'

'My own shadow?' Eider ventured.

''Tis a shadow,' Merle nodded. 'But still we take it for substance,' he explained, making illegible markings in the margin of the book.

'Then it is not real?' Eider quizzed.

'Aye, it is real, if you think it so,' said the wise one.

Eider watched the scratchings of the quill and though he tried he could make no sense of the spoken or the written word.

'Is it death?' he asked at last.

The Ancient looked up at him. 'Aye. That too,' he said. 'The time is close.'

Eider felt his face turn pale, 'I am ready.'

The Ancient smiled gently. 'We are never ready. But you have learned much and take with you the power to fulfil your destiny.'

'Yet I know not the way. Tell me how to find it,' Eider urged him.

The frail sage got to his feet and shuffled across the flagstones to the stone stairway. He turned back to Eider. 'Take up the amulets,' he instructed. 'Take up all that time has bestowed on you and follow me.'

Eider watched him ascend the deep-cut steps and, fearing he might fall, he followed close. On and on they went towards the tiny dome of light that shone so very high above. Eider counted the steps, climbing and

141

climbing, counted them all until he ran out of numbers and still they climbed on. Then at last the stairs ended and opened out on to a circular platform surrounded by a low and crenellated wall. Instruments of heavenly observation were positioned on its edge.

Here the black winds raged like a tribe of banshees and Eider had to fight to keep his balance on the exposed summit. Looking out from the watchtower he saw the billowing dark of storm clouds stretch like a voluminous black cloak far below. The base of the tower was veiled from sight, giving the impression that it was suspended in mid-air, lost in an endless sky and separated from all other worlds.

At Eider's side the Ancient stood, legs apart, arms akimbo, the patchwork cloak flapping about his willow frame like a gaudy banner, his long white hair streaming out like skeins of silk. Master of the tower he was, and like it he had weathered all time, and the endless dark.

Eider staggered in the gale and the old man clutched his cloak to steady his stance. 'From here I saw the prism fall and knew you came,' he shouted against the raging wind. 'Keep safe the heart of light, protect it from Dark at all costs.' He held Eider by the shoulders. 'You are the agent of transmutation, mediator between all that has vanished and all that is to come. Look . . .'

He pointed a steady finger, tracing a line from east to west over the vaporous black sea of cloud. Eider watched in awe as the moving heavens poured forth violet and delicate rose, the colours of a summer dawn. His cheeks flushed with overwhelming joy as the serene spectrum dazzled him and displayed itself before him conducted by the Ancient's magic hand. Then through the pulsing cloud cover, an outline could be glimpsed and Eider strained his eyes to see. As the clouds drifted away, it became clearer. A dark, distant contour fixed against the moving sky. A barrow grave.

The Ancient Merle turned to him. 'On you all depends. But mark me well: use not the sword of gold until you find the tomb of Rhion.'

Eider drew breath to speak, to tell the old man that he was not ready, that the sword he held was tainted; that it was not gold but sullied silver. But the Ancient raised an authoritative hand.

'Find Manannan!' he commanded. 'Spirit of the Bearded Lake.'

Eider's anxiety grew and he started a question but the clouds began to churn and then to race and Merle's old eyes were filled with sudden panic. 'Starfire?' he cried, his wide arms flailing the air. 'Away, away, I smell the day!' he bellowed, launching himself forth with the power of a thunderbolt.

Eider cried out as the Ancient pushed him and he fell backwards; backwards over the tower's edge, backwards through the dark cloud banks into the nothingness beyond.

— 17 —

The chill of bitter frost trickled over his skin and Eider opened his eyes – to a shining veil of silk. Its rainbow weave hung between his body and the roots beneath which he lay, and he tensed with sudden panic, unable to move or even raise his head. He glanced left and right, he saw his own arms and legs, fingertips and even the ends of his hair tethered by a million of the tiny strands of silk. The shape of stars, the shape of pyramids and fans, the delicate network of silken thread was strung with droplets of crystal dew. Eider blinked and with the movement of his eyelids felt the most fragile networks snap softly across his skin. He shivered in the frost-edge. He had fallen . . . or had he slept? Had he been saved by the gossamer net? He frowned, was this cocoon of silken webs a prison, or a bed? With sudden decision he sat upright. Millions of the tiny strands broke apart as he moved and pushed his face through their delicate veil. The gentle motion of their barely visible arteries cast rainbow lines and waves against a dark grey backcloth. Eider felt the miniscule ribbons of warmth fly away as he stood to his feet.

Glancing down he saw the shape his body had made in the undergrowth, a faint indentation where he had lain. An ice-blue aura edged the form until it seemed that the impression he had left was one of light. Dew drops fresh fallen from the veil of his cocoon had seeped into it, creating a still rainbow pool. Its beauty held Eider entranced.

He turned about, seeking the dwelling of the Ancient Merle from whose tower he had fallen, but found nothing of stone in all the place. The sudden cry of a rook overhead made him start, and he searched the sky for sight of the bird. He saw the motion of wingspan, saw it carried to the tall boughs above. The rook folded its wings and waited.

Eider shuddered but though he sensed danger still he clambered over the ridge of roots to scan the landscape. So it was he missed the shimmering of the magic pool of dew, and the blossoming of the pure white lily at its heart. Instead, from on top of the ridge he saw the rook's dark brethren gathered upon the sharp crenellations of a castle tower. His fear-filled eyes took in every line and formation of its walls, followed the iron grey of its drawbridge.

The black citadel stood in its sombre landscape exactly as Rhye had done; its turrets identical, its buttresses and its towers. Yet where there had been white in Rhye, here all was black. Where there had been embellishments of silver and gold, here all was lead. Where crystal had shone, now all was jet. Where stained glass had reflected light, now nought but rough hollows gaped like eyeless sockets.

The rook's cry pierced the silence like a spell and though Eider took but one small step, he found himself upon the drawbridge. The sleek wings flexed and the rook's black head bobbed as it gave a throaty cry. Now Eider was beneath the crumbling belltower. From their roof-top perch stone-carved heads of unseelie creatures gazed down in silent observation. Eider took another step and the pitch wood of the inner gate creaked woefully upwards. He heard the distant shift of stone, caught the movement of a grucsome head, saw the raw red tongue slip hungrily from the grey lips and realised that these were not gargoyles of stone, but living grotesques. Steeling himself, he took a third step and he was within the Castle Darke.

He felt his way along the first of many passageways, all lit at odd intervals by guttering torches. In the dim light he could make out nought but long shadows and cold stone, the occasional flurry of tapestried walls, the scrape of leather on uneven flags. He could find no end and soon realised that he walked along a network of identical corridors that threaded like dark arteries towards some secret heart. He knew this was the place, the setting wherein he would find the Feared Thing, where he would confront the Scath. He followed on, keenly alert to imminent danger, his senses strained for the merest footfall. He knew it was only a matter of time, knew that soon the thing he feared the most must reveal itself. He was ready for that moment. Thus he made his way along every passage, fearful yet eager to face his greatest enemy.

Then he heard it. The thud-thudding of stone worked in treadle motion. The screech of dull steel. The scream of steel honed sharp. Eider ventured closer and the sickening sound was amplified. Ahead, a narrow shaft of light sprang from blackness, from a fissure in a well-hid doorway. Eider pressed close to peer within.

The windowless chamber was sparse and grey like the room of an ascetic, or the cell of a condemned man. A rough blanket covered a hard pallet that was dotted with morsels of stale food. Flies buzzed about an overturned goblet. In the tallow light a hunched figure sat with his back to the door. Eider started. The meagre glow reflected upon golden hair and a small, wiry frame. There was something familiar in the demeanour, in the brisk movement of the head, the quickness of the hands. Something that reminded Eider of someone from the past. A memory of elfin-kind. Eider's heart leapt with joy and then with fear. What was his friend doing here? How had he come so far, and alone?

'Regor?' he barely spoke the word before instinct restrained further greeting, for the leather-clad figure had turned from his task. In the flickering light Eider saw him clear and his blood ran iron cold. Here was no lost friend of youth, no round and open face, but a brutal visage with chiselled jaw and skin the pallor of death. The cruel mouth was slightly agape and the large teeth clenched in a menacing sneer. Eider felt disappointment flood through him and then revulsion as

146

he watched the creature set down the candle and resume his task.

In the arc of light that enclosed him, Eider could see that the golden hair was violently cropped and stuck out from the square head like sharp corn stalks. The figure bobbed excitedly over the object of his intense fascination. Eider heard saliva rattle in the throat before it was spat forth, saw the glint of a blade and a globule of greasy spittle run the length of the dagger. He saw the shaft quiver as eager fingers pressed steel to whirring stone and sparks showered the ill-lit chamber like diamond jewels.

'Make it gleam, make it scream!' came the awful pitch of the voice, as the whetstone pounded on with renewed vigour and the blade wailed upon impact until its edge grew sharp and bright with bloodlust.

'Spikah's little beauty,' the figure drooled as he held up the dagger for inspection. 'Slit, snick, carve 'em up!' he gurgled, tracing a ragged fingernail the length of the hungry shaft.

Suddenly the breath in Eider stilled as Spikah turned abruptly from his task and rummaged beneath the blanket, casting it to the floor in search of something more important. Eider strained his eyes to see Spikah snatch up a leather bag and shake it with childlike glee. The contents rattled, though it was not the sound of coinage that brought the grin to Spikah's face, but that of bone on bone and opening the bag he poured all forth into his palm. Teeth. Teeth of every size. Teeth of every shape. Milk teeth, wisdom teeth. Canine and feline. Incisors and molars. An endless, gruesome array. Spikah gave a convulsive laugh and the white flecks of saliva that had clung to the edges of his mouth trickled into the hollow of his jaw and hung there like an opaque tear. He fingered the molars in silent adoration as if each were a rare gem and then as if recalling with an ecstatic shudder the manner of their acquisition.

'Bite and chew, rip and tear!' he enthused, the azure eyes bright with madness. 'Spikah's little beauty carves

'em out!' The bloodless fingers tightened about the hilt
of the dagger as Spikah swept the still air with gleaming
blade, making long, slow curves and figure of eight
designs on imaginary foes. Then he turned and strode
towards the door, hyena laughter breaking from the thin
mouth. His trance-like desire for blade on bone made
him oblivious to the onlooker pressed flat into the
shadows of the corridor wall.

Eider's body twitched in nervous spasm as Spikah
passed directly in front of him, looking neither to left
nor right as he made off down the passage, the hideous
rattle of molar trophies echoing in the dark. Who was
this creature? What was he? How did he come to be
here? Eider could make no answer to these thoughts.
He had felt fear, but it was not the same suffocating
threat that the Feared Thing had engendered, and he
knew for sure that Spikah was not the Scath. He knew
also that Spikah was en route somewhere and wherever
that was Eider felt the need to discover. He must do as
Merle had bid him, find Manannan and the Bearded
Lake, find the path to Phoenix Fire. Wherever Spikah
was going, Eider would follow.

He could still see the haloed outline as Spikah raced
on ahead of him, a puvvering torch held aloft. Eider
tried to keep pace along the narrow corridors, tried to
measure his steps lest his footfall alert Spikah to the fact
that he was being followed. On and on they hurried, the
torch sometimes almost extinguished in the draught of
movement. Spikah's boots pounded the flags as if he
were crushing the very stones into submission. Eider
glimpsed the dazzle of torchlight reflected on buckles
and sharp-edged steel, saw Spikah lurch on, dragging
the blade along the cold walls, saw the line of ice-blue
sparks, heard the murderous laughter. Suddenly, Spikah
stopped in his tracks and wheeled about. Eider threw
himself against the wall, clamping his teeth together so
that his gasps for breath could not be heard in the terrible stillness. Spikah held the torch in front of him but

its light did not penetrate the cover of shadows wherein Eider was hidden.

Spikah turned and ran on. The pace was relentless. Corridors turned left and right with increasing regularity. Some narrowed whilst others opened out into spacious galleries or became steep in gradient. Surely he must reach his destination soon, Eider thought, having noticed that the torches were growing farther apart and that Spikah's flame was fast becoming the only means of decent light between. Then, quite without warning, without sound, without reason, the torch and its carrier disappeared. Eider stopped dead. He listened intently. No sound carried to him; he strained to see, but the only source of light was far off and the darkness between, profound. He turned back from whence he had come. There was nought but shadow. Yet surely Spikah had a destination? Eider moved cautiously along the passage. What door had Spikah found? What secret corridor had he slipped into?

Suddenly, a powerful arm locked about Eider's neck and he started as a dagger was thrust at his face. Above the drumming of his own blood-rush came a madman's laughter and Eider responded on reflex alone. He dug both elbows hard into the abdomen of his attacker, winding him and breaking his hold. Struggling free, he turned in the dim light to meet the killer's azure gaze. Yet something in the eyes stirred compassion in him, prompted a memory, rekindled a doubt, and Eider hesitated. With a savage grin, Spikah lunged at him with all the fury of a maddened beast. Eider side-stepped, instinctively grabbing for his sword, but he had barely touched the hilt when the words of warning flooded back to him. To use the Triad blade here would see it doomed forever and he with it. But how to fight a madman without it? How to save himself from certain death? He was no wizard, had not the means to summon occult forces to his aid. The powers of Magus provided only a shield. Without the aid of the Triad blade, Eider could do no more than fight instinct with instinct, and given the odds against him, his instinct was to run! A leer of cruelty spread Spikah's ghastly face, but Eider was too quick and his well-aimed kick to the groin sent Spikah sprawling. He crumpled to the flagstones and Eider made off in search of safe refuge.

In his haste, torches became a blur of flame and Eider ricocheted off the walls as the desire to evade capture propelled him on. But all too soon Spikah was in pursuit, gurgling his bloodlust through the echoing corridors.

'Gouge out eyes, rip off ears! My little spike does the business!'

Eider's chest was drum tight, his face awash with sweat, yet he forced himself on: left and right, right and left again. But unlike him, Spikah knew the corridors well and as the scavenger's laughter grew in pitch and volume, Eider saw the jerky shadow of his pursuer cast upon the walls and knew he gained on him. Then, at last, he saw a glimmer of light ahead – he was saved! He threw himself towards it with all the strength he could muster, sending the door crashing back on its hinges. Panic! The chamber was windowless and grey, sparsely furnished like a cell and at its centre stood a whetstone ready for use. It was Spikah's chamber: he had come full circle! The door slammed at his back, and the key was turned emphatically in the lock.

The brutal features of the executioner chilled Eider to the core and he snatched recklessly at the sword hilt. He would use it and be damned! But the blade locked firm within the scabbard and would not yield to his needs. He backed away aware that Spikah too had realised he was helpless. Spikah approached, his large teeth flashing with demonic glee and Eider saw his left hand slip inside his jerkin to extract a second gleaming dagger. He circled them provocatively in the air, then holding both up he rapped them together. Their blades glinted slowly as he drew them one across the other in preparation for his gruesome banquet.

'Delicious pearlies. Shiny – like a necklace!' Spikah drooled his appreciation of the prospective spoils.

He stalked Eider, taunting him with random thrusts and feigned strikes, then, grown tired of the granted reprieve, his expression stiffened into unflinching cruelty. Suddenly he ran at his victim, pinning Eider to the chamber wall. But the lethal daggers were thwarted by the wood of the stool which Eider had snatched up in an effort to parry the blows. The pale eyes bulged, the leering mouth began to slaver and Spikah tried to tear the weapons free and strike again. As quickly, Eider thrust the stool between them, knocking one of the blades from his grip. Eider seized the hand that clutched the remaining weapon and tried to wrench it from Spikah's grip. They tumbled headlong. Spikah's madness stimulated a superhuman strength which sent Eider crashing against the chamber wall in its wake.

Now the lethal blade trembled less than a fingernail from Eider's cheek, keen for the taking of flesh and bone. Eider's arm began to weaken with the strain and realising he could no longer stay the deadly steel, he pulled free his right hand and shoved his fingers deep into Spikah's eye sockets. He clawed the saliva-ridden features in a desperate effort to save himself. Spikah retreated, clutching at his blooded face. Eider took his chance, butting his opponent in the stomach and forcing him back against the whetstone. It toppled beneath Spikah's weight and Eider fell upon him, seizing the stalk-topped head in both hands, yanking at it, smashing it against the wall, smashing it against the solid wheel of stone. He smashed it so hard that Spikah screamed with the agony, smashed it harder, and harder, until it cracked open like a brittle shell and Spikah lay still, his life trickling away.

Eider retched as he staggered to the door. He snatched at the key and fell out into the corridor where waves of terror made him vomit once again. He steadied himself against the wall, tried to breathe, tried to control his racing pulse. He listened to the silence and fell back to take rest.

But then, a lone and elongated screech shattered the

stillness, followed by the rhythmic sound of steel being worked on stone. Eider tightened . . . it could not be! He turned in utter terror, to see Spikah hunched over the moving whetstone, as first he had seen him, straight shouldered and intent upon the task. Eider released a gasp as the whetstone stilled and the blonde head turned slowly to glance towards the door. He stiffened with terror for the azure eyes that met his were strangely soft, compassionate, and the face that stared back at him was that of a friend.

'Regor?' Eider felt certain recognition and with the speaking of his name the elfin grinned in welcome. But Eider had seen the snarl that edged the corners of the mouth, had sensed the demon likeness and recognised the shadow, the dark twin. In a second he had slammed the door and feverishly turned the key, imprisoning the dark soul forever. Now he must escape from this nightmare place: he must find the right door.

—— 18 ——

He ran from the rusted iron of the door so fast he considered no direction, so fast he lost the comforting rhythm of his own gasping lungs as they struggled for air against the mounting heat. Now the Feared Thing was close . . . close enough to touch, to be touched by. He fought for air, he must keep moving, keep running. But then, in the putrid green smoke of the torchlight he caught sight of the ceiling above him. It glistened and he watched irregular rivulets trickle down the walls until, as his eyes became accustomed to its contours, he discovered a small door cut into its slant. The handle hung like a great brass earring. Eider's heart raced as he sensed possible escape. He would climb, would find a foothold on the torch-sconce, would push his way upward, away from the tunnels, from the dark and the horror. He drew closer and the outline of steps became clear. Three of them, cut cleanly into the wall gave access to the dark slab of the trapdoor. Eider leapt at them, preferring the unknown beyond to the terrors below. He twisted the ring and pushed his shoulder against the wood, opening a gap in the ceiling.

Beneath him the hiss of the dying torch forced him on and he climbed up and out into spreading magenta light. Soon he had crawled free of the door and as he found his footing he looked cautiously about. He was aghast. The space in which he stood was boundless. Roofless and wall-less. A space so wide and so long that he could make neither beginning nor end to it.

He strained his ears but heard only the distant howling of the wind. He strained his eyes in the curious light, certain only of the floor on which he stood, its vast tiles of white and black spreading in horizontal, then vertical, then diagonal design. He narrowed his eyes; at varying intervals giant structures rose up from the monochrome floor like massive pillars of ivory and obsidian. Eider moved closer to inspect them. Their sculpted forms were awesome chess-pieces, though unlike any he had ever beheld. To his left, an upright Tower of ivory, and on the square next to it the distinctive crown and cope of a Queen. Several black Pawns had toppled about a black Knight and Eider struggled hard to find the significance of the pieces. A white Wizard remained standing though its form was rent in two, whilst nearby a white Queen stood in fearless defiance of her black opposite. Two Knights provided escort though both bore the ravages of battle use, their features obscured and mildewed. Scattered across the chequered floor lay four white Pawns, while four more held battle stance, undisturbed. So many time-worn faces and yet Eider sensed an eerie familiarity as he moved amongst them. He shuddered. Whatever they were meant to represent they had been set out by some mighty hand and he had climbed in upon the game in progress.

Eider turned about, he searched above and below, yet found no sign of the players, giant or otherwise. He looked again upon the two white Knights – the first stirred memories of Lehon, the brave mortal who had never belonged in the seelie realm yet had given his life for it. Then feeling the presence of the second Knight, Eider scanned its mouldering form. The mildew scarred the face and twisted the smile upon the lips into a savage leer. Uncannily he saw in it both the roguish grin of his elfin comrade Regor, and the snarl of the maniac he had encountered below. A sudden flash of insight revealed at last the true nature of the ivory pieces and his mind reeled with macabre possibilities. Having reached the fearful conclusion, he turned to view the white Wizard. Could this piece that gazed on him so tragically be all that now remained of his own dear friend?

'Nairb Horatious?' he whispered. The words sounded like a prayer, or else they were some spell for with them came the flurry of ice draught, the sudden sensation of movement above and about him.

'Welcome.'

The disembodied voice shook Eider to the core and he ran from vulnerability into the elongated shadow of a taken Pawn, pressing himself against the wall of its upturned base.

'Welcome, prisoner of dreams and fantasies.' It was the voice of vile contempt, of hatred, of Dark personified. It was the voice of the unseelie, the voice of the Feared Thing.

Eider's face ran with the cold sweat of fear as he heard sound amplify and reverberate until it pained his ears.

'Time passes,' the Voice proclaimed. 'Play on.'

Eider heaved for air against his panic. He looked desperately about, but could see no one. 'Play on?' he cried into the terrible emptiness. 'With no knowledge of the game, or the opponent I face?'

An iron-cold wind of hatred cut deep into Eider's bones. 'The pieces are scattered. We have played together long, white King!' the Voice stated.

Eider scanned the chequered floor. The pieces were indeed set in combat and to his desperate relief he realised that white was winning. Yet where was the game-master?

'Too many of Dark's ranks have fallen to your strategies,' the echoing Voice shuddered as if in spasm.

Eider braced himself against the smooth wall of the Pawn. 'Then so shall you fall!' he cried out, hoping to lure his adversary into sight.

'Dark? Fall? Dark spares your life only to win! Dark shall be Grand Master of the final game!' the Voice vowed.

Eider's heart beat heavy in his chest. The baneful presence was dangerously close and he gulped air knowing it was the Feared Thing that drew near. With sudden decision Eider darted from cover, traversing the black and white until he reached the board's edge. He pressed himself against the face of the game clock, its huge hands halted at the middle hour.

'Time passes,' the Voice repeated. 'Play must resume.'

Laughter rose and fell about him like a tide and gave Eider certainty of his judgement. He was here at last, here in the presence of the Scath, and he was being challenged to . . . a game of chess!

'Play on!' the Voice commanded. 'While ever you hold out to Dark, you live.'

Eider closed his eyes and shivered as if in fever. He tried in vain to moisten his dry mouth, his lips parting in speech. 'Yet give me a name. Against whom do I play?' he demanded, slyly.

'Scath it is. Grand Master!'

The sound of the hateful word took Eider's breath. It was as he had suspected: the demons he had thus far faced in hand-to-hand combat, even in war, had been but minions of the all-consuming Dark he now faced. Now at last the wielder of the Triad and Lord of All-Light was to do battle with the Master of Dark, champion of all that was unseelie. The chequer-board on which he stood would provide their battleground and here Eider would discover at last his ultimate fate. Here too, in the winning or the losing of the game, was held the future of seelie lore and the fate of all seelie kind.

'Have you come for me?' Eider asked calmly.

'Dark has long walked beside you,' the Voice replied.

'Then show yourself!' Eider growled against fear of oblivion. He would display no fear before that which had haunted him since the day of his birth! Now the strange whirring rhythm of the blackness had begun to make Eider's blood tingle. 'Show yourself!' he demanded again. He looked anxiously about but could distinguish nothing. 'You see me. 'Tis gamesmanship I see you likewise!'

'You? See?' the Voice stated, gloated.

'Yes!' Eider frowned persistently into the dense emptiness. 'If I must be white's champion I would have some likeness of black's King.'

'Forced to play?' the mighty Voice replied. ''Tis the game to be finished, not begun!'

Eider felt an icy draught of movement. Above him the personification of evil emerged and he staggered backwards beneath the vast shadow of a massive hand that levitated above the board like some dark spell. At the sight of it Eider once more ran for cover, secreting himself in the shadow of the white Tower. This was unexpected. How could he deal with it? If Lumin had prepared him for this moment as she told him she had, then he had not grasped even the rudiments of the lesson. What was this that he grappled with? A feeling, a symbol of his terror? A malevolent shape-shifter? What should he do? 'Or undo?' Eider said to himself with a tremor.

His decision was to dart across the chess-board, hurling himself at every chess-piece that remained standing. Some swayed precariously, others tilted, a few toppled and crashed to the tiles as Eider pushed at them until his limbs ached. In the black heat he grew too exhausted to move, to breathe, to think. The emptiness above revealed no hand of Darkness, yet he was sure that he had seen it. In that moment all about him began to vibrate, to shake violently as the humid winds whipped into a violent gust, first hot then ice cold. He saw frost coat his skin and hair, his eyelids stiffen and freeze, his fingers turn blue. Fearful that he would be frozen to the spot, he ran, ran for the white King's file. As he criss-crossed the black and white squares he felt dangerously conspicuous, his robes of white and royal blue forming stark contrast against the board. He clasped the Triad hilt, desperate for the security of the magic blade yet knew he could not employ its power here. Steadfastly Eider watched the black King's file awaiting the first sign of his opponent. His wait was but short.

A pinpoint of Dark appeared on the square of white. Eider watched it until his eyes were sore; then it began to expand both left and right, above and below, until it rose and fell like a giant dark wave. Black as night it was, boundless and fathomless yet held as if by spell upon the square of white. Eider watched it oscillate then fold and unfold like skeins of black silk. It was energy, unseelie power, it was of every shape and size at once; it was forever changing, becoming, of every shade of black and of every texture. And there at its dark nucleus a baneful hand spread out its five fingers, clenched them into a fist; a hand at first the size of a man's, then growing full and wide until it consumed Eider's field of vision. The shifting contours formed into a palm, and the palm bore strange tattoos, deep blue lines and circles, bold inscriptions and symbols known only to the seer's eye. Eider read them all, seeing black knowledge in their gruesome design. With this hand of Dark Fate, the Scath would manoeuvre its pieces. Eider watched the pulsing mass hover: more fearful than the endless folds of its blackness, more sickening than the grotesque pattern of the palm, were the arthritic joints, the nails that circled and twisted in colourful spirals, chafing against each other as they noisily scratched the tiles of the board floor. With these talons the Scath would direct its commands, would prod and poke. Eider shuddered; with these he might be pierced to the heart.

His fingers tightened about the Triad's hilt, feeling the heat of the pommel, yet knowing he could not use the weapon in his defence. He inched backwards caressing the sword for comfort's sake; he saw the gold sheen of the scabbard remained, but now the gem at the centre of the hilt emitted a light of sapphire blue. Yet there was no such light in the place and Eider gazed at it, unsure.

19

Eider trembled as the voice of Dark commanded him.

'Begin!'

Swallowing back his wildest fears, Eider spread his arms over the chequered floor and gave a laugh of false scorn. 'I forget how the pieces stood,' he said. But the hand of dark opened its fingers and the pieces that Eider had deliberately scattered were returned by dark magic to their former positions.

'Con . . . trary to you, white King, Dark has forgotten nought!'

Eider felt a fury rise within him. He saw the pulse of blackness that was the Scath's evil core and knew that Lumin had been right – no form of combat would solve this impasse. Nothing less than inner strength and the wisdom of the Magus would grant him victory here.

'Your move white King!' the Voice insisted.

'Yet a King may move but a pace,' Eider argued, stalling for time in which to think, to plan.

'Your pieces, novice! There's the choice!' The Voice replied. There was a slight pause. 'But first the mystery!' the Voice added.

'Mystery?' Eider repeated to himself, his pulse beginning to race.

'That's the thing!' the Voice was emphatic. 'Cast it! Cast a rhyme!' the Voice provoked and the massive forefinger was raised, the twisted nail pointed squarely at Eider's chest. 'Your white wit is no match for Dark.'

Eider fought down the bewilderment that washed over him. He wracked his brain for some mystery or motto to appease the ghoulish mind.

'*A shoemaker* . . .', he began.

'Shoemaker . . . yes?' the Voice repeated, the

arthritic joints cracking as the fingers clenched and unclenched.

Eider steeled himself, hoping that the childhood rhyme might suffice. '*Makes shoes without leather. Yet with all the elements put together.*'

The resonating voice of Dark finished the verse. '*Fire and earth! Water and air, and every customer takes two pairs! Farrier!*' The Voice mocked and Eider felt his face flush with anger and humiliation, felt the sudden shock as the golden twists of a talon sent white heat skimming across the board to strike the Pawn at his side. It split neatly in two.

'Dark spares your fragile white bones one time more! Do you suppose its knowledge is no greater than a pea?' The hand clenched into a fist and smashed down towards the board. Eider stood rooted to his King's square, mouth agape.

''Tis a farrier!' the Voice repeated across the silence. 'A child could make it out!'

Eider felt ridiculed and pathetic, yet Dark's embodiment did not advance even though it clearly had power enough to snuff him out.

'Testing the Scath!' the Voice grew louder still. 'Dark knows all your white and wily ways. Your seelie stealth!'

With neither warning nor provocation the gnarled forefinger cast forth a lethal bolt, but instinctively white's champion held up both palms as a shield. The barrier was forged of seelie power and the shaft of Dark energy was retarded, its power diffused until it fell well short of its target. Eider glanced at his hands, amazed at his new found gift and gave thanks to the Gods for Lumin's sake.

'Tell it!' the Voice commanded him again. 'Tell the mystery! Lose fairly!' the Voice quickened.

'I shall not lose!' Eider countered, seeing in his mind's eye Lumin's bright face, hearing afresh her song in his heart.

Now the Voice encircled him. 'You have squandered your treasures and must forfeit all!'

Eider was defiant. 'Never!'

'Idiot boy. Must Dark take first turn? Show him how 'tis done?' The great palm opened as if in offering. 'So be it . . . yet there is but one answer boy. If that be wrong your precious piece is lost!'

Eider shuddered, sensing something familiar in the deft and certain action of the slender hand and bony fingers. He frowned, for what was at once familiar was foul and twisted, and though he thought of him he dare not speak the wizard's name for fear some dark damage be done to Nairb's wandering soul.

'*Geometrically I ride,*' the Voice began. '*But find only time's dark impasse. I shall not move again.*' A terrible silence fell as if the Scath awaited some response, but then the words began to flow once more. '*A finger stops the latch, and every track is blind. The bird so valiant in flight has left my banner, and my bright spurs flash in a world I cannot see . . . Answer?*' The ugly forefinger pointed at its opponent and in the ensuing silence Eider sensed a horrible defeat.

His mouth had turned dry. What could he answer? Though strangely woven the words seemed to mean so much to him, yet he could find no reason, make no reply. He frowned. Could it be the journey of the sun? Could the needed word be 'sol'? He watched the gnarled fingers spring against the shifting light and thought again . . . or else it was the phoenix insignia, he considered, grasping at one fleeting image from the strange rhyme.

He heard the hiss of suppressed mirth, then the sudden scrape of fingernails as he gave answer. 'Seelie Kingdom!' he guessed. Yet even as he spoke he knew the answer he had given to be wrong.

Dark flew about him as a suffocating wind. 'Knight!' the Scath revealed with spite-filled relish. ''Tis a Knight . . . 'tis your Knight!'

Eider felt bile rise in his throat as the power of Darkness held him firmly on his white King's square.

161

'Knight. The only piece to leap across all boundaries,' the Voice of the Scath explained.

Eider gasped. Of course, Lehon was his own brave knight. Had he not crossed the borders with him into the seelie realm forsaking his mortal home? Thus did he ride now, set in motion by the twisted nail, chasing against the time-clock in continuous diagonal across the board. Eider cried out, recalling the vision of Lumin's mystic pool, knowing his mortal friend would find no destination in the time lapse. 'Lehon!' he pleaded, yet in that moment the rider returned to inanimate ivory and at the Scath's command diminished to the size of a chess-piece.

Eider shuddered as he saw the mortal's frozen effigy snatched up and dropped into a wooden box at the board's edge. Lost forever, as were the others therein, to Dark. Where he had stood a void had opened up and Eider knew it to be the abyss of souls. The mortal's quest had been in vain, as his father's before him. As his would also be? Eider gritted his teeth, tears of sorrow tightening in his throat as he saw the shadow of deepest dark move one square closer to him.

'Your move!' came the command and the palm of the gruesome hand emerged from the dark core.

Eider could barely keep a grip on his senses for vengeance but knew he must. 'The song,' he whispered to himself, his teeth chattering with fear and the awful cold. He had once memorised Lumin's song as a shield against such fear, it had protected him, nourished him in his time of need. He would recite it now, rekindle all her love and warmth for comfort in his final moments. He looked to the white Queen that stood between him and the pulsing shadow mass. The piece reminded him of Lumin. Her voice had been soft as a mother's. Her words a vision of a white Queen's fate: Rhye's Queen, his mother, had fallen like a fragile leaf at the touch of Dark. So too had Lumin, his own white Queen, been lost. Taken, by Dark, in full bloom.

'*The broken crown sits on frosted hair,*' he began,

fixing the wedge of Dark power that was the Scath with his unflinching gaze. '*A bitter sun has ripened me. Last leaves are shaken from me, and I fall in the rains of spring. Who am I?*' Eider closed his eyes against the ridicule he felt was sure to condemn him. But no sound was made and he glanced at the game-clock, marking every second of silence that passed.

'Such words . . .' he heard the Voice of the Scath murmur low. 'Such sounds. Such . . . complexities!' The twisted nail of vermilion flicked the gleaming tile, squeaked against the white tile of the board as the Scath considered. 'Willow'. The word cut the stillness.

Eider shook his head, his dark orbs glinting as he heard his adversary's wrong reply.

''Tis a tree!' The savage voice insisted.

Eider tapped his foot against ebony black. 'Hold Scath! Your stated rule of game allows one answer only. The first you spoke was wrong!'

'Rule?' the Voice boomed. 'Darkness obeys no rule!' The spike-tipped forefinger traced circles on the air in a complexity of ruminations. 'A sheaf of corn!' Came the third attempt.

'Wrong!' Eider growled as he glanced at the shifting hand of the game-clock. ''Tis white Queen!' he cried triumphantly. 'White of hair, yet fruitful and ripe. My Queen fell young, sacrificed for her King!' He took his stance against the spreading mass of blackness. 'Yet her loss was not in vain for now I take black Queen!'

The twisted nail halted him, a bolt of Dark power released from its tip to crack at Eider's feet like a shimmering whip and prevent his stride towards the ebony piece.

'You took her in Bethalon, white waster!' the Voice accused.

'Then why is she upon the board?' Eider protested into the unfolding blackness.

'She lives on!' the disembodied voice declared.

'Not so!' Eider rebuked. 'The Bloodseed is dead.' He

relished the slight withdrawal of Dark energy at sound of his old victory.

'Her black heart beats still!' the Voice insisted.

'Then I shall destroy her again. Now and for all time!' Eider reached out and touched the black effigy that was his prize. Yet as it diminished in size it was not the face of the demon queen that he saw, but another's. A face more beautiful than hers. A face that smiled at him with a strangely familiar desire. Could it be . . . 'Baob-hanshee?' he whispered, but the glint in her eye held him from his task for only a moment: then he diminished her size, certain of white's triumph.

Here at last was revenge for his white Knight's loss. Determinedly he took up the new-won piece and deposited it in the pouch at his waist. As he did so the vast hand that embodied the Scath's dark core, stroked the air between them and the square on which the black Queen had stood vanished. Eider cried out, he teetered on the very edge! His balance lost, he felt himself falling, falling towards oblivion. But the instinct of Magus soared within him, alerted him to possibilities, to all impossibilities. He turned upright the palms of his hands and in that moment the weight of his body was lost and the power of spirit drew him forth until he levitated above the vanished square, exerting no greater weight than dew.

Vile curses were borne on the ice-draught, yet with regained self-possession, Eider took his stance upon a new square. One step closer to his hateful adversary. As he looked upon the lined palm with its gruesome mounds and baneful symbols he felt the terrible silence grow, knew that at last he met Dark on equal terms. Lumin had indeed granted him the power of Magus and now the Scath's anger turned to rage with the same realisation.

The hand of Dark enwrapped itself, its core changed shape: rectangle, square, then cone. A spiral of folding and unfolding, of power diminishing and then expanding. 'Another!' the Voice demanded. The Scath's wit must be proved the greater. The Scath's cunning the wilier. The Scath's heart of Dark superior. 'Another! Inferior wit shall never checkmate Dark!'

Eider shook his head adamantly. 'Your move.'

The core of unseelie power oscillated with the pleasure of demonstrating the superior force of Dark logic. 'Here Dark lore shall vanquish White,' the Voice declared. 'Always has. Always will.'

Eider flourished a provocative hand, listening close as the Scath delivered the new rhyme.

'Processions . . . winding through the veins of Time. And I at the heart of it . . . at the altar! My heart swings like a censer, but no incense clouds the mirror now.'

'Seer?' Eider thought, sensing the pulse beat of ancient ritual, the vows of Elders, as the overpowering voice of Dark spoke on.

'The book of hours gleams like a jackdaw's tail and lore is but a white window. Tall tallows dull the moonsong and I . . . fall to my knees. Shadowless! Who am I?'

Eider saw the pulsing core of Dark spread and then contract in an agony of suspense. He trembled as a sense of recognition overwhelmed him. In his mind's eye he walked again the corridors of Rhye. Yet who did he follow? 'Elder?' he said, unsure.

'Wrong answer!' the Voice declared and its pulsing mass advanced.

'Dark takes white's Wizard, does it not?' the Voice prompted almost delicately.

Ice chill flooded Eider's skin as he saw the piece in question and recognised the meaning of the Scath's words. He thought on the ancient rituals of seelie lore, of processions upon the winter moor. He thought of Nairb his wizard, he who had stood at the very heart of it all. Had Dark stood there with him? He recalled the moon's white face and the words Nairb had dedicated to her beauty. He thought of his wizard's black bound volume, and of the pure crystal sphere he had named his window on Time. Eider shuddered to recall its destruction. Was it true? Was Nairb no more than shadow and this chess-piece all that now remained? He watched its features slowly thaw, saw Nairb's crescent face look wistfully out as if waiting, as if watching from the confines of some ivory tower.

'Nairb!' he shouted desperately, but too late for the image neither saw nor heard his plea and the Scath's twisted finger struck the blow.

'Wizard!' Eider cried again, remembering at last the first of three words taught him by Lumin. As he spoke it out he hoped against hope that some small atom of the good man might be saved. But his hopes were dashed as Dark's hateful touch made the white piece shrink and Nairb's serene visage was lost to him again.

Eider's heart was heavy with sorrow as he watched the terrible void where his dear wizard had stood. How he had prayed that the circle of white lore had delivered him from harm on that most terrible day of misdeed, prayed that he would somehow find the kindly man again held in some sliver of time.

He swallowed back his grief, perhaps it was better that Nairb's span had been brought to merciful conclusion on their last day together, as had that of his mortal comrade Lehon. Better by far than left to wander some endless corridor of Time as Regor's dark soul did now below. Or, like himself, be forced to face the trial of black and white. He it was who must fight. He it was who must win the game and forge a union at last. Eider frowned. This very union of good and bad, light and dark, black and white, the union so talked about by Elders, so longed for by wizards, so sought after by the ageless prophets of seelie lore . . . might never be achieved. What then? What if he were to lose?

He watched the Scath's newly won piece fall into the wooden box and shivered. Magus! What did the title mean? A little knowledge here . . . a little magic there. How to fuse them? How to win without the Triad's aid? How to win this game of games? He stroked the pommel of the great blade longing to tap its power, but knowing he must not risk it here. He shook his head, was there power enough in it to kindle the mystic fire? His heart raced with anxiety and fear as he sensed the Scath's oscillating form halt its mesmeric dance.

'Fire?' the discarnate voice quizzed. 'Fire you say?'

'No!' Eider gasped. 'The trier! I said I am ever the trier!' He forced a laugh of scorn. 'Give me more mysteries.' He baited: 'I would find answer to your mighty wit!'

The five twisted fingernails of the Dark hand splashed hectic colour against the blackness. Eider concealed a smile, had he found Dark's weakness at last?

'Pit your simple wit against Dark, would you? Again?' the Voice declared and in its wake there raced a draught more bitter than hemlock. 'You came to do combat, not be polite! Play on! Prove the blade of your mind to be sharper than unseelie knowledge!'

Eider stiffened, sensing that this most feared of feared things might consume the gameboard, and all it held with it. His mouth grew suddenly dry and he could do no more than offer up the final lines of Lumin's song as a shield against destruction.

'*I fall through blustery air into the light and the dark. Finding no shelter in the black, no refuge in the white.*'

'Chess-board!' the Voice of the Scath responded immediately, eager to take a pace and the piece that stood between it and checkmate.

Eider held up a hand and bade Dark wait on his rhyme.

'*Where once my turret was, a bell tolls on the time-tide bringing new Dark.*' His eyes widened as he watched malevolent fingers stroke the air between them then dissolve into a wedge of black energy before reconstructing itself as the baneful hand.

Eider shook his head impatient to be done, eager to move forward to face his enemy.

'The wind, the Black Wind!' came a second guess. The Voice continued its listing.

Eider saw the elongated nails flick sparks on to the blackness in an agony of rage and suspense. How long would mighty Dark hold back? Why did it not simply swallow up the board, the pieces and the white King of seelie lore?

''Tis the Rook!' Eider pointed emphatically. 'Black rooks thrive in Rhye's tower. Creatures of light they are, flying on blustery air. Creatures of dark they are, their presence announces ill omen.' He paced forward triumphantly. 'Black Rook is mine!' As he touched the ebony piece its bright earring gleamed and Eider recognised the slanted eyes of an old adversary. With the power of Magus he shrank the effigy to a mere talisman and dropped it into his pouch. There it would remain and the black rook Taekhor would be lost forever to the game of Fate.

Cries of overpowering rage flooded the endless chamber until a mangled finger thrust out over the diminishing space between itself and the champion of white lore.

''Tis but a word,' intangible force was channelled into the thunder Voice and its spell held Eider fast. '*A storm of trumpets blew it through the time crevice! Yet learn this one truth: palm of the hand was all thy father saw, is all you shall see. Until the game's folded up in Dark. Until the dice is cast and hollow lore rolls to my feet.*'

In the ensuing silence Eider froze in the ice breath of his dark opponent, a look of timeless hatred chiselled on his bone-white face. For the rhyme was a vow, and the vow was a spell and Eider would move and speak no more.

'Checkmate,' the Voice whispered, certain Eider could do nought. 'Checkmate!' the Voice announced as Dark relished the eternal manipulation of this most beautiful of all chesspieces. The endless game Dark would make it play, the tortures it would endure, in perpetuity!

20

The game-clock was stopped on the hour of twelve, but Eider's keen eyes shone like jet, glittered with the quicksilver of the life force. He had seen meaning in the words, had seen the vision of his own coronation, and had fresh sight of past victories over the unseelie. The palm of this dark hand was the Dearth Hand, that which he and his father before him had seen prior to calamity. It was this dreaded hand of Fate before which he stood and this, the game of games. To lose here was to forfeit seelie lore's white King, was to cast Ancient Lore to destruction.

''Tis but a word!' the Voice taunted and the wedge that was Darkness moved in upon him.

Eider could not speak the word. But though his skin ran with ice and turned ghostly blue, and though his face was a frozen grimace, there at the core of him a throbbing heat kept him alive. Its pulsing rhythm sent the noble blood of his seelie line coursing through his veins. Kept him whole, kept him safe from harm, from the destruction of Dark force.

'He has it not?' the Voice said, and the wedge that was Darkness moved closer still. 'Check . . . mate.' The voice pierced him to the heart. 'Checkmate. Check. Mate. Game's won . . .'tis Dark victory!' the Voice stated. 'Game to Black!'

Eider's ashen face did not move, his mouth remained firm closed, yet the chamber space resounded with the force of the white King's voice. 'Wait upon my answer! No move is to be made without my answer!'

The great hand wrapped itself in a blackness made more dense by rage. 'Wait?' The Voice of the omnipresence echoed in the void. 'No waiting where there is no time! You lose! White King is taken!' The undulating folds of blackness spread out to engulf him but Eider had summoned enough strength to whisper the final word from Lumin's store.

'Regal!' Its sacred potency halted the advance of Dark and Eider shouted out once more. ' "King!" The word is "King", 'tis the white King – it is I!' He fixed the core of Darkness with his glittering eye, all fear was gone. 'Stalemate,' he declared with the authority of a seelie Magus.

The terrible shadow that was the Scath spread across the width of the board before him. 'Then embrace me brother and we shall be one.'

Eider felt the sudden weight of suffocation upon his chest. 'Equal we are, he heard his own voice reply. 'But if I embrace you I am lost.'

'Then we are at stasis and shall remain so,' the Voice declared.

'I . . . must not remain,' Eider blurted his resistance against the enfolding Dark. 'Be done I say! Let the game begin again!'

The core of blackness contracted, and then pulsed again with unseelie power. 'The move is mine. 'Tis Dark shall embrace you!' the Voice announced.

With gleaming eyes Eider watched the aura of vile energy spread out from the Scath's black heart and thought again of the orb of jet that he had once smashed to pieces on the day he had freed Rhye from its bonds. Now he stood helpless before the all-consuming vortex into which Dark's cohorts had been cast on that day. The wedge of Darkness challenged him anew, distorting from a thin line into a flat plane, and then a square which moved forward consuming one white square after another. Eider watched it compress itself once more into a spiralling cone, its nucleus skimming the shining surface of the board, forcing him to raise his hands, fearful that he could not halt its flight. Was the end now come? Would blackness envelop him and he be lost to that which he had denied for so long? Would this Feared

Thing take him at last? That which had consumed Lumin, would it also consume him? And yet, could it be that he might find his beloved somewhere deep within the tomb of Dark, and Nairb and Lehon, might they also await him there?

Light had sprung Dark's elaborate trap and was caught forever! Now he could be no help to his loved ones, no use to Triad force, no King to seelie kind. Eider heard the omnipresence utter unfathomable sounds, like one asleep, like one in trance. The words of some vile curse? He shuddered as the shadow of shadows passed over him.

Yet with it came sudden inspiration. Here was some choice to be made. He could do as the Scath had bid him, could live on in stasis and in so doing prevent the working of Dark in the world. Yet would not the force for good be thwarted too? He could do as the Gods bade him, could defeat Darkness, turn from stasis and fear new fears. His heart raced with fresh vigour and he felt the core of him throb with a new life. The will to complete the task burned inside him with the force of an inferno. Now his frozen limbs began to thaw, and as ice-crystals twinkled on his skin Eider cried out his defiance.

''Tis stalemate,' the Voice reminded. 'Here in stasis we shall remain.'

'No!' Eider was defiant. 'Stasis holds Dark and Light alike!' He recoiled aware that he must fight on but knowing not the means to do so. He shrank back to the narrow parameters of his King's file but as he did so the prism, the heart of pure light he thought held firm within his shirt, fell from safety. Calamity! Wild-eyed and disbelieving he watched it slide across the board-floor with uncanny ease. His blood ran cold as the fragile pyramid of colourful light halted in tranquil beauty on the very edge of the void.

The Scath spread out its fathomless cloak of night. 'Embrace me, I say. There can be no winner.'

Eider hesitated. Had the Scath not observed the thing

of brightness lying there? Did it not know of its existence? Eider thought again of Lumin and of the song
trilled by her bird-voice.

'Vanissan deorc!' he cried in her loric tongue. 'Fire-
carrier fears thee no more!'

At his words the ebb and flow of the Scath's dark
power metamorphosed before him, turned to black
matter, hard as a lance, swift as a thunderbolt. The
deadly mass struck the prism hard.

'Never shall that flame be lit!' the Voice decreed as
Darkness struck the prism of crystal once again.

Eider took his stance, intuition raising his hand. Now
the power of seelie Magus was with him, and the
accumulation of Ancient Lore made impotent the Dark
attack. At the moment of impact no harm befell the
prism and the intangible force of malevolence was fused
into vulnerable matter. Now it was not the Scath that
confronted him, not the all-consuming Feared Thing.
Eider was aghast. Dark force had been made tangible
and rolled towards him as a fragment of blackest ebony.
A mere chess-piece. A black King.

So this was all his fear had come down to, a simple
chess-piece, a black King now fallen at the feet of the
white King, at the feet of the Magus. He who had power
over all the elements, he who had dominion over all
matter! White King had elected to replay and the Scath
had been forced to retreat.

Now Eider's heart beat fast, though not with triumph.
He had withstood the tests, had not endangered the
Triad blade, nor any amulet of the lore. In his moment
of greatest need the powers of Magus had not deserted
him; he was free to fulfil the quest once more, and he
gave thanks to the Gods for new life, gave thanks for
his insight and for sweet Lumin's sake.

In the oppressive stillness he trembled in a spasm of
relief and glanced at the sacred prism. It remained still,
unmoved, unharmed but teetering on the very edge of
black eternity. Eider panicked. He must rescue it! Carefully he edged across the path of the dwarf King of

ebony that he had made, hardly daring to believe that the dreaded Scath had vacated its form. Timidly he reached for the prism, barely breathing as he deftly snatched the fragment of crystal to safety and embraced it as if it were Lumin's own heart. It bore no mark upon its sheen, and Eider breathed a silent prayer . . . no harm was done. But then, as he watched its facets gleam, he saw the hair's-width of a fine black line drawn deep within its reflecting planes. A line like a stroke made by a quill.

Eider narrowed his eyes. What was this stuff that seemed to trickle, to spread from the base of the prism like ink, or sand? Anxiously he watched its course. The motion of the black particles was barely noticeable, yet how long before they filled the prism completely? How soon? How soon before Light's perfect star was changed to impenetrable obsidian? Once black it would not gleam, once black it would not reflect. Once black it could not cast the spark needed to light the mystic flame . . .

Eider was wracked with sudden grief. He had won the game, conquered Darkness on equal terms. 'Stalemate!' he cried aloud but the word only returned to him a thousand times. Where was that perfection so long awaited by Elders, the perfection so talked about in the scripts of seelie lore? Eider lowered his eyes, there was none. There was nothing, nothing but the prism and the slender, living line of Dark within it. At the realisation of his burden, the true heart was wrenched and Eider wailed his grief aloud.

Then from the abyss of all-Darkness a thin light, the colour of luna rays began to rise. It hovered momentarily until as Eider blinked he saw its shape and knew it well.

'Wizard!' he breathed, astounded at the sight. He saw Nairb stand tall and gaunt upon the chequer-board floor. He wore the gown of Horatious Thor and in his long and delicate hands he clasped the red wood box as if it were some ancient hope. Eider watched him in awe and disbelief.

'Nairb,' he said again, and reached out to embrace him. But though the wizard smiled, Eider knew he had not been seen for the mystic stepped forward as if he would walk straight through him.

Eider could do no more than long for the touch of his dearest friend. But his was another place in time, and Eider could only watch him pace the endless dimensions of the chamber. The dark curls fell in youthful abundance and though the face was pale it shone with bright hope and firm resolve. Eider's heart ached as the apparition passed close by. He felt compelled to follow and as he did so he saw at last the chamber door. Even as the ghostly Nairb moved towards it, the heavy door opened of itself and Eider followed in the gentle man's wake. He had to find a way in this unknown place, had to speak somehow with Nairb and gain answer to all his questions.

As the white robes of the wizard flurried ahead of him, so Eider's pace quickened, eager to catch up with him. Yet as he crossed the threshold into the gloom-filled corridor beyond he felt the compulsion to turn, to see the way that he had come. And so he turned but saw behind him only dark. Momentarily, he glimpsed the pitted texture of the stone wall, finding no trace of a door. He trembled at the realisation, for he had passed cleanly through the wall as only a wizard can. Eider smiled, for he knew that his powers were complete at last. Turning back to his ghostly companion, eager to impart his happiness, he found no one ahead of him. No edge of mystic gown or wizard's cloak had stirred the dust however far he stepped in search. Yet the faint glimmer of light just ahead made him squint. Was it merely made by rising smoke veils adrift in the aura of torchlight? Or was it some fleet movement of a white robe's trim, a flash of sacred light against the dark walls as his dear wizard led him on? Eider stepped up his pace. Nairb must not be lost again. Yet however quickly he moved the twists and turns of the stone corridors, the faint glimmer of that ephemeral light remained always too far ahead of him, always just out of reach.

Eider began to run. He would halt the wizard, would halt him and ask his questions! The sudden shock as he hit the door stopped his breath and he cried out with the pain of impact. His cry returned to him in muted tones but he was quite alone. He felt warm blood trickle down his forehead and slumped against the wall. He had reached impasse with no clue for direction, no comfort from his long lost friend. His power would carry him no further.

Despite his frantic pursuit the vision of his beloved wizard was gone and now without the spectral aura the corridor seemed blacker still. Eider clutched at his breast and felt the gentle life pulse held therein. Did he dare to take out the prism to light his way in this terrible dark? He shook his head; he would take no risk with it but stumble on following the dim lit walls with careful fingertips.

The corridor sloped steadily downwards and as Eider followed it the air grew heavy and ice-edged. His footsteps echoed in the yawning emptiness as the passage turned and twisted, winding back upon itself before intersecting with another identical tunnel. A zephyr of cold raced past him and Eider halted abruptly. He could feel a gust of frosted air force its way upwards into his face and instinct told him to move no further. Could he be on the edge of another dark abyss? With sudden decision he took the prism from its place of safety. The facets reflected serene blue and rose pink as they edged the sapphire heart and cast forth narrow shafts of ghost-light. Eider held the prism aloft and it rested on his palm as a tiny, vibrant star. He caught his breath. He stood between two giant pillars on the topmost step of a deep-cut stairway, every cobweb and every wedge of stone lit sharply by the prism's light. He was awestruck by its powerful, mystic glow. But his heart lurched, for the fine line of blackness trapped within it had begun to fill the prism's base.

'So quickly?' Eider said incredulously. His heart pounded with sudden panic; soon he would lose the light completely, soon the dark would be all there was, forever, and he left to roam eternal night. He felt the pulse of the prism warm against his hand and he straightened determinedly. While there was light within he would complete his task. He must journey on and since there was no other route to follow, he began the final descent.

At the base of the steps Eider found a gate of wrought iron. It stretched from floor to roof and the chain that secured it was loose and rusted with time. He rattled the solid links but knew that they would not yield to any amount of strength he could exert and to risk the power vested in him by transmuting spiritual energy into physical prowess was too dangerous an act. He dare not sublimate his higher self and attempt to overcome Dark in a physical encounter lest he relinquish some facet of mystic knowledge gained from bitter experience, knowledge he might yet need to reach Phoenix Fire. Yet if he pressed himself against the wall he might be able to slide within . . .

He peered through the bars into the impenetrable dark, knowing that his route was therein, and wrapping his cloak tight about him he stood in meditative silence, mouthing Lumin's mystic mantras, until he felt his limbs relax, his muscles grow fluid, his bones become soft as pulp, until he was no more than elementary particles that passed between the wall and iron post, and then fused together as matter as his form was reinstated. Eider whispered ritual thanks as he set out upon the final part of his quest.

He had found some disused cellar, a dungeon or else a vault. He narrowed his eyes and tried to see in the deeper dark. He caught a quantum of light. Perhaps a torch burned farther on, if he could find it he could use it to make the pathway less hazardous and could then move with utmost speed. Stealthily he pursued the glim-

mer until its source became recognisable as small terra-
cotta lamps positioned along the walls.

Eider could see stairs and arches, tunnels that
ascended and passages that wound away. Cut into the
stone were tall vertical recesses and as he approached
the gold-green lamps lit up the eerie outlines held fast
therein. He saw the shape of inert limbs cocooned in
silken webs, saw the unseelie symbols carved upon the
walls, recognised the putrid stench and realised he stood
within the womb of Dark. Or was it a tomb?

Eider frowned. 'Catacombs,' he breathed, barely
daring to make a sound. A resting place it was, the
burial place of baneful souls. Yet as he walked along
the silent files he realised the place was both the first
and the last, a place of death, and a place of birth. For
though he saw the regiments of corpses suspended in
clear membranous sacs, they were not held in the rigor
of death but were vile embryos awaiting rebirth. Within
the sacs Eider glimpsed the foetal repose of limbs, head
and torso and each bore a feature fully formed. Where
in one the tip of a scarab sting was clear, in another the
black cowl of a demon queen; in one the heavy brow of a
mountain warlord could be seen, in another a deformed
yellow fist pushed for freedom against its membranous
womb.

Eider raised the prism and its reflected light gleamed
upon a death mask. He shrank back in terror, yet the
blood pulse of Magus bid him hold the prism higher
still. Only light would terminate this endless becoming,
ensure the pure heart's passage to the sacred fire of the
phoenix and the defeat of Dark forever. He held light
aloft and an arc of purity was cast about the webby files.
Eider shuddered, hearing the muted cries echo round
the chamber as the embryonic sacs wizened to nought.
He saw them wrinkle, dwindle and vanish, their deadly
seedlings to rise no more.

Soon there was nothing to see save the strange ethereal light of the prism shining above his head like some
will-o'-the-wisp, urging him ever on. Then as if by some

magic sight Eider suddenly noticed the vast stone coffer which loomed up in the darkest corner of the dank chamber. His eyes grew wide with painful curiosity. What could be within? The coffer was cold to his touch, but still, as he drew closer he leaned over its rim eager to view its contents. As he did so he could not mute the anguished cry that escaped his throat. Within the coffer there lay a giant shard of glass, its edges jagged and unfinished, its facets half concealing, half revealing that which it held deep inside. The beautiful form that lay cocooned slept peacefully, wrapped in her endless black hair. She was at once breath-stilled and glowing with the rose tincture of life.

'Baobhanshee!' Eider cried aloud and the name rebounded from the iron-cold walls. Why was she here, here in this accursed place, and thriving still? Was she a victim, or a creature of unseelie kind? Torn between love and hate, Eider recoiled, cast himself from her sleep-held form, and ran from the chamber. He ran blindly, ran heedlessly, ran desperately, ran along the low passageway until his lungs ached, until his face streamed with sweat, until his heart beat wildly in his chest. He ran until the last breath in him was spent, until he could see at last an exit from the nightmare place, a skeletal gate – a portcullis of bone.

Eider pushed against the gate but the ropes and chains that held it in place would not be triggered into movement. He scanned the jigsaw of human remains searching out the means to prompt the mechanism. He followed the gruesome pattern of femur and humerus, of tibia and clavicle, dozens of them locked together to provide an impenetrable barrier. He traced the largest and the smallest. The bones were white and gleaming, smooth as polished ivory. He ran his finger lightly across them and halted. His touch had found an irregularity, a brittle edge, and looking closer he saw that one of the bones set amid the pattern of digits had been lost or broken off. It was no more than the length of a forefinger but its omission quite clearly broke the unity of design. A flaw, a minute weakness.

'A solitary bone,' Eider considered for a moment and then with a secret smile he took from his pouch the gift that Merle had given him. A bone, a forefinger in length, with jagged edges. A solitary bone. 'This bone.' He stated it plain as he pressed the phalange into the waiting space. It slotted perfectly and the pattern of a hand was at once complete. Instinctively, Eider pressed his palm against the skeletal equivalent and the gate rattled ominously. His touch had released it.

He passed beneath the gate and heard it close at his back. A sudden rush of wind pre-empted a gathering of tremendous force. Behind him he heard the bones echo in an eerie death-rattle and as he turned saw the gate of bone recede at white hot speed, though he himself appeared not to move an inch. It fled from him as if attracted to some nucleus of magnetic force, until it became the smallest pinpoint and disappeared from his sight.

Now with trembling hands Eider held up the prism and groaned with despair. The dark within it was growing still and had now covered more than a third of its volume. Eider could barely swallow so great was his panic, there was yet so much to do, so many things to set right, so little time left to him. He called out to Lumin to nourish his breaking heart, called on Nairb to aid his soul in the moment of his deepest despair, called on the time-held keepers of the Ancient Lore to protect the pulse of life he carried forth, called on the Gods themselves to grant him the final redemption. And when he turned away from all that had gone before, he saw the symbol of his hope rise up as an arch of blazing light.

21

The arch was of no substance but light and a white ethereal curtain of fine water which cast itself in perpetual crescent from right to left. Eider felt its warm coolness cascade about him, felt its dry wetness alight on him as dew. He stood before it in silent euphoria, delighted by its beauty, awed by its very existence.

With its millions of tiny droplets a strange sound ebbed and flowed as if it were the sound of its motion, a sound high pitched and so pure it caused no tremor in Eider's eardrum, yet penetrated to the very core of him. It was the sound of the smallest bells, some distance off but then all around him, as if only the bow of the arch obscured it.

Eider's heart was suddenly at peace and he stepped into the white shadow of the crescent arch in search.

. . . And the rhythm of the bells was like a tide, rising and falling. The rhythm was of ankle bells, of finger bells, of temple bells that tremble as one passes. The shimmering bells rippled upon the surface of his soul, rippled upon the surface of water and the water was ice blue. Eider raised the prism for light and was dazzled. He was in a cavern of clear ice and as he narrowed his eyes he saw four perfect reflections dancing in the water like slender candle flames. At last, when his eyes had grown accustomed to the brightness of the light he saw their cause. At the water's edge four maidens danced and their voices were as light as the four winds interwoven in harmony. Their endless song was a timeless chant, its circling melodies spreading through the ice cavern as ripples spread across the surface of a calm lake.

They sang of the shimmering arch that held them safe

within, and all Dark out. They sang of the beautiful wanderer who had found his way. With raised arms they sang of their cavern of clear ice, its vaults and pillars of vast icicles. Then kneeling at its edge they sang of the bottomless lake and spread out their arms to encompass its icy boundaries.

Eider scanned the motionless lake and saw the small boat at its edge. It was time-battered and oar-less but the lamp that glimmered at its helm was the sacred blue of his cloak. On the farther side he saw mist, a swirl of amethyst light, but though he strained his eyes he could make out no thing of substance from its shape. He scanned again the spreading waters . . . yet was it water, or ice? Could he safely walk its span? He drew closer to the edge and crouched to test its substance. At the touch of his fingertips a gentle wave danced away over the lake's shining surface and Eider saw green ropes of waterweed rise from the depths in its wake.

So the water changed its hue, as ice blue gave way to green. Now the maiden's ancient song told of their sorrow, of the black gusting squall and how they, the four winds, had taken flight to the shelter of the Bearded Lake. Eider gasped, he had found it! He had reached the Bearded Lake, and was close to the fount of the sacred fire.

He frowned, for the wave that he had cast met the farther bank as a flash of white water and at its touch the amethyst haze took shape. It appeared to be a long way off, perhaps a world away. Eider blinked hard, for before his eyes a light-edged triangle rose up from the water's edge to the roof of icicles. He saw its sides shine like crystal and like steel, and watched the pure blue and white of a summer sky race diagonally away from base to apex. He shivered with ecstasy and knew that he had not seen such a sky since the day he had lost Rhye.

Entranced, he drew closer to the water's edge, yearning for its colour, for its light, for the touch of warmth on his bloodless skin. His dark eyes narrowed abruptly, catching tracers of silver, then of gold as they flashed across the surface of the triangular monolith. What strange geometry was this? Could it be he had triggered some exit by his presence?

Now the maidens' chanting weaved in intricate harmony and suddenly they called out to him.

'Water-strider, embark!' They pleaded on and on. 'The Spirit of Water shall speed you forth.' And their chant became a mantra, its rhythm like the motion of time-worn oars.

'Spirit of Water?' Eider repeated, holding aloft the prism to make a wider arc of light. 'Manannan!' he cried aloud and the holy name filled the ice-cavern. As if by his spell the waterweed grew faster and spread until green of every hue drifted in pennants upon a surface of white water. The motion of its sudden surge carried Eider's spirit forwards and he leapt into the waiting boat, clinging fast to its old timbers as it began to glide away over the silky ripples. Soon the mingle of voices and of bells had carried him far across the lake and he could see shoals of bright fish swimming among the waterweed. The weed grew like hair and as the boat drifted to the centre of the lake Eider caught his breath. Just beneath the pale green surface he had spied a white expanse. It was shaped like a great face and the weed that flowed from it formed its hair and beard. Eider raised the prism aloft the better to see the elongated features. The rose light it shed made clearer the dark hollows of the eyes, the long jaw, aquiline nose and the mournful mouth of one long held in torment. An ancient form now filled the lake, body, arms and legs drifting with the gentle current. The weed of hair and beard cascaded down his entire length and clung to the flowing robes of white and ice blue. Here and there water violets decorated their folds and in his green hair a crown of water forget-me-nots clung. Eider shuddered, was this he? Could this be Manannan? Had he arrived too late?

'Stasis, stasis,' the maidens chanted, their song undulating like the drifting of the ancient form itself. Eider grew heavy with sadness as he heard their song, for they sang of the victorious Dark, how the Arch-Wizard Manannan had been rendered lifeless before it, frozen, and cast to the ice depths of the Bearded Lake. Banished from the rivers, outcast from the streams, exiled from the Seven Sees of seelie lore. Eider buried his face in his hands. The seas had run dry at his misdeed! The hope of all his kind lost! Yet the song of the maidens soothed him, drifted all about him, drew him on.

'The advent of Light-Carrier has healed his soul. The coming of Light-Carrier will set him free.'

Eider leaned over the edge of the boat and saw in the prism's light the colourful fish that weaved through Manannan's hair and beard. He watched the old eyelids ripple, and though he feared the great Spirit of Water, he longed for his eyes to open, to see him and the talisman he held.

'Speak his name,' urged the maidens in tones both desperate and gentle. 'Raise him up.'

Eider's blood raced. 'Manannan!' he cried. 'Manannan, come forth!' he commanded the waters, and the eyes of the Spirit of Water flickered open. Eider's heart leapt with joy for the eyes that looked upon him were the blue of Rhye's sky, and he smiled, unafraid of the quietness of ageless kind.

The placid waters grew active and bubbles broke against the sides of the boat as the great palms turned upwards, and from their hollows perfect water-lilies sprang, of red and white. Eider's jet black eyes reflected their fragile beauty as the maidens cried out in worshipful praise.

'Hail, Magus. Hail, Master of the Elements!'

In reverence Eider too made oblation while the Spirit of Water cast the fragile lilies adrift.

'Hail, spirit-freer!' the maidens sang and Eider raised his head to see them on their knees, whilst below in the watery depths the old hands of Manannan were pressed together in prayer. It was then Eider realised that it was he they honoured and as the maidens rang their finger bells in union, they sang the praises of Eider, the beautiful wanderer who had restored the gift of life to Manannan.

Eider sat in the boat bewildered by their praise, his heart full of joy at the sight of the blossoms that sprang forth about him.

'Hail, Magus.' The sonorous voice of Manannan arose from the glassy lake. 'Hail, Fire-Carrier.' The vibration of his voice gently rocked the boat and set waves lapping at its sides.

Eider nodded proudly into the great smiling face that rippled below him. ''Tis true, I carry the light,' he confirmed, and held the prism aloft. 'And shall return it to the barrow grave,' he vowed.

At the sight of the mystic glow Manannan's wide brow creased and the look of sadness returned. 'Hurry,' the echo-voice pleaded. 'Blackness overcomes.'

Eider scrutinised the prism and was pained by its near-dark state. 'The light shall soon be spent!' he gasped and turned in desperation to the ancient spirit of the depths. 'Manannan, I shall not reach the tomb in time!'

The long hands of Manannan swept the waters of the lake until a gentle current began to rise. 'While one atom of light remains may the spark be struck.'

Eider's frightened face broke into a smile. 'Then speed me quickly on!' he urged.

'Once the core is black,' the ageless voice rippled on the quickening tide, 'the dominance shall be forever Dark.' Manannan's speech was punctuated by the small shrill bells of the maidens as they began their song afresh. Eider felt giddy as the waters began to speed by, the current quickened by their song, and soon his tiny boat was carried away over the folds of Manannan's flowing robes.

He watched the transparent waters glide and saw in their sheen the setting of a thousand suns. Then, through the night-crossing, he witnessed his own fall and the falling of all he had lost. And he saw there all ugliness and all beauty. All false and all real. All evil and all good. All darkness and all light. He saw it all and knew it all inextricably bound. He had discovered the truth of all things. Like life itself the water continually flowed, was gone but was always there. As if in a dream he saw the possible and the impossible, saw the unimaginable towards which he sped, and saw perfection, saw the gauntlet and sword engraved with new design, the likeness of the flowers of the water, their tendrils weaving about the golden scabbard, the sword-hilt, the gauntlet and the sapphire cloak in delicate barely visible design, yet Eider saw it all.

He saw too the insubstantial triangle towards which he sailed, its rose and amethyst light reflecting on every rivulet and candle of ice. He turned back to see the maidens kneeling beside the lake, to see the white and pastel green form of Manannan swimming in a slow circle of joy with the fish of his life-given waters.

Eider brimmed with new-found happiness, for he knew now his purpose and his sacrifice. He waved his hand in farewell. 'Manannan!' he cried. 'When I stand before the sacred fire, I shall give thanks for your freedom and mine!'

The waters parted at his words and the great white face of the Water Spirit thrust upwards toward him. 'Light the fire and thanks enough be given!'

Eider watched in silence as Manannan sank below, there to wait until Phoenix Fire released pure waters into the world, until Manannan would swim forth once more and create new life.

Behind him the maidens were silent as they watched him approach the point of departure and as Eider gazed upon the glistening haze of the vast ethereal triangle, his skin flushed the colour of amethyst. He held up the prism, aligning its glassy substance with the insubstantial nebulae of the mystic doorway. The conjunction cast forth rods of bright light and at their axis Eider found the opening. The heat of the magical entrance pulsed with the colours of the spectrum and as a curtain of icicles rained down from the vaulted heights and acti-

vated the pure waters, Eider stepped from the boat and
vanished into the molecular pyramid of light.

22

His lungs expanded with the taste of musty air and his skin felt the edge of ice, though there was no frost. He stood in a corridor. The walls sloped on each side and at its end a triangle of blue-white light drew him on though he could not see the ground beneath his feet. Still he could feel its gradient, feel himself gradually climbing towards the triangular gap of light. In the distance behind him he could still hear the maidens' chanting: 'Fratakara,' they sang. 'Fratakara, Fratakara,' they echoed on and on.

Eider felt the heat rise at the core of him, felt the lifeblood rush through his veins, felt the glow of the prism on his palm. 'Fire-Maker,' he gave whispered reply to their chant. 'I am He,' he vowed, taking the seven steps which rose up before him.

They led into an ante-chamber of coarse stone. The strange light of the prism arced through the emptiness and Eider frowned. Here was nought but a solitary chair. A chair of stone it was, set before a wall of pictures. Eider entered, hearing his own footfall, and drew closer to the chair to view the ancient ritual taking place within the drawings of the frieze. A line of penitents stood before a set of scales, yet what their Elder weighed upon them Eider could not see. 'The chamber of the Two Truths,' he whispered, reading from the scrawled lettering of the frieze and understanding its meaning. Like the penitents, he must submit to the judgement of his life's deeds. Only then would he be granted entrance to the chamber of the mystic fire. He moved to place the prism on the rough floor, his dark eyes saddening to see its vibrancy defiled by the thickening line of Darkness at its core.

How many more such trials as this before he reached the ancient altar? The prism would be obsidian black by then. He would be lost, and the white lore with him. He tightened as sudden fear gripped him, but then gathering firm resolve he seated himself and began the ancient ritual of the Two Truths:

'I, dutiful son of Eyre, have not failed to show mercy to those who have opposed me,' he whispered to the listening walls. He had indeed been a King of mercy. Had he not spared the life of the Usurper, casting him as a changeling to the void? But then he saw the crystal of the prism gleam and remembered his impatience with Nairb his loyal wizard, with the Elders who had taught him all of seelie lore . . . with Darius. He bit his lip, there he should have shown mercy, and had not. Fine beads of sweat laced his brow as he returned to the ritual.

'I have not allowed Dark to gain victory over me,' he vowed. In truth he had not, for here he was, still battling to overcome. Yet, the Bloodseed had corrupted him, had defiled Rhye, tainted the Triad amulets and sown the seeds of distrust where harmony and love had thrived. How quickly the death-seeds had flourished in the land. Once his corrupt vanities had opened his eye to the mysteries of artifice and the sheen of the looking-glass, they closed it to the needs of his people and the ruin of his lands. He shuddered in the stone-cold chamber.

'I have not denied sustenance to any who stood at my gate,' he gulped, his mouth turning dry. In that deed there was both good and ill. His heart raced with fear . . . what would happen if the Gods cast him out?

'I have not wilfully tainted the Triad, nor any object of the Lore,' he held his breath, knowing it was both true and false. 'I have not sought to avoid my fate,' he offered as his fifth Truth. He felt the sweat pour down his face. 'I have not wielded Triad Force as a God, but as a man of seelie-kind.' He thought on the words, knowing he had felt mortal fear in the sacred forcefield of the Great Sword's power, knowing he had felt the elation of immortality at the axis of that power. Had that been arrogance? He swallowed hard. 'I, dutiful son of Eyre, have never denied the dictates of seelie lore.' He fell silent, his body wracked with uncertainties. Here, alone with himself, with his life's truths, he began to know the mystery of his journey past, and the gravity of his journey to come. The hollow chamber was filled with his whispered words, and Eider heard them returning to him over and over until it seemed the static figures of the frieze murmured them in echo.

He raised the Gauntlet-clad hand, his palm extended towards the light of the prism and began the seven positive Truths.

'I, dutiful son of Eyre, have obeyed the calling of my line.' He thought of Rhye, of the Kingship he performed there, thought of how he had cast out Dark. Then he remembered Dark's terrible revenge, recalled the fractured orb of light and his fall from grace. He stammered as he began his second Truth.

'I . . .' he swallowed hard, 'I have returned the Triad to its source.' He closed his eyes, if nothing else he had retrieved the amulets, brought them here, back to their origins. Here they would be reforged. He glanced at the darkening prism . . . he must perform this ritual, must press on towards the sacred chamber!

'I have cherished seelie lore, and all of seelie kind; I have nurtured mortal-kind.' He frowned in deep earnest. 'I, dutiful son of Eyre, have obeyed the calling of manhood.' He thought of Lumin and their marriage in the shining bower. How he longed to see her again. He looked again at the line of blackness caught within the prism and thought of Baobhanshee . . . which of his two Queens would the Gods approve?

He lowered his eyes. 'I, dutiful son of Eyre, have accepted the task given over to me, have dedicated myself to the Quest . . .' He straightened his posture bringing the ritual to its close. 'I have satisfied the Gods in all their commands.' He held his breath, hoping against hope his words were not in vain.

With one swift and reverential motion he rose from the chair, then cast himself to the gritty floor, arms outstretched, to await the judgement of the Gods. He felt the sudden draught, heard the harmony of the four winds speeding towards him from the distant ice-cavern. Their words were old as the Ages, yet he knew them from childhood:

'Heart of thy mother. Heart of thy father. Rise not against thee in the chamber of Judgement. Send not the balance against thee before the Scales of Light and Dark, lest thy name be blotted from the Book of Time, be cast from the grace of the Gods.'

Eider trembled, waiting. Waiting for the sign of absolution. Yet from where would it come? No Elder stood beside him here as they had stood beside him at Rhye, as they had stood beside his ancestors. He felt the lightest breeze, heard it rush through the passageway, heard the words 'Seed-Carrier' speed upon it to his chamber.

'I once carried seed,' he whispered to himself sadly, recalling the rye-grass that Lumin had plucked from his threadbare cloak on the day he had found her. 'Rye-seed . . .' he said again. 'Rhye's Seed,' he repeated over and over again. Yet what of the seed of Eyre? What of his line? His heart ached with sudden remembrance of Darius and the prophecy he made: 'And you shall have no issue in this realm . . .' Eider trembled. What of Baobhanshee and the lost fruit of her womb? Yet, what of Lumin? Of their union? Had he not seen her plant the rye-seed he had carried to her bower? Where was she who carried his seed? Where hid their progeny? The chanted whispers of the four winds reached his ears afresh. 'Seed-Carrier,' they called him. 'Seed-Carrier! Seed-Carrier!' And he felt his heart-beat race, felt its faintest echo make reply at the core of him. And as the second heart-beat grew strong, he knew that the fruit of their union lived indeed. It lived in him and of him would be born! 'Seed-Carrier!' he cried aloud, and knew that it was he.

Yet suddenly the song of the chanting maidens changed its pace, changed its rhythms, changed its words. He felt his silken hair fly as pennants on the gusting air, heard the chanted cry come to him on its flight. 'Maakheru!' they named him anew, and the Gods granted him absolution at last! In that moment he saw the arc of white light above his head, saw the glowing nimbus vanish, then as quickly materialise in the shape of a torc of bright silver. At its centre a heart-shaped garnet was cast, and from the heart wings in flight were spread. Eider watched entranced as the wondrous thing fell through the ancient air towards him.

With sudden magical force it had possessed him. He felt it band his forehead, saw silver and gem-red pass before his eyes, felt metallic cold about his neck, felt its unrelenting hold on him. He closed his eyes, hearing the echoed cry: 'His is the Torc of Sight. His the Garnet Heart on wings of mercurial flight. His the Pure Heart.' Then he knew he was Maakheru . . . knew he was judged and found to be whole. Knew he was the One of True Heart. He stood to his feet, his heart filled with joyous thanksgiving as he cast his arms wide.

'Praise to the Gods for the gift of wholeness. In homage I return the elements into Their keeping: Soil of Rhye. Water of Manannan. The Four Winds that attend him, and Fire. Fire of seelie lore, the Sacred Fire of the Phoenix!'

As he spoke, he felt the second pulse within him grow, felt the shudder of the rich earth, heard the winds blow and knew they flew free. He heard the rush of waters, and knew Manannan to be free. He closed his eyes and cast back his head in a triumphal cry: 'Earth of my body and fruit of my self. Water of my blood and line of Eyre. Spirit of air and of great Rhion's tomb, carry me to the chamber, to the sacred fire of the phoenix.'

His invocation rang the chamber round and the gap through which he had entered punctuated its sound as it closed and sealed at his back. Eider's dual heart-beat pounded at the thought that he would never leave the tomb towards which he moved. His heavy eyelids raised, and with them a new door opened, at the heart of the frieze.

23

The light towards which he strode shone sapphire blue, and washed his skin with its serene hue. Yet, he had moved mere paces when he caught his first glance of the chamber beyond and the figure who stood at its centre. His twin heart-beat fluttered weakly below his own in sudden fear. Who was it awaited him here? Some God in the guise of seelie-kind? Some guardian of the tomb? He halted before the threshold unsure, the palm of his hand instinctively clutching at the Triad's hilt. He felt the Sword's heat, and knew he could not use it. Was this his final trial, set 'twixt him and the sacred fire? He waited for movement, for sound, but none came and so he moved forward.

It took but one step and Eider was over the threshold. He took firm stance gladly awaiting that which the Gods had preordained for him. 'Who is there?' he demanded of the staunch back of the chamber's occupant. His dark orbs detected no tightening of muscle, no slight motion of one who had been disturbed. Yet they widened at the beauty of the garments of blue-royal and white, marvelled at the sight of delicately worked silver and gold. He gasped at sight of the helmet with its bright plumage and could not prevent himself from drawing closer. Yet still the figure towards whom he so stealthily crept made no move, and as he stood at its side Eider's body relaxed at last. For he had spoken warning to no man, no vestige of seelie-kind, no guardian of the tomb, but to a suit of armour!

Bright, gleaming silver armour, its breast-plate decorated with a phoenix of gold. The bird was surrounded by fine engraving of wild flowers and grasses. At first he thought of Rhye then of the strange tracery that had magically appeared upon the scabbard of the Triad blade. He drew closer . . . yes it was so, the engravings not merely alike but identical. He felt a tremor course through him, a surge of joy and fear mixed. The armoured suit stood before him like a second skin, yet he could see no mannekin beneath, no spine-rod to hold it thus. It simply levitated there. Levitated as it had since the Elder's spell had left it there. So it had waited, like a silent ghost. Waited how long? Waited on and on . . . for him.

The helmet gleamed invitingly, its crown adorned with a fleur-de-lys of bright plumage. The feathers were white, yet in the strange light they reflected every colour of the rainbow. His eyes widened as he reached out his hands to take it up. In moments he had it in his grasp, and as he placed it on his head he felt his man's heart-beat join with the child's, his boyish grin returning memories of his first trophy to him. 'First and last,' he whispered, yet he had barely uttered the words when the draught of sudden movement took his breath and he both heard and felt the sudden bindings of armour fasten tight about his limbs. He gasped at the brightness of the shimmering breast-plate. At the sight of the gauntlet, how perfectly it fused with the whole, its feathered wristlet layering as feathers over the shimmering armplate. In ecstasy he felt his dual heart-beat race, realised his mouth formed mantras too old for him ever to have learned. They rose from spirit to his lips as the breath of healing warmth, spiralling with his speech to the ceiling.

At the sound of his voice the door through which he had passed shut, its closure reverberating in ever-deepening tones throughout the hollow system of underground chambers in which he stood. Eider's pulse-beat froze his blood . . . now he knew he was the Blessed One, knew he would find the altar, light the sacred fire. He glanced at the prism, seeing its crystal light diminished to a mere triangle at its apex by the rising Darkness at its core. Now his whole being trembled. 'Let me not fail!' he cried out, his desperate plea filling the chamber. Suddenly the heart-beat deep within him flooded his veins with regal blood, granting him fresh vigour. With it came Eider's final resolve, 'I shall go forth, light the sacred fire. And should I fail, the Triad blade shall be my merciful executioner!' He turned to the steadily rising opening of the eastern wall, seeing the triangular light take shape. 'I leave it . . . in the lap of the Gods,' he vowed, and having given himself up to divine dictate, he went towards his fate.

The passageway through which he passed was but three paces long, three paces that led him to seven steps, and upwards to a new opening. Passing through, the light of the prism arced, and caught within its span of illumination the massive dimensions of a burial chamber. Eider caught his breath, for its eternal grandeur, its majestic beauty overwhelmed him. At the chamber's heart, three guardians of seelie mythology awaited him, guardians not of flesh and blood but of ebony and ivory, of silver and of gold. In time-held perfection the like-nesses of Rhion, the great king; of Rhia and Rhys his tragic offspring, were caught in the sleep of death upon ornate sarcophagi which held their ash and bone.

Eider bowed reverently, knowing the tomb as well as if he had been present at its making. This was the ancient barrow-grave of kings, that sacred place first described to him in times long past by Nairb Horatious. Here, in this most sacred of all sacred places, the bodies of Rhia and Rhys had been laid. He had seen it all with the story's telling as if it were real. He saw it all now as if it were a dream, a mystic vision.

The likeness of Rhia was beauty itself. Carved of ebony, the detail of her body, face and hands were etched in silver, whilst blue-green porcelain was set in mosaic between two gilded hawks, to form the decor-ation of her coffin. Along its side, a gilt-scaled serpent coiled away into the blackness of the marble slab on which she lay. There was her name inscribed, and below, a solitary eye was carved, its lid closed to sight. 'Eye of Eternal Dark,' Eider whispered hearing his own words return as loudly as if he had shouted them out. He looked upon her tragic beauty, she the innocent foil for Dark, and thought of another . . . thought of Baobhanshee. The knot of love and hatred twisted deep within, and he turned from the pain to look upon the resting place of Rhia's twin.

The sarcophagus was of ivory, inlaid with gold leaf. Here, aqua-blue porcelain was set between gilded lilies. Along its side, a dove of mother-of-pearl carried the laurel of peace. Here lay the passive Rhys, his name inscribed above a magical Eye, its lid raised, its iris wide open to light and to all sight. Eider marvelled at the youthful faces of opposing kinship, glimpsing in their features a trace of his own line. He felt their ancient enmity, felt grief for a brother and a sister, the terrible grief of a father.

'Rhion, the great king, founder of the line of Eyre,' he murmured as he looked upon the tomb of the ancient patriarch. The ornate robes of gold bore silver design, symbols of the four divine ones: Michael, Uriel, Raphael and Gabriel. Along the side of the tomb, the gilt-winged phoenix was engraved. Eider traced its form, brushing the raised feathering of its wings with reverent fingertips. Yet suddenly he frowned, for the bird's red eye was missing. Nought remained but a niche, the size of a teardrop. Or was it the shape of . . . a heart? Eider clasped the smooth garnet of the torc about his neck. Firestone had been returned to him! He smiled in new certainty. Thus would all the sacred talismen of seelie lore be saved, thus would they be reforged and cast into the future time: by his own hand! By the hand of Maakheru! The hand of Fratakara! By he of the pure heart, he the fire-carrier!

Eider looked upon the gauntlet and saw the prism held firm within its grip, its glittering light now but a dwindling triangle at its apex. Fool! He was so taken by the ancient myth he had forgotten all else! He turned to the great altar stone. There the prism must be placed. There the sacred fire lit. He bowed before the rugged stone of worship. Its octagonal shape bore a solitary design on each of its sides and as he traced each in turn he named the symbols of the four elements: the lines of water . . . the cup. Furrows of earth . . . the coin. Flames of fire . . . the baton. Spirals of air . . . the sword. The altar had been fashioned into even planes, until the table itself was a smooth and perfect triangle. Of ancient stone it was, carried here, sheltered here, deep beneath the timeless moor. The carved table bore a heavy book with a cover of purest white. It lay open. There was also a cavity, a perfectly cut square in the smooth stone, of size and shape exactly akin to the base of the mystic prism. Eider hesitated: should he slot it into the cavity? With firm resolve he elected to take the risk and aligned the cool base of obsidian, his keen eye fixed firmly upon the triangle of white heat at the prism's apex. Its tremulous light steadied, then intensified to illuminate the pages of the open book and Eider saw the words inscribed there. Their colourful lettering mesmerised him, words written in the Loric tongue, indecipherable to all but a Magus. Eider looked on them and understood them well.

''Tis the ancient tale . . .' he said, almost in a trance, remembering the wizard and the story he once told before a winter's fire, '. . . a story with no end and no beginning'. He could almost hear Nairb whisper in his ear as he stood entranced before the gilded lettering of the script. His dark eyes recognised every phrase and silently read the ancient prophecy:

> From every compass point I come
> Summoned here by Ancient Lore.
> Bearer of the Sacred Key
> With which to unlock future deeds.
> I come, the Sower's Seed
> Witness of those who came before
> And call upon the ancient light
> To charge this crystal with the sight

That all may be revealed,
And in the past, the future sealed.

Eider read the words and knew he read the fateful course of his own life. He glimpsed the prism, Dark still raced against him, suffocating the heart of light like black sand! And Manannan's words returned to him, *'While one atom of light remains may the spark be struck.'* Eider threw back his head in anguish. 'Let it be so!' he cried, knowing he must act, must set the words of white lore in motion! And so he spoke them out, knowing something of their power:

The branch, the twig, the woven bier
A king of light begets a fire.

He thought then on the ancient burial rites, of Rhia and Rhys. Of Triad wielders who came before. Of the sacrifice that he must now make for Triad wielders to come. He remembered the artefacts of Triad Lore and straightened with pride. He it was who gathered the sacred amulets together and returned them to their source. He, the two in one, was come! His the touch that would ignite the spark of seelie lore afresh. His the flame that would rekindle sacred fire. In Phoenix Fire would the amulets be reforged, and from the flames be cast to the four winds. In Phoenix Fire would his own progeny be born and from the flames go forth into the future.

He clasped the Great Sword's hilt and the sapphire gems of the Gauntlet shimmered. Its forceful grip released Triad's blade at last and it slithered into the light as a shaft of gold, no longer tarnished or corrupt, no longer prisoner of the heavy scabbard. Eider cried out for joy and, as if possessed, he raised the blade high above his head for strength. In the blink of his dark eye the Gauntlet-clad hand had thrust the Sword into the ancient granite, had plunged it to the heart of the sacred stone. It unlocked both time and space. It was the key that freed light from the bonds of Dark. It was the golden blade of the Gods whose divine light sprang from the heart of the firmament . . . slowly, and from the east it came, the rebel spark, the pulse of solar energy, a lateral beam of light that sought the secret shaft, that pierced the sacred chamber and fell with the force of a silent thunder-bolt upon the waiting prism. And Dark had drained all but the smallest particle of light, had claimed all but a fragment at the apex. Yet in the moment of Dark's triumph, in the moment when black would eclipse white for all time, one speck flared defiance. It was enough. For light begot light, it reflected on hard steel, it bounced off gilt-edged sarcophagi and ricocheted off his sacred armour. Its narrow parallel beam criss-crossed back and forth, then soared to its point of origin, its fiery path engraving a mystic pentacle of light on the time-held air of the tomb.

Eider named the design of which he was a part. 'Spirit,' he said, as he traced its first line. 'Earth,' he followed the second. With his keen eye he traced the third and fourth, 'Air . . . Water.' Finally, he pressed the Gauntlet-clad fist against his breast-plate. 'Fire!' he stated triumphantly. At his acceptance the thin beam intensified and struck him afresh, struck him as a shaft of lightning from the Gods, struck him as the first spark that lights tinder. Eider cried out with an unknown agony, wept with euphoria, laughed against his pain. He felt solar force wash through him, saw the slender flame ignite, carried from his heart into the prism's core. He felt the heat-pulse of his veins, saw fire dance in the crystal womb. He raised his arms in homage to the Ancients, in homage to the Gods of seelie lore. Then it was he saw his limbs ripple as white heat, like ivory wings sweeping with the fire-current in long ellipses. He saw flame lick the base of the prism, saw the sudden flare at the centre of the ancient stone and knew the sacred fire was lit!

The red flower of fire grew and blossomed until within its flames he saw all. Saw the faces of all he had loathed, all he had loved. Saw Mother's tears and Father's sorrow. Saw the young boy's vow and the triumph of the grown man's quest. He saw the minions of Dark, the shadow of shadows, saw the battles, the victories, the recklessness and the heroism. He saw dual nature in firm embrace, and knew each moment that he glimpsed was once his own. The fire combusted, yet he felt no heat, saw in its pulsing colours the luminous wings and tasselled tail of the Bird of Paradise hover over the pure flame. He heard its sweet call, saw it alight in the bough of the spring-woken Tree of Life and knew her name. He saw the Trinity of comradeship: mortal-kind and elfin side by side with the wizard. He watched them bow low in homage to him, Fratakara, saw their raised eyes look upon him, smile upon him. It was then he made supplication to the Gods, that each one be redeemed, saved from the time of wandering by his deed. Saved from Dark. Like the Triad they too could be healed, made whole, and like him find new life in the living flame. They opened their arms to him, to worship and to greet him. They spread their loving arms to welcome him.

Now the living pulse within him throbbed, discordant rhythms in direct counterpoint to his own heart-beat. Eider felt its struggle for light and life, felt it surge upward from the very core of him. His own heart-beat raced to keep pace, raced with the intensity of revelation, the intensity that precedes death . . . that precedes the promise of birth.

'I come, the Sower's Seed!' he cried aloud, and a way opened for him in the flame of the blue fire, a way that led him to the Tree of Life. Unflinching he mounted the steps of the altar towards his vision. On the first step he blessed all selfless deeds and selfless hearts that had led him to the Sees of Rhye. The second step he dedicated to white lore, and to the sanctity of friendship. The third step he dedicated to knowledge, and then to love, and their combined qualities he gave to the one who would follow. Now blue fire had changed to gold and with his hair aflame he gave his whole being to solemn invocation: 'Triad amulets may the Gods reforge, and cast to the four winds for the one who comes after!'

He steadied himself before the heatless flames at whose centre his beloved Nairb awaited. As their eyes met Eider smiled the smile of All-Knowing, moved to embrace, to be embraced. It was then that the great cloak rippled as fire, its voluminous folds spread as wings, silk turned to feather and Eider leapt into the heart of Phoenix Fire . . .

 . . . *and he felt no heat on his fair cheek. He felt no fear in his pure heart, for there was nought in the fire but spirit. There was nought in the heatless fire but joy. Nought in the sacred fire but certain hope, born upward on vigorous wings. Soon there was nought to be seen in the fire but feathers, nought to be seen but a fabulous bird, a phoenix of red-silver and blue, spiralling heavenward through the flames. The eye of it was red, and the song that it sang was of the Loric tongue.*

Then did the sacred song vanish on the four winds. Then did the westering moon fall to the new horizon, scattering stars, changing the prism from black to white, and as the sweet smell of wood-smoke and resin caught his nostrils the eyelids flickered open.

'We shall read no more this day,' the Ancient One said.

The boy glanced up from the great book. He saw the white hair and beard illuminated by the shimmering pages, saw the trembling fingers brush the parchments edge, saw the strange key turned and the visions locked from sight. The apprentice moved not, his keen eyes still fixed upon the cover of blackest black.

The scrape of wood against flagstones caught his ears, and he noticed the misty chamber once again: still there the Harlequin and his Columbine; still there the twin cats caught in play before the glass . . . and the chess game still in progress. Obediently the boy took his seat to await the Ancient's move. Yet, though he watched the squares of the board, though he glared at the pieces, glared at the old hands, no move was made. He thought again of the great book, of the Sight he had been granted, and turning to the blazing hearth the boy whispered it, knowing little of its power: 'Gold of feather, then of mane. Ice of water, heat of flame . . .' The wide eyes ignited with the sudden flare, for it was then red fire leapt from the coals, burned sacred blue. It was then the fiery bird spiralled in the churling flames and changed to gold. 'Gold!' whispered the boy, seeing feathers of burnt amber splash the fire, seeing vast wings spread and carry a golden eagle from the ashes of the Phoenix. He caught his breath, 'First, then last, then last again, gives the Wielder his name!'

The thin line of the mouth quirked in a smile of secret knowledge and in unison the clocks of the chamber struck the middle hour.